REMORSELESS

JC RYAN

BOOKS

By JC Ryan

Rex Dalton K9 Thrillers

The Fulcrum

The Power of Three

Unchained

Sideswiped

The Inca Con

The French Girl

Duty of Care

Donna Teresa

Under the Pope's Windows

The Shanghai Strain

The Delphi Technique

Holes in the Wall

The Abyss

Unearthed

Remorseless

The Message

Dedicated to my good friend Mitch Pender, a military dog trainer, for giving me the idea for this series and guiding me through the intricate and amazing capabilities and psychology of those majestic four-legged soldiers.

Mitch has a lifetime of experience and an exceptional depth of knowledge as a military dog handler and trainer.

Vinci Books

vinci-books.com

Published by Vinci Books Ltd in 2025

1

Copyright © JC Ryan 2023

Major characters

Rex Dalton: Former black operations specialist working for CRC.

Catia: Married to Rex. Former Mossad mission support specialist.

Digger: A black Dutch Shepherd. Former military dog. Rex and Catia's companion.

Josh Farley: Black operations specialist working for CRC. Friend of Rex, Catia, and Digger.

Marissa: Married to Josh. Black operations specialist working for CRC. Friend of Rex, Catia, and Digger.

John Brandt: CEO of CRC (Crisis Response Consultancy), a private military contractor specializing in black operations on behalf of their clients, such as the CIA and other US security agencies.

Christelle Brandt née Proll: Former deputy director of the DGSE, the French equivalent of the American CIA. Married to John Brandt.

Greg Wade: Team leader of CRC's small but highly skilled group of IT specialists.

Rehka Gyan: IT expert. Greg's love interest. Friend of Rex, Catia, and Digger.

Jessica Lloyd: Rex's love interest, whom he was about to get engaged to when a terrorist bomb killed his entire family on March 11, 2004, at Atocha Station, Madrid, Spain.

Howard Lawrence: Director of the CIA.

Martin Richardson: Deputy director in charge of CIA operations.

Harrison Douglas: Director of the FBI.

About Remorseless

For over sixteen years, John and Jessica have been hiding a secret from Rex. But secrets have a way of finding a path to the light, and when that happens, Rex's life changes.

The changes will come gradually but will be irreversible.

The turmoil is immediate, and it has end-of-days, as in full-scale war with Russia, type consequences.

Prologue

There was more than one hell. In her short life, Abbie had been through several, and she was about to go through another.

"You knew what she'd planned. You didn't tell me," hissed the man she only knew as TJ.

Theirs was a world of fake names and a strict prohibition against sharing personal information. Notwithstanding, before Chrissy had escaped, she and Abbie had exchanged real names and personal information.

Abbie's real name was Eva Hansen. She was nineteen, born and bred in Orlando, Florida. She ran away from her abusive parents at age fifteen. Her parents never reported her as missing; Child Welfare did, weeks after she'd disappeared. That was it. That's what the entire United States law enforcement system knew about Eva Hansen.

Chrissy's real name was Elizabeth (Beth) Clayton. She was sixteen.

"I've put *you* in charge of them. Your job is to supervise and control them. Watch them. Maintain discipline among them. Prevent them from escaping. You were supposed to report to me that she'd left. You helped her get away."

Abbie was shaking her head violently. "I didn't…"

"Shut up, bitch! She was in your room less than an hour ago. She told you where she's going."

Abbie bit her nails and stared at the floor.

"You're not their mother. You're their supervisor. Supervisors don't fraternize with subordinates. I'm going to teach you to remember that. Where is she?"

"I don't know. She didn't tell me!"

TJ took two steps and struck her in the face. "Okay, in that case, I'll beat it out of you. And you'll never lie to me again."

At five-foot-nine and only a hundred- and thirty pounds, Abbie was on the verge of being underweight for her height. Her unkempt blonde hair was natural. Although she was still beautiful, four years in this hellhole as a sex slave, a bad diet, the physical abuse, smoking, alcohol, and drugs were ruining her looks rapidly.

Her broken nose was bleeding profusely when she got back to her feet. She was dwarfed by the thirty-something six-foot-two, obese, beer-bellied bully in a stinking black wife-beater vest.

"I don't know anything! I was with a client. When I came back, she was gone."

"You're lying!" A punch in the gut threw her to the floor in a sobbing heap, breathless.

"She was in your room." A vicious kick to her side cracked two ribs.

She was delirious from pain when he ripped her mini skirt and scanty underwear off. Removing his belt, he said to Johnny, one of his henchmen, "Get the other bitches in here. It's time for an obedience lesson."

Nude from the waist down, her body was shaking with fear, and tears were streaming down her face as she whimpered softly. She had been the subject of such a lesson once before. The scars and welts were permanent reminders. That time it was for being disrespectful to TJ in front of the girls. Abbie had witnessed such lessons many times. She knew begging wouldn't help. Even if she told him everything right now, it wouldn't stop the beating. He had a lesson for the teenage girls.

Besides, TJ found erotic pleasure in inflicting pain. The more pain, the more satisfying for him. As Abbie heard the whistling sound of the metal-studded leather belt traveling through the air, she was terrified of the pain she knew would come. But overriding the fear of the pain was the fervent belief that Chrissy had indeed escaped the abode of the condemned. Which meant the police were on their way already. She only had to hold out until they arrived.

She gave up the information five minutes later. Her escape from hell came a minute later when TJ kicked her in the side of the head, which mercifully rendered her unconscious.

The police never came. Chrissy was back in perdition less than two hours later and was killed two days after that.

Chapter One

It was an old couple out on an early morning walk with their dog that made the discovery. The dawn, pre-breakfast stroll was a daily ritual, even when it was a cold, bleak morning like this. On their route was a dog park where their little Jack Russell Terrier could run free. He had his favorite copse of small trees on the bank of the creek running through the park where he performed his daily toilette. This morning, as always, when they got to the park and unleashed him, he headed straight to his 'bathroom.' Usually, as soon as he was finished, he would let them know with a few short happy yaps and set off exploring while they performed the poop scoop regimen.

By nature, Jack Russells are happy, energetic dogs. Playful and noisy. But this morning, instead of the usual cheerfulness, his yapping signaled distress. The old couple hastened their pace. When they arrived on the bank of the brook, they drew a collective sharp breath as they laid eyes on the source of the little dog's anxiety.

Completely naked, her bruised and battered body lay in

the motionless pose of death, half in and half out of the water.

The 911 call made by the old gentleman from his cellphone was logged at 7:12 a.m. The nearest police patrol car was two miles away and arrived on the scene at 7:17 a.m.

Within minutes of their arrival, the two patrol officers called in the experts.

Forensics, Homicide, and the Medical Examiner were onsite thirty minutes later. By now, the entire area had been cordoned off with crime scene tape. It was a formality for the ME to declare the life of the young Caucasian female to be extinct. Lieutenant Benson Harris of the LAPD's 77th Street division and the forensics team quickly established that death had almost certainly occurred somewhere else and the body dumped in this location.

An ambulance transported the body to the state morgue, where an autopsy was performed to establish identification and the cause and time of death.

The old couple and occupants of nearby houses were questioned by the police, but no one had heard or seen anything suspicious.

Twenty-four hours later, Lieutenant Harris arrived at the morgue to get an update from the coroner.

"I found no jewelry, no tattoos, no distinguishing marks to help with identification. She's around sixteen, about two years past puberty," he told Harris.

The detective shook his head. His job was sometimes a thankless one, sometimes it was a rewarding one, but when an innocent child was murdered, his job was downright galling.

"This is one of the most brutal cases I've ever seen. A pack of wild dogs could hardly have done more damage to her," the coroner said as he led Harris into the cold room and retrieved the body from the fridge.

The man had not exaggerated; the broken, beaten, abused body of the young girl made the hardened homicide detective queasy. The face, back, and buttocks bore cuts and bruises, evidencing a brutal beating with fists, canes, and rubber hoses. Burn marks caused by cigarettes and lighters covered her stomach, arms, and legs. Bruises and lesions of the pelvic area, plus excessive vaginal and anal dilation, indicated she had been gang-raped and sodomized repeatedly. But despite the horrific suffering, death had not been caused by the beatings. According to the lab report, it was the lethal dose of fentanyl in the cocaine cocktail that killed her. The multiple needle marks on her arms indicated she had been injected with drugs regularly for an extensive period. Whether it was administered by herself or someone else was impossible to tell. At least the last jab would've been administered by someone else.

Harris knew it was wishful thinking to hope that she had been pumped full of drugs before she was tortured. The monsters who did this to her wouldn't have had much 'fun' otherwise.

The coroner had taken fingerprints and a DNA swab, then he'd restored the facial damage as best he could with sutures and make-up before taking photographs.

He uploaded the photos together with the forensic evidence to the computer systems of law enforcement agencies across the country. If there were a match in the databases, the computers were supposed to find it.

After the autopsy, the body was placed in the cold room while the search for identity continued. Until then, she would be Jane Doe.

Chapter Two

IN THE MISSING PERSON DATABASE

The computers remained silent. Sometimes it took up to thirty-six hours to find a match. Often, there were no matches at all.

Three days later, when it seemed as if Jane Doe was going to be just another number among the more than 100,000 annual drug overdose fatalities in America, Harris reviewed the evidence gathered. There wasn't much; in fact, there was nothing more than the information collected by the coroner. Without identification, it was only by luck or coincidence that he'd find the killers.

According to the National Missing and Unidentified Persons System (NamUs), 6.5 out of every 100,000 Americans were missing. Annually, about 600,000 people go missing, and approximately 4,400 unidentified bodies are discovered. About 1,000 of those bodies remain unidentified after a year. No wonder it was referred to as the Nation's Silent Mass Disaster.

The perpetrators of these types of sex crimes had the same modus operandi. Young children, some as young as ten, were shanghaied, hooked on drugs, and used as sex slaves to service pedophiles and other lowlifes of deviant sexual behavior up to ten times a day. This scenario was an everyday occurrence in numerous locations in numerous countries across the globe. Many of the children were snatched in the countries of their birth and smuggled across the borders into foreign countries. Wherever they ended up, their godforsaken lives were short and inhumane.

The punishment measured out to anyone trying to escape this hell was diabolical. The gang rapes, brutal beatings, and forced participation in unimaginable perversions, even bestiality, served a dual purpose: One, money. There were creatures prepared to pay to participate or watch this —therefore, there were creatures prepared to provide it. Two, it was a deterrent to the other children.

Jane Doe had been the recipient of such punishment.

After more than four decades in the police force, almost all of it on homicide and vice, Harris had seen some of the worst of humanity.

Sex trafficking, the second-fastest-growing crime in America, had reached epidemic proportions. The United Nations' International Labor Organization estimated it to be a $99 billion-a-year global industry. Some experts thought that number should be tripled, maybe even more. And law enforcement was losing the battle, big time. Prosecutions that ended in convictions were few. The word of a drug-addicted prostitute didn't sit as well with jurors as the word of sober, well-spoken pimps defended by clever, unprincipled lawyers.

Within the sex trafficking industry, according to the

United Nations' International Labor Organization, there was an international niche in which one million children, child sex slaves, were exploited for commercial purposes. They generated about $19 billion per year for their masters, about twenty percent of the total sex trafficking industry. Within the borders of the USA, it was estimated there were about 10,000 child sex slaves. In America alone, adults were purchasing children for sex at a rate of two-and-a-half million times per year.

To Harris, one of the big frustrations was, on the odd occasion when they got a conviction, the buyers—the pedophiles and sexual degenerates who fueled the child sex trade, were seldom held accountable. Their names and crimes were almost never made public. They just blended back into society, their families, jobs, and neighborhoods. Until the next time. The buyers faced little risk. "You're unlucky if you get caught," said Bjorn Sellstrom, the head of INTERPOL's Crimes Against Children unit in Lyon, France. "It's fairly free of risk to travel to another country and abuse children."

Harris clicked through the list of 'matches' produced by the facial recognition system. The system would read a photo of a human and map more than eighty different features, aka nodal points, i.e., distance between the eyes, size and shape of the ears, size and shape of the nose, depth of the eye sockets, the shape of the cheekbones, etcetera.

When asked to find a match, the system would read the photo and set out to find the best match in its database. The results were listed by the number of points that matched and expressed as a percentage. If the quality of the photos were good, the matching could reach up to ninety-nine percent. Anything over eighty percent was a bullseye. Anything below fifty percent was not worth looking at.

The highest score Harris had for Jane Doe was forty-eight percent. For no reason, he clicked on it anyway. He blinked a few times as he looked at the photo on the screen. "So much for the infallibility of computers," he mumbled. "The geeks would probably call it a glitch in the system."

He didn't need a computer program to tell him he had a match. His eyes told him so. The girl in the pictures in this database was Jane Doe in the morgue. The matching photo was a high-quality image of a teenage girl found in the missing persons database. Just to make sure, he asked the system to compare the fingerprints. It returned a hundred percent match.

Her name was Elizabeth (Beth) Clayton. About seven months ago, shortly after her sixteenth birthday, her parents had reported her as being abducted. She was in her second to last year of high school. The police treated it as a missing person's case. It was not an abduction—there was no forceful removal or detention. Her parents reported that it was a sleazy Hispanic man about fifteen years her senior who "abducted" her. However, all evidence indicated she had eloped with the man. The legal age of consent in America varied between states from sixteen to eighteen. In California, it was eighteen. In the neighboring Nevada, the age of consent was sixteen.

But that was irrelevant now; Lieutenant Harris had the unenviable task of breaking the devastating news to the Claytons and asking them to identify the body of their daughter.

Chapter Three

HOW?

Lieutenant Harris arrived at the Clayton house shortly after six o'clock on Friday evening with a heavy heart. There was never a good time to tell parents about the death of their child, and the circumstances of the death of Beth Clayton didn't make it any easier. Benson Harris was a decorated and honorable cop, a descendant of three generations of reputable law enforcement officers. Situations like these always made him feel as if he'd failed those he was supposed to protect.

The Claytons were a hardworking, middle-class Christian family in their early forties. Anthony was a human resource manager, and Emma a primary school teacher. They had three children, two girls, and a boy. Beth was the middle child.

Harris couldn't help but think about the so-called middle child syndrome. It was the hypothesis that middle children were excluded, ignored, or even outright neglected because of their birth order. Despite that, apparently, middle children were good mediators who wanted fairness in all situations. However, they were not as family oriented as their siblings and didn't have the same strong sense of belonging their brothers and sisters had. Those who claimed to know postulated the reason for it was that middle children often drew the short stick when it came to parental attention.

The Claytons were devastated by the news. They had been hoping their daughter would quickly overcome her idolization of that slimeball and return home. But seven months later, they'd given up on trying to find her. The motto no news is good news became their straw to cling to in the middle of a raging river. They were clinging to that straw until that fateful Friday night when Lieutenant Harris arrived on their doorstep and ripped the straw away from them.

On the way to the morgue, the grief-stricken silence in the car was broken when Mr. Clayton uttered one word. "How?"

After almost half a century on the police force, Harris had seen countless people reacting to the news of the death of a loved one. Yet, after all those years, he still didn't know how to tell loving, shocked, grieving parents how their child had been beaten, raped, sodomized, and murdered. There was no way to soften the news unless he lied—just a little. He started with the truth. "She died from a drug overdose. Fentanyl mixed in with cocaine." He knew they would soon see the body and the damage done to it by those animals. "She was assaulted, but I can assure you with the drugs in her system, she wouldn't have felt any pain."

Emma Clayton started sobbing softly again.

A catatonic stare out the window was all Anthony Clayton could muster.

At the morgue, he held his wife in his arms as they

stared down at the once lovely face of their beloved daughter and nodded in silence to Harris as the tears streamed down their faces.

Harris was relieved that they didn't ask to see the rest of their daughter's body.

Afterward, he took the Claytons to his office and went through the statements they gave when they reported their daughter missing and added any new information.

About ten months ago, Juan Garcia, a Hispanic man with the looks and swagger of a film star, purportedly born in Columbia but grew up in America, appeared on the scene. Both Beth's parents and her siblings immediately sensed he was trouble. They pleaded with Beth to stay away from him. She refused to heed their advice. She told them when she was with Juan, for the first time in her life, she felt a sense of belonging, appreciation, and worthiness.

The thought that maybe there was an element of truth in the middle-child hypothesis passed through Harris's mind, but he shook it off. The Claytons were a loving and caring family.

Juan Garcia was obviously a master manipulator.

Seven months ago, two days after her sixteenth birthday, Beth and Garcia disappeared. All messages to her mobile phone, email, Facebook, Twitter, and Instagram went unanswered. Within a week, all her social media accounts had been deleted. Emails sent to her bounced back undelivered. Then about three weeks after she'd disappeared, they'd received a one-line email from a Gmail account they'd never seen before saying that she and Juan were having a wonderful time in Cancún, Mexico, on the Yucatán Peninsula bordering the Caribbean Sea, known for its beaches, resorts, and nightlife.

The police's computer experts quickly confirmed that

the email indeed originated from an internet café in Cancún. They couldn't confirm if the email was sent by Beth, though.

The Claytons had no photo of Garcia. They'd seen him with their daughter only a few times and then only for short periods. It was as if he deliberately tried to avoid them. Now they knew why. But his face had been etched into their minds. They could help the police artist draw a detailed identikit.

Chapter Four

THAT'S THE SAME PERSON

Jane Doe had been identified. The missing person case of Elizabeth Clayton had been closed. Now Harris had to find the killers. He sighed deeply. With more than four hundred and fifty active gangs with a combined membership of more than forty-five thousand, the county and the City of Los Angeles had well and truly deserved the title Gang Capital of America. Most of the gangs were involved in both drug and sex trafficking. Many of them were extremely violent and utterly ruthless human beings, the kind that would butcher an innocent, defenseless teenager for the entertainment of a psychopathic audience.

The first person of interest to Harris was Juan Garcia. His name was as common in the Hispanic community as John Smith in the English-speaking community. A fake name, surely. Therefore, he'd distributed Garcia's identikit among his street networks. He got two replies. The first informant said the man in the sketch went by the name of Marc—no last name. He was some kind of pimp or something. The second informant had it on 'good authority' that the man's real name was Marc Martínez, nickname Rigoberto. It was only marginally less common than Juan Garcia. Another alias, no doubt. According to the informant, Martinez was rumored to be a freelance sex slave recruiter selling his 'merchandise' to the highest bidder.

When it came to computers, Harris was not exactly what one would describe as a power user. He had a certificate somewhere in a drawer that proclaimed him to be proficient in filling in electronic forms, writing reports, getting answers from search engines, writing emails, and so forth.

He started Googling for Juan Garcia, Marc Martinez, and Rigoberto but surrendered fifteen minutes later. A little frustrated, he walked over to one of his young detectives, O'Neal, who had proven himself a prodigy with computers, told him what he wanted, and went to the cafeteria to get a coffee and a bagel.

On the way back from the cafeteria to his office fifteen minutes later, O'Neal waved at him. "Got a result for you, boss, if you want to have a look."

Harris made the detour. He looked over O'Neal's shoulder at his computer screen. As soon as the young detective had his boss's attention, he launched into a technical soliloquy about how he queried the various social media and law enforcement databases, talking about strings, concatenations, lookups, primary keys, SQL queries, etcetera.

Harris interrupted. "O'Neal, you're a wunderkind. I'm a sixty-five-year-old fart. I retire in a few months. It's impossible to teach me anything because I know everything. But if perchance, there's anything I don't know, it's only because it's not worth knowing or too late for me to learn it. So, cut the verbal diarrhea and show me what you've got."

O'Neal mumbled something about grumpy old men, old dogs, and new tricks and opened an image of a young Hispanic-looking man who could've been in his late twenties or early thirties and possessed film star looks.

"I found this image in the National Missing and Unidentified Persons System under the name Marc Martinez. Unbelievable as it may sound, the facial recognition system found about ten percent similarities between the face on the identikit and this photo." He opened the image of the identikit of Juan Garcia, dragged it next to the photo of Marc Martinez, and looked up at Harris. "I don't know about your sixty-five-year-old eyes, boss, but my twenty-five-year-old eyes are telling me that's the same person."

"Son of a gun," whispered Harris as he stared at the screen. "I'm impressed, O'Neal."

"You're welcome."

"Let me guess, this scumbag's name and face came up because another young girl has eloped with him. Right?"

"Yes, sir. Courtney Lloyd. According to her mother, she was abducted by this guy a few months ago. However, the police established that she was not abducted. She went with him voluntarily."

"She eloped?"

"Precisely."

"Good job. Thanks for the help. Email it to me."

O'Neal smiled as he clicked the mouse twice. "Doneski."

"Who the hell is Doneski?"

O'Neal was shaking with laughter. "Not who, what."

"Okay, boy genius, what?"

"The Urban Dictionary says doneski is the state or aura of being done—"

"The Urban Dictionary?"

O'Neal was grinning. "Yes, kind of like the Oxford Dictionary for modern man."

Harris slowly raised his middle finger at O'Neal, turned, and left, shaking his head and mumbling something indecipherable but easy to guess.

Chapter Five

AN URGENT PHONE CALL TO MAKE

Lieutenant Harris arrived at Ms. Lloyd's house shortly after ten o'clock the next morning.

Ms. Lloyd's caregiver, Anne, forewarned him about her medical condition and was very reluctant to agree to a visit from the police.

"It's about her daughter," said Harris. "I must see her in person."

That was enough to swing Anne.

The moment Harris laid eyes on Ms. Lloyd, he knew she must have been a beautiful woman before cancer and chemotherapy had ravaged her body. She had an unnaturally pale complexion, was in a state of near-anorexia, and her blue eyes were almost lifeless. A colorful headscarf covered her head, which he suspected was hairless. The ravages of chemotherapy.

Harris could see Ms. Lloyd didn't have long to live and was seriously wondering if he should continue with the interview. But then there was a chance her daughter might still be alive. No matter how small the chance, as long as it existed, it had to be pursued.

Yet he had to be careful not to create false hope. Ms. Lloyd was in no condition to receive bad news. However, Harris had the hard-earned experience of knowing that it was always best to be honest, even if it hurt. He'd explained to her how he came across Courtney's case and the photos of Martinez while looking into another case. He didn't give her a name but told her the victim had been killed. Although he could see that the news shocked her somewhat, her strength surprised him when she told him the whole story of Courtney's abduction. Her voice was stronger than he'd expected. Her mind was clear and coherent despite the massive doses of painkillers coursing through her veins.

Ms. Jessica Lloyd was thirty-nine years old. The father of her twins, Reece and Courtney, left her more than sixteen years ago to join the Marines. At the time they broke up, she didn't know she was pregnant. She never contacted him after he had left, never told him about the children, and never got married. She didn't give him the name of the twins' father.

The children were her pride and *raison d'être*. They were the most respectful, loving kids any parent could dream of. At school, their teachers and peers loved them. They had many friends, and both excelled in academics and sports.

They loved and respected their mother, and for the past seven years, as she had been fighting a losing battle with breast cancer, they had doted on her and cherished her. But the cancer had defeated all treatments deployed against it until she finally realized she was on death row, only awaiting the date of her execution. Four months ago, when her oncologist told her there were no more treatment options, she knew her date with the

Grim Reaper was near. Nothing but a miracle would stop the cancer. She believed in God, and she believed in miracles, and she believed until the miracle happened, she had to prepare for her death. At least she had time to get her affairs in order.

After that verdict, she went home and told the twins. The news was hard on both, but it was as if something had snapped in Courtney. She started crying, stormed out of the kitchen, and locked herself in her room for two straight days.

When she came out of her room, she had changed. She had turned into a rebel. Against God. Against Reece. Against her mother. Against society, authority, humanity, and everything in between. Within weeks she had to get psychological counseling for bulimia nervosa, an eating disorder.

By now, Jessica's condition had deteriorated so much she was practically bedridden and required a permanent live-in caregiver.

Soon, Courtney got mixed up with the wrong crowd at school. Her schoolwork suffered. She got in trouble with the teachers. She lost her friends. Reece tried to help and cover for her. Then she started smoking marijuana, and soon after, she moved on to cocaine. She used all her pocket money to buy the stuff. She borrowed money from Reece and her friends. Then she started stealing Jessica's jewelry. Reece knew about it, and he tried to stop her and reason with her, all in vain.

About two months ago, Marc Martinez, a Hispanic man with the looks and swagger of a movie star, started dating Courtney. Reece took an instant dislike in him. Jessica only met him weeks later and immediately disliked the man, too. But she didn't dare say a word about the relationship for fear of alienating her daughter even more. As long as

Courtney didn't run away with the man, there was hope that she might come to her senses.

Reece pleaded with her to break up with Martinez. She refused. She told them when she was with him, for the first time in her life, she felt like she belonged. She needed psychological help, but she refused to admit it.

Clearly, Martinez was a master manipulator.

Four weeks ago, two days after her sixteenth birthday, Courtney and Martinez disappeared. Jessica's hands were shaking when she showed Harris the handwritten note from Courtney.

"Mom, I'm leaving you and Reece. If there is a God, he has declared war on our family. It is my presence that's causing all the pain and suffering. I can't watch you die. This vengeful God might leave you and Reece alone when I'm gone. Marc will take care of me. He's the only person in the world who loves me. Courtney."

"Ever since she got involved with this man, Reece, Anne, and I have been hoping and praying that Courtney would overcome her idolization of that creep. That was until four weeks ago when I found that note on my bedside table when I woke up in the morning.

"I yelled at God to get it over. To rather let me die and spare my daughter. But instead of God, Reece and Anne rushed into my room."

All messages to Courtney's mobile phone and social media accounts went unanswered. Soon, all her social media accounts disappeared. Emails sent to her bounced back undelivered. Then, about two weeks ago, they received a short email from a Gmail account they'd never seen before saying that she and Marc were having a wonderful time in Cancún, Mexico.

The police's computer experts confirmed that the email indeed originated from an internet café in Cancún. But they couldn't confirm if the email was sent by Courtney.

Reece had three photos of Martinez, which he had taken covertly. When Harris asked him why he felt it necessary to take the photos, Reece shrugged. "I had a bad feeling about him. I wanted to check him out online."

"And did you?"

Reece nodded. "I found many people with the name Marc Martinez online. There are many social media profiles for the name. A lot of them have no photos, but none of them was the man who took my sister away. There are also many Google images for that name, but none of them was this man. Of course, he could've given us a fake name."

"You're right. He gave you a false name." Harris couldn't help but notice the boy's dark, penetrating eyes and, for a sixteen-year-old boy, a respectful yet confident disposition.

"I told Courtney I'd checked him out online, and he was nowhere to be found. She was furious that I had done such a thing. She didn't talk to me for three days."

"Did you ever get an address for him? Did he have a job? What about a car?"

"No address and no job that we know of. He had a motorcycle. Courtney was almost as smitten with that bike as she was with him." He pulled up some photos of the motorcycle on his cellphone and showed them to Harris. One of them displayed the license number.

Harris didn't tell them that he was almost sure the registration would be in the name of someone who didn't exist. "I will check out the bike and upload the photos to the system. Hopefully, we'll find a match and track him down. But don't expect a speedy resolution. These cases take time." He didn't have the heart to tell them that most were never solved.

On the other hand, he didn't know that Jessica already knew all those statistics, that she knew much of the horrific details of the child sex slave industry. Since reporting that Courtney was missing, she firmly believed that the police had been working day and night to find her daughter. Her hopes were shattered as she listened to Harris explaining why he was there.

They've made no progress. This is the first time Courtney's case is getting attention, and only because they accidentally stumbled across a connection between her case and that of a murdered child.

Jessica was relieved when Harris finally left. She was drained, but she had an urgent phone call to make to a lawyer in Washington, D.C., before she could rest.

Chapter Six

I HAD NO IDEA

It was early morning on the Ranch, a twenty-thousand-acre property in Yavapai County in the western part of Arizona. The property had been in John Brandt's family for four generations. He had turned it from a cattle farm into CRC's headquarters and training facility. It was a secluded place, pristine and beautiful. The air was clean, the spring water fresh, and the climate perfect. With arrays of solar panels, a few wind generators, and banks of Tesla batteries, the Ranch was self-sufficient in electricity. The homestead comprised three beautifully remodeled homes and two barns converted into offices, a mission control center called the Ops Center, a communications center called the Cyber Room, and a lecture room. There were also three helipads and a landing strip long enough for most small jets to take off and land, including CRC's Dassault Falcon 2000 DX private jet.

John Brandt stood at six-foot-two in his socks. A handsome man with gray hair and hazel eyes, stately comportment, and in excellent shape for someone of seventy-odd years. He was a veteran of the Cold War, which the politicians officially declared over in 1991 when Russian communism collapsed. John and other Cold War warriors were told that their skills had become obsolete, and they had to take desk jobs or early retirement. John thought they were making a big mistake and told them so. He was right. By 1995 he had enough and left the CIA.

Six years later, in 2001, after the 9/11 attacks, the CIA came knocking on his door, begging him to establish Crisis Response Consultancy (CRC), a private military contractor specializing in black operations on behalf of the CIA and other US security agencies.

Rex and John were out walking with Digger and Cupcake. The latter was a short-haired, brindle-colored Dutch Shepherd. She was a gift to John and his wife Christelle from Rex and Catia when John got out of the hospital after brain surgery a few years ago.

Rex had inherited Digger from his friend, Trevor Madigan, a former SAS operative from Australia who'd been killed in an ambush in Afghanistan. Digger, an Australian military dog, had been his companion since Trevor asked Rex to take care of him with his dying breath. Rex, mortally scared of dogs ever since one had attacked him when he was a small child, had agreed. He and Digger had become inseparable mates. Rex never learned to give Digger proper commands like military dog handlers do. But working as a team on many missions over the years, they had developed a unique communication system between them. Some of Rex's colleagues thought the two spoke some kind of 'language' only they understood. The reality was Rex had learned to be very attentive to Digger's behavior.

They were less than a mile from the homestead when John's phone rang. He looked at the caller ID. A call from his lawyer in D.C. was not an everyday occurrence, and never this early in the morning.

It must be important.

He answered and dropped back so that he could have a private conversation while Rex and Digger kept walking. Cupcake stayed with John.

The conversation was about half an hour in duration. John Brandt had one of the biggest, if not *the* biggest, dilemmas of his life.

When Rex returned, he found the Old Man sitting on a big rock staring at the eastern horizon. John was not a man who wore his heart on his sleeve, but now disquiet was plastered all over his face. In the fifteen-plus years Rex had known the Old Man, he had seldom seen him like this. "What's wrong, John? You look like you've had an encounter with a ghost."

"It's a long story, son. I want you to sit down and hear me out." He motioned to a nearby rock.

Rex sat down.

Digger and Cupcake stood around for a few minutes until they realized they were going to be there for a while, then plonked themselves down on the ground between John and Rex.

"Way back in 2005, shortly after you joined the Marines, one of my talent scouts brought you to my attention. I followed your progress throughout your training. By the end of your Marine training, I was sufficiently impressed with your attitude and abilities. I pulled the necessary strings to get you transferred to Delta Force. Again, I followed your progress until I was satisfied that you would be an asset to CRC. I started making arrangements to bring you over. But before I did that, I ran a comprehensive background check on you. And that's when I found out about Jessica Lloyd." He paused as he tried to find the right words.

Rex opened his mouth but closed it again. Jessica, or Jessie, as he called her, was the girl he fell in love with during their university years. After completing his master's degree in 2004, he and Jessie accompanied his family on vacation in Europe. He had already bought the engagement ring and was planning to propose on March 11, 2004. But that very morning, at Atocha Station, Madrid, Spain, tragedy struck. A terrorist bomb killed his entire family, parents, and two younger siblings, while he and Jessie were at a nearby coffee shop buying coffee for everyone.

That incident transformed the peaceful young man who'd looked forward to a life with the woman he loved and a career in the US Foreign Service into an emotionally damaged, brooding, angry man. For months after his family died, he was a directionless, self-pitying drunkard. Then he got a purpose. He broke up with Jessie and joined the Marines. He had only one mission in life—to avenge his losses. From the Marines, he was recruited into Delta Force and trained as a Special Forces operator and from there into John Brandt's black ops outfit, CRC, where he was trained as one of the world's most lethal assassins—a capacity in which he'd rained terror, destruction, and death on the enemies of the US. There was no place for a woman, let alone children, in his life then.

Now, it felt like it was in another life, someone else's life. Rex wasn't that man anymore. He'd burned out the anger in rooting out terrorists and drug and arms dealers who supported and financed them.

John continued in a whispered voice. "When I learned about her, you were in the final month of Delta Force training, and she was a mother of twins—"

"She got married?"

"No, Rex, there was no one after you. She has remained single to this day."

Rex's face turned paper-white.

Digger was on his feet and next to Rex in two steps as he sensed the anxiety in his alpha. He nuzzled Rex while making soft, comforting noises as if to say, "Don't worry, buddy. I'm here."

"Are you... I... I am..."

"Yes, Rex, you're their father," John spoke softly as he looked Rex in the eyes. "I'm..."

"My God, John, what have you done? Two innocent children. Fourteen years you've known!"

John held his hand up to quiet Rex. "Let me finish."

"Don't say another word, you son of a bitch," Rex hissed as he stood. "I've worked for you all these years, John Brandt. I've been loyal to you. I've respected you. But you lied to me, you bastard. For fourteen years, because of your underhandedness and selfishness, two children grew up without a father."

John didn't interrupt. Rex's reaction was justified. He'd always feared this day would come, and he'd feared how it would impact the man who'd become like a son to him.

"Do you have no conscience? Is there not a shred of decency in you? Forget about loyalty. You wouldn't even know how to spell it."

John made no reply.

"Answer me! You piece of shit."

John stood and looked Rex in the eyes as he spoke measuredly. "Okay, I'll answer you. Now sit down and shut your damn mouth until I'm finished."

Rex remained on his feet. Unspeaking.

"You've got no idea what's going on. If you've got the

guts to hear the truth, sit down, shut up, and listen. Or get lost. What's it going to be, Dalton?"

Rex sat down slowly.

"When I learned about your relationship with Jessica Lloyd during the background check on you, I had to do a background check on her as well. That's when I learned about the children. I couldn't ignore that. I regarded it as my duty to ensure that she and the children would never fall on hard times. Therefore, I instructed my lawyer to set up a trust fund for her and the children. Her late father was a Vietnam veteran. We used that to make up a story about this anonymous person who served with him in Vietnam and how they made a pact to look out for each other's families if it ever became necessary. She believed the story.

"I've never met her. My lawyer has always been the go-between. He knows your name and that you're the father of her children. He doesn't know you work for me but knows he can contact you through me. I hired private detectives to keep me in the know about her life. I instructed the lawyer to let her know from time to time that he could track you down and let you know about your paternity. But, over the years, she steadfastly refused to have anything to do with you until a few years ago. It was after she'd been diagnosed with cancer that she wanted to know what had become of you. The lawyer told her you were serving in one of the military's special forces units but didn't know which one. She didn't want to know more than that and remained adamant she didn't want to make contact with you.

"But that has changed. Last night she phoned the lawyer. She wants to see you. She said she has something very important to tell you and very little time to do it."

"I'm sorry, John." Rex was shaking his head slowly. "I had no idea."

"Of course, you didn't. There's more. She was diagnosed with stage four breast cancer at age thirty-two."

"Seven years ago," breathed Rex, shaking his head slowly.

John nodded. "The twins were about nine. Since then, she's been through the chemo and radiation hell more than just a few times. Every time the cancer went into remission just to return with a vengeance—always more aggressively than before. A week before her thirty-ninth birthday, the cancer was back. The treatments resumed but to no avail. Six months ago, her oncologist told her there was no more treatment. She has less than a year. In the last month or so, the cancer has metastasized to her spine and brain. She now has a full-time caretaker to help with the children and household chores."

Rex nodded slowly as he stared into middle space. "What are their names?"

"Reece and Courtney. Beautiful and exemplary children."

"My grandfather's and her grandmother's names," murmured Rex. He looked Digger in the eyes as he scratched his ears. "Do you believe this, buddy? I've been a father for sixteen years without even knowing."

Digger whined softly and put his head on Rex's lap.

Rex stood. "I need to talk to Catia."

John remained seated on his rock. "Yes, you have to. Be honest with her and yourself, and it will all work out well."

Rex replied with a nod. That was exactly what he'd intended to do.

Rex met Catia Romano, an Italian Jew, in 2010 when she provided him with part of his European tradecraft training. At the end of Rex's training in Rome, he and Catia, although they didn't say so, knew much more than a tutor-student relationship had developed between them. They got married in May 2016.

Catia was an only child. Terrorists had also killed her parents. A lone assassin working for the Jihad Council, the military wing of Hezbollah, poisoned them while on holiday in the Caribbean. The official version was they drowned while on a boat trip. It happened in 2005, the year after Rex's family was killed. Mossad recruited and trained her as a mission support specialist—a *sayan*—the Hebrew word for helper.

Chapter Seven

THE FORMER KILLER

Walking back home with Digger next to him, Rex's mind was bombarded with what felt like hundreds of thoughts, all ending with question marks.

He wasn't worried about how Catia would react. She knew all about Jessie. Undoubtedly, she would be surprised, maybe even shocked, to hear about his fathership. But she could hardly be more surprised or shocked than he was.

He pushed those thoughts aside to attend to the nagging question flashing through his brain.

How do you feel about Jessie?

I don't know.

You've never dealt with it, have you?

I didn't have to deal with it because the Rex Dalton who loved Jessica Lloyd died in the bomb explosion with the rest of his family on March 11, 2004, at Atocha Station in Madrid. For many years after, the Rex Dalton that walked out of the station that day was incapable of love. The Rex Dalton who died was a diplomat—a man of peace. The one who survived was a killer—a man of violence.

What would you've done if you knew she was pregnant?

I would've married her, of course. What a stupid question. I'd never have forsaken my parental duties.

Says the killer—a man of violence. The man who lived for revenge. What would you have taught your kids? How to hate? How to seek revenge? How to be heartless killers?

Digger yelped. It was enough to pull Rex out of his brown study. It was as if Digger had eavesdropped on Rex's thoughts and was telling him, "Ease up on yourself, buddy. There's no sense in beating yourself to a pulp about conjectures."

Digger's tongue was lolling out, his lips curled slightly upward at the corners. Digger's smile.

Catia was in the kitchen making breakfast when Rex and Digger walked in.

At five-foot-nine, Catia was tall for a woman. She had shoulder-length waves of stunning auburn hair and a scattering of light freckles across her nose attested to the natural red in her hair. A near-constant dazzling smile lit up her face—she was breathtakingly beautiful. Rex would tell anyone who wanted to listen that her eyes were the color of the Mediterranean at times, blue and aquamarine at others; they changed with her mood and what she wore.

"What's wrong?" were her first words. She handed him a cup of espresso. "Do you want to talk about it before, during, or after breakfast?"

"During breakfast, I am too hungry to wait."

Rex was right. Catia was surprised, not shocked, though. And she had only two questions.

"What would you have done if you knew about the children?"

"I honestly don't know, Catia. Part of me wants to believe I would've married her and tried to be a good father. Another part of me knows I would've been incapable of it."

"How do you feel about her?"

"You know the story. There was a time when I loved her. I was going to ask her to marry me. It was a long time ago, in a different epoch, in another life, when I was a different person. Now, I only have deep feelings of sorrow for her. She had hell on earth. Single mother of two. Cancer at thirty-two. A few months to live. I can't help but think the only thing I could've changed in her life would've been to be there as a husband and a father."

"That's speculation, Rex. You could only have been there if you had known and if she would've let you marry her. None of that happened. And according to John, that was her choice."

Rex nodded contemplatively. He told her about the debate with his alter ego on the way home.

"So, I'm married to the killer version of you, the violent man?"

He noticed the fleeting smile in her eyes. "No, Catia, you're married to the *former* killer. You made me human again."

Catia got up from her chair, walked around the table, pulled Rex up from his chair, and put her arms around his waist. "Rex, I know this is a difficult time for you, but I want you to know that I love you, and I will always support you."

Rex pulled his beautiful wife forward and kissed her. Six years after getting married to her, Rex was still madly in love with this exceptional woman.

Chapter Eight

A LOVABLE PERSON

On the ninety-minute flight from the Ranch to Los Angeles in the CRC jet, early the next morning, Rex was nervous. Catia could see it. She nudged him. "C'mon, talk about it. I'm just as nervous as you are."

"How does someone prepare for something like this?"

"I don't know, but I'd imagine honesty with her and with yourself will be the best approach."

He regarded that as wise counsel that he intended to follow, just like he'd followed the same advice from the Old Man the day before.

"I guess she wants to tell me about the children. But I think it's more than just introducing me to my children. They're minors. If she dies, I'm probably their legal guardian. How do you feel about that? Two teenagers in your life?"

Catia smiled. "I've been thinking about it since yesterday. And, ignoring the tragic circumstances, I'm excited. They might not be *our* children, but I'll love them as if they are."

"Did I ever tell you what a remarkable human being you are?"

Catia laughed. "Never."

Rex took his cellphone out and scrolled to the pictures John had given him the night before. He connected his phone via Bluetooth to the big screen in the cabin and started scrolling through the pictures taken over the years of Jessie and the twins as they grew up.

Strangely, the moment the screen went on, Digger opened his eyes from a deep sleep. He jumped off his chair and went to sit next to Rex on the floor, facing the screen.

Contrary to popular belief, dogs recognize a face on a digital device if the screen is big enough. On the screens of mobile phones and tablets, they struggle. But this was a big-screen TV. Digger's wagging tail and soft yelps told them he must've sensed what was coming would be important to Rex and Catia.

After a few photos of the twins, Catia said, "Obviously, they've inherited their good looks from their mother, yet there could be no doubt who their father is. Especially the boy, he's going to be one handsome *cavaliere*. Just like his dad."

Rex smiled. "I think it's time for your visit to the optometrist."

She punched him in the shoulder playfully. "There's absolutely nothing wrong with my eyes."

There were a few pictures of Jessie and the twins when she graduated from Yale with a Ph.D. in History. The twins were four years old then.

John's trust fund had paid for her studies. His contacts in high places got her an interview at UCLA, where she secured the lecturer's position. The trust fund had also paid the deposit and half of the monthly mortgage payments on the house in which she and the children lived in Glendale. It was not only one of the safest areas of LA but, according to the FBI, one of the ten safest cities in America. The best place to raise kids without having to worry about safety.

But then, as Jessie would've been able to testify, the kind of safety the FBI referred to didn't prevent scum such as Marc Martinez from seducing underage girls from that neighborhood.

Rex couldn't help but feel embarrassed about jumping to the wrong conclusions the day before when John broke the news to him. John had really taken good care of Jessie and the children in the material sense of the word.

He did what I was supposed to do.

Rex went quiet as he pondered parenthood. He knew absolutely nothing about children except that he'd heard that raising teenagers could be a real challenge. Apparently, they were controlled by hormones which made them moody and rebellious. And, from what he'd heard, there was no cure for it. The parents just had to tough it out. Having two of them sounded daunting. How Catia could not be horrified about the prospect was beyond him.

Starting with a newborn baby and raising it suddenly looked a lot easier than starting with two sixteen-year-old 'newborns.'

He sighed. He didn't even know what he had to do to love them like a father is supposed to love his children. He stopped himself from thinking how on earth they'd get themselves to love *him*. They would love Catia, no doubt. She was a lovable person.

Me? — not so much.

Chapter Nine

THE MISSING SIXTEEN YEARS

Rex left Catia and Digger at the hotel and took an Uber to Jessie's home in Glendale.

He arrived at her front door at 10:00 a.m. as per the lawyer's instructions.

There was nothing that could've prepared Rex for the sight that met him when Anne led him into Jessie's bedroom. There was a modern hospital bed with white linen sheets. Next to the bed was a portable oxygen generator that was connected to a long tube ending in a nasal cannula, a small tube that split into two prongs from which a mixture of air and oxygen flowed into each nostril of the pale skeletal female, blending in with the white sheets on the bed. She was asleep. The ravages of cancer had left only small hints by which Rex could recognize the woman he once loved—in another life. And he was about to learn that cancer was not the only thing to blame for her condition.

Anne went to the bed and took Jessie's hand. "He's here," she said softly.

Jessie opened her eyes and removed the cannula. "How

are you, Rex?" Her voice was strong, and she had a little smile on her lips.

"I am good, Jessie. It's good to see you again. I just wish it was not in such dreadful circumstances." Rex was about to find out just how dreadful they were.

She pointed to the easy chair next to the bed. "There's a lot to talk about."

Rex nodded but remained on his feet. "Jessie, before we start, please allow me to ask your forgiveness for—"

Jessie raised her hand to stop him. "Let's not go down that road, Rex. I forgave you a long time ago. I hope you can do the same."

"I'm not aware of anything I should forgive. You've done nothing wrong. I'm—"

"As soon as you shut up and listen, you'll know I have."

She sounded a bit like John the day before. "Sorry, I'll be quiet."

"Shortly after you left me in February 2005, I discovered I was pregnant with twins. At that stage, I hated you so much I wanted nothing to do with you. Withholding the pregnancy from you was my revenge. It took me years to get over the hatred. It took much longer to get over the love. I was too proud to go looking for you. Besides, if you loved me, you would've returned to me. Five years down the track, the children and I had our lives. I presumed you had yours. We were happy. I was not going to ruin that with a man who didn't love me."

"But... I... I loved you, Jessie. I had an engagement ring with me that day in Madrid. I was going to ask you to marry me when we were in Barcelona. But—"

"I understand, Rex. It took me a long time to realize that those terrorist bombs didn't just physically kill and

41

maim all those people. They also killed and maimed many more people psychologically."

Rex nodded slowly. "Jessie, I want you to know I learned about the children only yesterday. I'm still trying to come to grips with the idea."

"Would it have made a difference if you knew about them before?"

Rex was seriously tempted to tell her he would've returned to her if it had happened before he had met Catia. But he stuck to his resolution to be honest even if it would hurt. "I've been asking myself the same question since yesterday. Honestly, I probably would not have returned to you, Jessie. But I'm sure I would've wanted to meet the children and build a relationship with them."

"Thank you for being honest, Rex. Who told you about the children?"

"The man who has been your benefactor all these years. I only learned about that yesterday, too. I've been working for him all this time, but he only told me about you and the children yesterday."

"What's his name?"

"John Brandt." Rex continued and told her everything John had told him, about the trust fund, about the ruse that he was an old war buddy of her dad, and how John had kept tabs on her over the years. He told her about his life after he left her, about the Marines, Delta Force, CRC, Digger, and Catia.

"I wish I could meet this John Brandt."

"He'd welcome that. I'll let him know."

"Good. Let's move on. There's still much to cover." She replaced the cannula under her nose. "The reason I made contact is about the children. Obviously, John Brandt's informants told him about my battle with cancer for the past seven years, and I assume he told you?"

"He did."

"Well, then you probably also know I got the death sentence about six months ago. The oncologist reckoned I had about eighteen months at most. He was overoptimistic —it will be much less. Maybe another four to five months."

Rex nodded.

"When I got the news, I came home and told the children. Until that day, no one would've convinced me there were two better-behaved kids on earth. Through the years, they've been my pride and joy. Through thick and thin, they've loved and supported me. They're disciplined. They respected authority. Their fellow students and teachers loved them. They excelled at academic work and sports. They were model children."

Jessie's body started shaking. Tears streamed down her face while she told Rex how Courtney fell into Marc Martinez's trap. She told him about Lieutenant Harris's visit and the realization that the police had done nothing to find her. They were hoping for a lucky break, hoping that she or Reece would have Martinez's home address or something. She also told him what Harris told her about Elizabeth Clayton. The same man who took Courtney away took Elizabeth Clayton away in the same manner. And Elizabeth had been murdered. Rex would soon discover that Harris had spared her the details of Elizabeth's killing.

Rex swallowed hard at the lump in his throat. There was no logic to it, but he couldn't shake the feeling that he was responsible for it.

If I were there for them like a real father was supposed to be…
I could have…

43

But you were never given the opportunity to be a father. Even if you were with them, it wouldn't have prevented the cancer.

Rex shook his head subtly, as if to shake the illogical thoughts from his brain. As those thoughts left, they made room for the first wave of anger about the unscrupulous reprobate who took his daughter away from her mother on her deathbed.

He couldn't explain how it was possible to love someone he'd never met. Yet, what he felt was love, unmistakably. He *had* to protect her. He *had* to find her. He *had* to rescue her or die trying.

The love for our offspring and the urge to protect them must be coded into our DNA.

Jessie's voice was soft. "I called you for two reasons, Rex." Her hand was shaking when she held it up, showing two fingers. "First, I want you to find our daughter and bring her back to me. The police won't. Not in the time that I have left on this earth. My soul won't leave this realm in peace unless I see my angel's face one more time. Two, when I'm gone, you'll have to take care of our children. Are you up to it?"

Rex was nodding slowly. "You have my word, Jessie. I *will* find Courtney." He took a deep breath, "Am I up to being a parent? I have no idea. But believe me, I'm going to do my best. I owe them sixteen years to start with."

Jessie nodded. "That's good enough for me, Rex. One more thing. I'd like to meet your wife if she's willing. I want to tell her about our children."

"I'm sure she'll be happy to meet you, Jessie."

"If you let me rest for a few hours now and come back at four this afternoon, I will introduce you to your son. He's a good boy, Rex, just like his father. You'll be proud of him.

I told the children all about you. Until you left me, that is. You'll have to fill in the missing sixteen years."

Chapter Ten

WHAT DO I CALL YOU?

Rex was back at four o'clock. He expected it to be awkward. What do you say to your sixteen-year-old son, who you didn't know existed until yesterday?

But it wasn't nearly as uneasy as Rex thought it would be.

When he entered Jessie's room, she was sitting up against a stack of pillows. She looked much better than when he left her earlier. Reece was sitting in the chair Rex had occupied that morning. There was an additional chair. Rex assumed it was brought in for him.

Reece stood when Rex entered. He was tall for his age, about five foot nine, with dark hair, dark penetrating eyes, and the build of a gymnast.

Jessie smiled. *He looks just like his father when I met him.* Her voice was strong again. "Rex, this is your son, Reece. Reece, this is your dad, Rex Dalton."

His son had a firm grip and looked him in the eyes when they shook hands.

Looking at him in real life now, Rex tried to see why

Catia thought the boy looked like him. He couldn't find anything. He'd forgotten that people usually couldn't see physical attributes of themselves in others.

Reece said, "What do I call you? Sir, Dad, or Rex?"

Rex was impressed. His son was a respectful and confident young man. "People called my dad sir; he was a teacher. Dad is a title a man must earn. So, until *you* think I've earned it, you may call me Rex, if I may call you Reece."

"You may."

Rex relaxed and smiled. *Things are going to work out well between us.*

Unbeknown to him, Jessie had similar thoughts, hence the little smile playing on her face.

"Rex, we grew up with Mom telling us you had left her to join the Marines before she even knew she was expecting us. She told me earlier you didn't know about us until yesterday?"

"Yes, Reece, it is true. I wish I'd known earlier."

The boy nodded. "I know Mom kept it from you... but she never kept it from us. She gave Courtney and me a choice. She was always willing to contact you if we wanted. We decided that if Mom didn't want to see you, neither did we."

"I understand... Well, I think I do."

Reece nodded and wiped tears from his eyes. "I wish Courtney was here; she is the best sister any brother could ever hope to have. I hope you will find the snake who took her away soon."

"I promised your mother I'll find her. I intend to keep the promise."

Reece nodded and took a deep breath to regain his composure. "Mom says you told her all about your life in the military. But she said she wants you to tell it to me in your own words. Will you?"

"Of course. You want to hear it now?"

"Yes, please."

Rex told his son about the killing of his family in Madrid and the aftermath when he left their mother to join the Marines. He was not making excuses, just stating the facts. Therefore, he didn't go into detail about his state of mind. Reece and Jessie had their own loss to deal with. Then he told his son the rest, which was what he told his mother earlier in the day, about the Marines, Delta Force, John Brandt, CRC, Digger, and Catia. He left out the secret stuff, which he hadn't shared with Jessie either.

It was almost six o'clock when Jessie told them she needed to rest.

Reece accompanied Rex to the front door. "I wish Courtney could be here. What can I do to get my sister back?"

"Well, a list of names of the friends she'd been hanging out with at school and elsewhere the last few months before she disappeared will be very helpful," said Rex.

"I think I can do better than that, but I am worried that I might get into trouble for what I did."

"What did you do?"

"I've been tapping her phone ever since she got mixed up with Marc Martinez. A friend at school helped me set it up. I have her address book, a history of all calls, a copy of all text messages, and a copy of all chat messages. She and her new friends used Signal. I didn't tell Lieutenant Harris about it; I was too scared. I have a friend at school whose dad is a lawyer; I thought maybe I could talk to him first. But I don't want Mom to go through more stress and hardship if I get in trouble with the law. And I don't want my friend who helped me bug her phone to get in trouble either."

"Have you tapped anyone else's phone?"

"No, never."

"Okay, in that case, don't worry about it. You won't get into any trouble. Where did you store the information?"

"On a USB flash drive. It's in my room. Shall I get it for you?"

"Yes, please. Would you perhaps also be able to get me a piece of clothing or something she wore often or always had with her, like a purse or handbag or something?"

"For Digger?"

Rex was surprised by the boy's sharp mind. "Yes."

Reece came back with the flash drive and a pink t-shirt. "I won this in a raffle at school last year. Courtney wanted it and kept on pestering me to buy a ticket; she reckoned it increased her chances of winning by a hundred percent. I didn't even try to explain to her that her math was wrong. Anyhow, I won, and she immediately confiscated it to sleep in. The day she absconded, she left it in my room. I've kept it in my drawer ever since as a reminder of her."

Rex could see that the boy was fighting hard against the emotions welling up in him. He put his hand on his son's shoulder. "Reece, I can't promise that I will find your sister, but I can promise you that I intend to move heaven and earth to find her."

"That's all Mom and I can hope for. It was a shock for us to find out how little the police has accomplished in all this time."

They spent a few more minutes talking about school before they exchanged phone numbers and shook hands.

"I'm glad to finally have met you, Rex."

"Likewise, Reece. Thank you for seeing me."

Chapter Eleven

I'VE EARNED THE RIGHT

It was eleven o'clock the morning after Rex had visited Jessie and Reece. Detective Benson Harris of the Los Angeles Police Department was in his office at 77th Street Community Police Station when the front desk buzzed to say a Mr. Dalton wished to see him.

"Tell Mr. Dalton to make an appointment."

"He says it's about the Courtney Lloyd case."

Harris sighed. The name Dalton didn't ring a bell. But he had struck out on Juan Garcia, aka Marc Martinez, his only possible lead. O'Neal had spent hours trying to find more photo matches in any of the other law enforcement databases. Zilch. He had neither fingerprints nor DNA. As expected, the registration number on the motorcycle was false.

Even if he managed to get hold of Martinez, the Lloyd girl would not be with him anymore. He would've sold her to some gang and moved on to his next victim. There was literally nothing he could pin on Martinez that would stick in court. The testimony of Ms. Lloyd and her son and caretaker would be truthful and emotional and prove nothing except that Courtney had left with Martinez out of her own free will. But Harris still wanted to find him.

After four and a half decades in law enforcement, six months away from retirement, his frustration was that very few of the sex trafficking bosses ever saw the inside of a criminal court. Not to mention the inside of a prison cell. The biggest issue was a lack of reliable witnesses. They were just too scared to come forward and testify. Those who tried often died, almost always in the most gruesome manner imaginable, such as Elizabeth Clayton. The scumbags seldom faced justice. Therefore, until Harris stumbled upon a lead, which he knew may never happen, the dossier of Courtney Lloyd had been moved to the bottom of the pile.

Harris knew it would be stupid to ignore a lead of any kind without due consideration. Who knows, maybe this Mr. Dalton knew something that could help him nail at least one of those animals. He'd retire a happy man if he could send a few of them straight to hell or put them behind bars. Preferably the former.

"Send him in."

Mr. Dalton was about an inch short of six feet, with penetrating dark eyes, black hair, tan skin, the physique of a gymnast, and a stern-looking facial expression. Accompanying Mr. Dalton was a big black Dutch Shepherd on a leash attached to a harness that displayed a service dog notice.

The men introduced themselves and took seats.

The dog, whose disciplined mannerisms reminded Harris of the police and military dogs he'd seen in action, sat next to Mr. Dalton. He had what looked to Harris like a smile on his face, but he was sure it couldn't be because dogs didn't smile. Or did they? Regardless, despite the Service

Dog label, Harris was sure this dog was not there to provide physical or emotional support to or detect the onset of a serious medical condition in Mr. Dalton. To Harris, it was obvious that Mr. Dalton was a fit and healthy man—more than capable of taking care of himself.

Mr. Dalton said, "I'm Courtney Lloyd's father. I want to know everything you know about Marc Martinez, the man who drugged, raped, and kidnapped my underage daughter."

"Raped? Kidnapped?"

"Isn't it rape to have sex with someone under the age of eighteen in California?"

"Yes, but—"

"My daughter was only fifteen when she was drugged and raped by Martinez. She was two days older than sixteen when that cold-blooded sewer rat, almost double her age, lured her away from her dying mother."

Harris drew a sharp breath. People who had harm done to their loved ones tended to be vengeful. They had his fullest sympathy but nothing else. They could be meddlesome, tiresome, and dangerous. He had to get this man and his damn grinning dog out of his office as quickly as possible.

"Mr. Dalton. I can assure you that every effort—"

"Relax, Lieutenant, I only want the details you've got on file, and I'll be on my way. Unless, of course, you have questions for me."

"Mr. Dalton, I understand what you must be feeling, but you have *no right*, and I have *no authorization*—"

Mr. Dalton held his left hand up. Harris stopped talking, and for the first time, he paid close attention to Mr. Dalton's eyes, facial expressions, and demeanor as Mr. Dalton put his right hand in his jacket pocket and pulled something out.

Harris's blood ran cold. *How did he get past security with a gun in his pocket?*

His own gun was in the desk drawer, which was locked. *Very inconvenient.*

He almost sighed in relief when a badge instead of a gun appeared. Mr. Dalton placed it on the desk in front of Harris. It was a shoulder sleeve insignia depicting a Fairbairn–Sykes fighting knife inside the outline of a red arrowhead. It was the crest worn by operators of the 1st Special Forces Operational Detachment–Delta, colloquially known as Delta Force. One of the US military's most secretive units. An outfit that instilled the fear of God in the enemies of the United States.

Mr. Dalton spoke in a quiet, calm, and measured voice. "Lieutenant Harris, for the past decade and a half, in places far away from here, fighting in shitholes you're unlikely to have heard of and probably never will, I've earned the right to know who raped and abducted my daughter. I paid with *my* blood for *my* right to know."

Harris's mouth was dry. As a detective, he dealt with dangerous people from the underbelly of society every day. He was no softie. But he didn't have to second-guess; Mr. Dalton was a dangerous man, capable of extreme violence. And that grin on the damn dog's face. The two of them gave him the jitters.

Before Harris could respond, Mr. Dalton's hand went back into his jacket pocket. When the hand came out, it held another badge, a metal one. He placed it next to the other. It was a silver circle with the words United States in the top half and the word Marshal in the bottom half. Inside the circle was a silver five-point star with the American Eagle in the middle. It was the badge of the United States Marshal Service. Created in 1789, during the Presidency of George Washington, they were the oldest federal law enforcement agency in the country.

The names of two of the most notable US marshals sprung to mind: Wild Bill Hickok and Wyatt Earp. Men who didn't take shit from anyone. To Lieutenant Harris, Mr. Dalton seemed to have been cut from the same cloth as those two gentlemen.

Again Mr. Dalton spoke in that unnerving quiet, calm, and measured voice. "And that, Lieutenant Harris, is *your* authorization."

Harris nodded in silence. The Marshal Service was responsible for apprehending wanted fugitives, protecting the federal judiciary, transporting federal prisoners, protecting endangered federal witnesses, and managing assets seized from criminal enterprises. They also managed the Witness Protection Program.

How Mr. Dalton, a Delta Force operator, happened to also be a US Marshal, Harris didn't even bother to ask. He concluded that the next time Mr. Dalton's hand entered his jacket pocket, it would come out with an FBI badge. For all he knew, there could be a DEA badge in the pocket as well, and badges for every intelligence or law enforcement agency in the country. It was also quite possible that there was a gun in one of his pockets. Harris had no doubt that every one of those badges and the gun would be legit because Mr. Dalton was obviously a special kind of special agent.

Harris didn't know that he was right; Mr. Dalton indeed had legitimate badges for the FBI, DEA, CIA, NSA, and a few others. Neither did he know that those badges were not meant to be used for conducting any of those agencies' official business. The badges, although they would stand up to scrutiny, were to be used only to get him access to people and places where he otherwise could not go. The thing was, those badges could only be used during properly sanctioned missions, definitely not for vigilante activities. Rex had committed his first crime on this mission. Fortunately, Harris was clueless.

Despite his initial unease, Harris slowly started to relax as he came to the realization that Mr. Dalton might actually help him resolve some of his job satisfaction issues by removing some unsightly garbage and weeds from the public lawn, so to speak. Garbage such as Martinez and the pimps and their enforcers—those who did the beating, raping, and killing. The filth of society, which he, as a policeman, couldn't remove from the garden because he had to do things by the book. Mr. Dalton was obviously not a by-the-book kind of man. With Mr. Dalton's help, he might just be able to make Los Angeles a safer place for young girls before his retirement in six months.

There was a stipulation in the Justice for Victims of Trafficking Act of 2015 that authorized the United States Marshals Service to assist state and other federal law enforcement agencies in locating and recovering missing children. It was that stipulation that gave Lieutenant Harris permission to ask for Mr. Dalton's assistance to find the long list of missing children in his 'books.'

"Mr. Dalton, you've *earned* the right, and I *am* now authorized."

Harris had a massive amount of information about numerous sex and drug trafficking gangs, but it was not enough to arrest any of the kingpins. On a USB thumb drive, Rex got an electronic copy of Courtney's dossier and witness statements obtained from Jessie, Reece, and Anne.

On the same USB stick, he also got the dossier of Elizabeth Clayton, witness statements, coroner's report, and pictures. On an external hard drive, he also got copies of the dossiers of every lowlife suspected of sex trafficking and drug dealing in Los Angeles and neighboring areas. There was more than one terabyte of data.

While the data was copied over, Detective Harris gave Mr. Dalton a short but very informative summary of forty-five years of experience with the vice gangs and drug dealers operating in Los Angeles and neighboring areas. "The details are in the files on the external hard drive," he told Mr. Dalton.

Before Rex left, they exchanged cellphone numbers.

One look at Rex when he and Digger entered their hotel room, and Catia knew Rex was in a murderous mood. She knew the kidnapping of his daughter would've brought back the memory of the senseless killing of his entire family in 2004. She understood how he felt; her parents were also killed by terrorists only a year after his.

Digger could sense the anger and disquiet in his alpha. With soft whines, he sidled up to Rex to comfort him.

Catia made Rex an espresso and quietly listened to him about his meeting with Harris and the information he got from the detective.

"So, what do you think it means? He kind of gave you the keys to the city, didn't he? I'm not ungrateful, but why? Is there a catch somewhere?"

Rex shrugged. "Nothing's impossible. But Digger was happy with him, and I didn't pick up any tells. He worked on the vice squad for most of his forty-odd years as a cop. He's six months away from retirement, but he's a frustrated man because he knows all the gangs involved in the child sex slave business in LA. He was instrumental in putting away only a few of them during his tenure, but the vast majority are still free. He could never lay a finger on them because he wasn't allowed to beat confessions out of them."

"So, he wants to use you to take his frustrations out on those criminals?"

"He didn't use those exact words, but that's my interpretation. He didn't exactly ask me to do anything, neither did he promise me anything, except to say that the information I needed is on the terabyte drive."

"Do you think he will blow the whistle on you when you take the law into your own hands?"

"Same as before. He didn't say so, but he left me with the impression that he wouldn't interfere with my investigation."

"Okay, where do you want to start?"

"Let's go back to the Ranch first," said Rex.

On the plane, his mind was working overtime. He had to break the news to his friends on the Ranch. It was going to be hard, but he couldn't see it happening any other way. He couldn't involve them.

Chapter Twelve

ALL FOR ONE AND ONE FOR ALL

When the Daltons arrived on the Ranch late afternoon, John and Christelle were at the landing strip to meet them. Christelle was a former deputy director of the DGSE, the French equivalent of the American CIA. She and John had worked on a few joint missions in their young days during the Cold War. There was a romantic spark between them back then, but the Atlantic Ocean and work had put it out. More than thirty years after their last joint mission, they caught up again. The old flame was rekindled, and two months after Christelle's retirement, she and John got married. Despite being over seventy, Christelle was still the personification of feminine elegance and class.

John steered them to the Ops Room, where the rest of their friends were due to arrive momentarily. None of them knew why John had called them to this meeting.

First to arrive were Josh Farley and his wife, Marissa. Josh was one of CRC's special operators. According to John Brandt, almost as good as Rex. Standing two inches over six feet, Josh was a pleasant-faced, All-American type with blond hair. Between him and Rex, they had more than just a few war stories to tell and the battle scars to show for it— they trusted one another without reservation.

John described Marissa as the best of CRC's handful of female agents. She was beautiful. Shoulder-length raven hair and azure eyes suggested French heritage. She was almost ten years older than Josh, but one would have to see her birth certificate to know that.

A few moments later, Greg Wade and Rehka Gyan walked into the room.

Greg, a tall, almost skinny, bespectacled man with long curly dark hair in his early thirties, was the head of CRC's IT team, a highly skilled band of seven IT specialists. Computer hackers, among the best in the business.

Rehka Gyan was a stunning but shy Indian beauty who could, if she wanted to, have made a career as a fashion model. She was the daughter of Rex's friend from Bilaspur, India. Rex and Digger had saved her from the claws of an illicit arms dealer a few years ago. She had a master's degree in computer sciences and exceptional skills in programming and online research. Since she had met Greg and worked with him and his team on several missions, her knowledge and abilities had gone from strength to strength, and so had their feelings for each other. The two of them were secretly engaged. Secretly because Greg still had to make the time and gather enough courage to travel to India to ask Rehka's father for her hand in marriage.

And, of course, no meeting was properly constituted if Digger and Cupcake were not in attendance. They were very busy trying to retrieve the peanut butter which Catia had stuffed into their Kongs; odd-shaped toys, part cylinder, part cone, with indentations that made them look like hard-plastic snowmen. A hole ran through them from top to bottom, which could be stuffed with delicacies such as jerky, peanut butter, and other treats. It was always a joy to see Digger and Cupcake losing all dog dignity and going into a frenzy when they saw their Kongs.

Rex and Catia had talked about Rehka on the way. They were worried that what Rex was about to share with them would open old wounds in Rehka's psyche. Greg knew the full history of how a scumbag, a Saudi prince, no less, had bought her in India from a lending shark and smuggled her into Saudi Arabia, where he kept her as a pleasure wife against her will. She was his sex slave. Greg had assured her it didn't bother him in the least. Well, maybe not entirely; what bothered him was that he couldn't bring the bastard back to life so that *he* could kill him at his leisure.

Catia, Marissa, and Christelle were her best friends, and they'd always kept a close watch. According to them, their friend had been doing very well. She was a strong and confident woman.

CRC's resident psychologist, Rick Longland, had been mentoring her and told Rex, "She will never forget it, Rex. The emotional scar is as permanent as the scars on your body caused by knives and bullets. It's not an open wound anymore. It has healed well. The scar has faded but will never completely disappear. I've made good progress teaching her how to live with it. That Greg loves her unconditionally, plus yours, the Farleys', and the Brandts' friendship has helped a tremendous lot to restore her trust in humanity again."

Nevertheless, Rex had asked Catia to have a private word with Rehka before the meeting to warn her about the contents of the discussions they were about to have and to keep an eye on her during the meeting.

For the first forty minutes, while sipping on their coffees

and teas, they listened in shocked silence, with empathy and growing fury, as Rex told them about Jessie and the twins. Learning of the abduction of Rex's daughter was as much of a shock to John and Christelle as it was to everyone else in the room.

Rex and Catia kept an eye on Rehka throughout and were happy that, as far as they could see, she was handling it well.

"I've made two promises to Jessie," said Rex when he came to the end. "I intend to keep them. I promised to find our daughter, and I promised to take good care of our children when she's... ah... after she passes."

Everyone was staring at him, waiting for him to continue. As if to say, "Ok, what's the plan?"

Rex took a deep breath and told them about his meeting with Lieutenant Harris of the LAPD that morning. He inserted Harris's USB drive into one of the ports on his laptop and showed them Elizabeth Clayton's coroner's report and the photos.

Over the years, as intelligence agents and black ops operators, they'd seen heinous atrocities, but this made their stomachs roil. They were seething.

"My daughter is in the hands of creatures capable of doing that to a child," said Rex.

Rehka was wiping tears from her eyes. Greg had his arm around her shoulder. But she was okay.

"Every breath those savages take is one too many," hissed Josh.

"We're going to find the scum and put them down," said John.

But Rex held his hand up to silence them. "Yes, John, that's exactly what I'm going to do. But there's no we or us.

There's only me. No one else. This is my battle, my promises, not—"

"You must be joking," interjected Josh. "We're your friends, man. Your battles are our battles. Your pain is our pain. We go where you go. How can you even—"

"Thanks, Josh, but you don't understand. I'm talking vigilante justice here. No government backing. A totally illegal operation. Stepping on the toes of the LAPD, the FBI, DEA, and others. If I'm caught, I'm going to jail. CRC can't be connected to this. None of you can be involved. Catia and I are resigning. We're leaving in the morning."

A stunned silence descended upon them and stayed for a long while.

Marissa recovered first. "That changes absolutely nothing, Rex Dalton. You need help, and you'll get it. From us."

"Damn straight," said Josh,

"Precisely," said Greg and Rehka in chorus.

"If you resign to go after those animals, so do we," said Greg.

"Exactly," said Rehka.

"'In the immortal words of that French dude whatchamacallit, 'All for one and one for all,'" said Josh.

Christelle smiled. "Alexandre Dumas," she said. "The Three Musketeers."

"Yes, that guy," said Josh.

Rex was touched by the loyalty of his friends. He tried to reason with them, but he soon realized he was wasting his energy. They wouldn't budge.

And for that, he was grateful.

When Rex had lost the argument, and they'd reached consensus that they were all in with Rex and Catia, John stepped in. "I'm not accepting resignations. We're going to help Rex get his daughter back and, in the process, eradicate any vermin standing in our way. If CRC's clients get their noses out of joint because we helped one of our own, I will deal with it when it happens. If it means the end of CRC, so be it."

Rex launched another stream of objections but with a lot less conviction. Fifteen minutes later, shortly after ten o'clock, they decided to base themselves on the CRC's luxury yacht, the *TOMATS*, which would be in Los Angeles harbor for a few more months before sailing back home to Rome.

It was the first time that the *TOMATS* had made the Atlantic crossing, not as a pleasure trip but for a major over-haul of its engines and upgrade of onboard technologies and systems used in CRC's missions.

Chapter Thirteen

SPOIL THEM ROTTEN

John and Christelle had retired to their house and bedroom when Rex and the team started packing. They couldn't sleep. The whole situation was an emotional mixture of sadness about Jessica's illness and Courtney's disappearance on the one hand, a lot of joy about the discovery of Rex's children on the other hand, and the uneasy feeling about taking the law into their own hands to rescue Courtney.

They decided to accompany Rex and the others to LA the next day so John could meet Jessica and Reece and help the team settle in on the *TOMATS*.

Later, their discussions turned to the future of CRC.

When John handed over the reins of Operation Peregrine, a Cold War-type group within the CIA established to contain China's world control ideals, he was hoping he could also retire from CRC. Rex had been the acting CEO while John was heading Peregrine and did a sterling job. John wanted him to continue, but Rex refused.

This handover of the command of CRC had been an

ongoing tug of war between them for quite a while with no resolution. Even about that, Rex and John disagreed. Rex believed the matter had been resolved; he said he was not taking the job. John believed as long as Rex refused, the matter was unresolved.

Nevertheless, every time Rex was ready to leave, another mission came up—untimely and unannounced—for sure, missions always did. But it suited John. The longer Rex stayed, the better the chance he'd say yes. After Operation Sierra in Namibia, during which Rex and his team had a run-in with the Chinese about a rare-earth mineral mine in this small nation on the southwest coast of Africa, Rex was determined that he and Catia would take a break from CRC for at least six months, in mid-April when the upgrades and maintenance on the *TOMATS* would be completed and ready to sail back to Rome, her home port. Rome was Catia's birthplace. They wanted to spend the summer in the Eternal City and sail around the Mediterranean aboard the *TOMATS*.

Christelle told John that Catia had confided in her that since the Namibia mission, Rex and she were having more frequent discussions about starting a family. Apparently, Catia was keen and ready, but Rex was afraid. He just couldn't bring himself to believe that, with his background, he could be a good father. Catia, on the contrary, believed Rex would be the best father her children could ever have.

"And she wouldn't be wrong," said John.

"I agree; Rex would be a great father," said Christelle.

John chuckled.

"Why are you laughing?"

"How would you feel about being a grandmother?"

"I can't wait." She giggled. "How about you?"

John laughed. "I've got many years of grandfathering to catch up on. I'm going to spoil them rotten."

Christelle was laughing out loud now. "Exactly what I had in mind."

Chapter Fourteen

YOU HAVE MY WORD

They left the ranch at ten o'clock the next morning in CRC's Dassault Falcon 2000 DX jet and touched down shortly after 11:30 a.m. at Van Nuys Airport, one of LA's most popular private jet airports.

Two o'clock that afternoon, Rex introduced John, Christelle, Catia, and Digger to Anne, Jessica, and Reece. Digger whined softly when he offered his paw to be shaken as he was introduced to Jessie and Reece. Rex knew it was Digger's way of sympathizing. Dogs can sense different human emotions, such as the grief he smelled among them. They're also able to sense physical pain and suffering.

Jessie had a big smile when she shook Digger's paw. Anne and Reece were laughing out loud.

Jessie looked well-rested, and Rex thought her eyes looked livelier than when he last saw her. Nevertheless, they kept the introductions short. John and Christelle stayed behind with Jessie and Reece while the rest of them moved to the family room, where Anne served refreshments.

Jessie assured John he had nothing to feel guilty about; it

was her choice not to let Rex know about the children. She thanked him for honoring her wishes and for his financial support over the years.

"Remember, Jessica, Rex and Catia are the children John and I never had. Reece and Courtney will be our grandchildren," said Christelle just before they said goodbye.

Jessica nodded and whispered, "Thank you, Christelle. You have no idea how much that means to me."

It was Catia's turn to talk to Jessie.

In the family room, Reece and Digger became instant friends. Only once before had Rex seen Digger accept someone into his pack so quickly and unreservedly; that was the day when Digger met Catia for the first time. It was on the Piazza del Popolo in Rome when they had rescued her and a friend from the claws of the mafia. It was as if he had instantly realized Rex and Catia were meant for each other and immediately accepted her into his pack.

Or maybe Digger recognized her from all the times I told him about this wonderful woman? Rex smiled when the thought crossed his mind.

Now, with Reece, it was the same. It was as if Digger could smell or sense the family ties—the shared DNA. Was that even possible? Maybe he just sensed his pack's goodwill toward the young man.

Or maybe he recognized the boy from all the photos he'd seen the last few days?

The meeting between Catia and Jessie was emotion-filled. It started off a bit awkward, almost tense. It was to be expected; they both loved Rex. But as soon as they realized that the conversation was not going to be about Rex, the tension evaporated, and it became a heart-to-heart between the two women. A mother in the throes of death, asking a stranger to take over her role.

An hour later, there had been a lot of tears, and pain, and grief, and Catia's solemn pledge. "Jessica, you have my word; I will love and care for them as if they are my own children."

Jessie was physically and emotionally drained but completely at peace when Catia left the room. A new friendship had been forged.

It was late afternoon when the CRC group arrived on the *TOMATS* at anchor in Cabrillo Way Marina, Los Angeles harbor. Declan Spencer and his wife of almost two years, Simona, were there to greet them.

The name *TOMATS* was derived from the first letters of Ernest Hemingway's classic short novel, '*The Old Man and the Sea*.' John Brandt was a Hemmingway devotee. The *TOMATS* was a three-deck two-hundred-and-seventy-foot luxury superyacht.

The *TOMATS*, under the command of John's bosom friend, Declan Spencer, had served as CRC's mobile mission control center for several major missions around Europe, Hong Kong, Vietnam, and now for the first time, the USA.

Many handshakes, hugs, and kisses later, Digger walked up to Simona and protested loudly about the fact that they had not paid any attention to him yet. It worked; he immediately got ear and back scratches from both her and Spencer.

The villains involved in Courtney Lloyd's case had no idea that their judge, jury, and executioners had arrived on their doorstep.

Chapter Fifteen

THE HARRIS FILES

The mood was subdued as they carried their stuff aboard and started unpacking. Absent was the usual nervous excitement and bantering when they were preparing for missions. Though, over the years, the media and Hollywood had kept them aware of the horrors of the child sex trade, never had they thought one day those horrors would strike in their midst. In the somber atmosphere, even Josh, the team's eternal joker and prankster, was quiet.

Digger knew his pack; he knew when they were excited, stressed, happy, or sad as they had been for the past few days. Which is probably why Digger took it upon himself to console them. He did the rounds, visiting everyone, sidling up, and 'encouraging' them to scratch his back and ears. It was as if he knew it was therapeutic for them to do it. Of course, it was also entirely possible that he was merely vying for their attention and see if he could score a treat to boot. Whatever Digger's agenda, his visits worked wonders for Rex, and it seemed to have had the same effect on the rest of the team.

As black ops agents, Rex and his team knew all about operating outside the law. But that was always in other countries and with the backing of CRC, which was backed by their clients such as the CIA, FBI, DEA, NSA, DNI, and others, who were backed by the President, their Commander-in-Chief. But what they had in mind now was different. They were about to launch an operation on American soil without the official support of CRC or any of its usual backers. In fact, those very people who were keen to keep them alive during missions in the past would now be keen to have them arrested and thrown into prison.

Among the tools and gadgets they brought with them were rolls of duct tape, sedatives, syringes, zip-ties, industrial strength flashlights, Tasers, tranquilizer guns, mini microphones, mini cameras, directional microphones, mini drones, and GPS tags for humans and vehicles. All of it was stored in the yacht's armory next to the engine room.

They were licensed under California gun laws to carry concealed guns, so each of them, including Rehka and Greg, carried one or another model Glock pistol and three spare magazines. Rehka and Greg were not nearly as skillful with guns as Rex and the rest, but it would've been a bad mistake to underestimate their abilities to use their guns, especially their willingness to do so on the scumbags they were going after.

Digger yelped excitedly when he saw Rex putting his canine tactical harness on the shelf. As if he was saying, "Action! at last."

It was almost 7:00 p.m. when the chef announced over the intercom, "Dinner in five."

Over dinner, they observed their standing rule of no shop talk. None of them felt much like chit-chatting. So, dinner was a quiet affair until Christelle announced that she and John had decided to stay for a few more days "to help you move in and settle in," she said.

Josh couldn't let that opportunity pass. "Yippee! Did you hear that? Mom and Dad are going to stay a while longer." Everyone was laughing but also knew Josh had hit the nail on the head; John and Christelle regarded the six agents around the table as their children.

The minute dinner was over, they moved to the Comms Room and started working through the information provided by Lieutenant Harris. As usual, Spencer and Simona were involved in missions controlled from the *TOMATS*.

Digger seldom missed meetings. He didn't contribute much, but he was available if they wanted his opinion. Rex had long suspected Digger's conscientiousness when it came to attending meetings had something to do with his Kong stuffed with beef jerky or peanut butter which Catia always gave him at the start of a meeting. Once he had managed to get the treat stuffed into the Kong out, he would give a loud sigh, close his eyes and go to sleep. And every now and then, to the utter disgust of the two-legged members of his pack, he would make a malodorous contribution to the planet's greenhouse gases. Of course, he was totally unaware that he was doing so—how could he when he was fast asleep?

The team knew they were not going to sleep tonight or tomorrow night and maybe not the night after either. The clock was ticking. Every minute Courtney remained in the hands of those demons was a minute too much.

In an article by IndyStar columnist Tim Swarens, which he

published in USA Today, he asked, "Who buys a 15-year-old child for sex?"

"The answer: Many otherwise ordinary men. They could be your co-worker, doctor, pastor, or spouse. More than one million children, according to the (United Nations) International Labor Organization, are exploited each year in the commercial sex trade," said Swarens.

"They're in all walks of life," said a seventeen-year-old survivor from the Midwest, trafficked when she was fifteen, about the one hundred and fifty men who purchased her per month. "Some could be upstanding people in the community. It was mostly people in their forties, living in the suburbs, who were coming to get the stuff they were missing."

From the US National Human Trafficking Hotline statistics, Rex and the team learned that there were 10,583 traffic incidents in 2020, of which 7,648 were sex-related.

"Trafficking does not happen in a vacuum," says an entry on the Polaris Project website. "Virtually everyone who ends up in a trafficking situation has a clear and identifiable vulnerability that a trafficker preyed upon. The top five vulnerabilities for sex victims were: Substance abuse, runaway or homeless youth, unstable housing, mental health concern, recent migration or relocation."

The Harris files contained a lot of information about prostitution which was illegal not only in California but in every state in America. Nevada, possibly to keep the gamblers entertained, was the exception. Buying or selling sex for money was a serious offense. In most states, a conviction could result in jail time and fines.

Notwithstanding the legal prohibition and heavy penalties, according to the Harris files, prostitution was a thriving industry. Prosecutions happened seldom, and convictions were rare.

Ever since some clever politician or bureaucrat or intellectual came up with the twisted concept that prostitution and drug abuse were victimless crimes and should therefore be decriminalized, law enforcement agencies became less interested in policing those crimes. That would've been fine was it not for underage children being victims of those crimes; some as young as ten were often found among the adult prostitutes.

Rex told them about the conversation he and Harris had and that Harris supported the idea of legalizing prostitution. "He reckons it's better to decriminalize and then regulate it. He says, for starters, they should register them all, and while they're at it, make sure they're over the age of consent. He told me he doesn't want to waste his time keeping adult hookers off the streets of LA while there are sex traffickers using drugs to enslave teenagers to satisfy the whims of pedophiles on the loose."

"Ok, where do we start? I am itching to get their names and addresses," said Josh.

"Let's get them for you," said Greg as he and Rehka started querying the files they had copied to the CRC server earlier.

The information on the sex crime bosses in the Harris files was extensive. Not only did Harris spend the largest part of his working life collecting it, but his colleagues also collected vast amounts of information. Apart from the large collection of news articles, white papers, political pieces, op-eds, and academic papers about child sex trafficking, there were also witness and victims' statements.

Some of those victims were plaintiffs and witnesses in criminal cases, forty percent of which ended in convictions.

But a significant number of the witnesses and victims died or simply went missing before the cases reached the courts. Often victims and witnesses would suffer from an incurable bout of amnesia, usually after receiving a late-night visit from men in black with matching ski masks carrying rubber hoses and batons.

Sometimes a sex slave was sold to a gang where she would be controlled and abused by more than one gang member. Sometimes they were trafficked outside the gang for money. Gangs were turning to sex trafficking in droves; it was not only safer, with less policing, but also more lucrative than drug trafficking. No wonder some gangs would tattoo their slaves with distinctive markings to establish ownership over them. Very much like cattle farmers of old who had their own unique branding irons with which they marked their cattle.

One of the rather pleasing pieces of information they came across was a news report about the trial and conviction of Rances Ulices Amaya, in June 2012. He was a leader of an MS-13 gang and got sentenced to fifty years in prison for child prostitution. He was caught trafficking girls as young as fourteen into a prostitution ring. They were lured from middle schools, high schools, and public shelters. Once in Amaya's claws, they were required to have sex with a minimum of ten clients per day.

One of the witnesses, Maryann Porter, whose battered body was later found adrift in the harbor, never got a chance to tell her story to a jury, but she told it to Harris, who duly recorded it and had it transcribed.

According to the late Porter's statement, the most prolific recruiters were women, colloquially known as groomers. They were usually in the young adult age bracket, eighteen to twenty-two, role models for susceptible girls in their early teens. They recruited them at schools, on playgrounds, at slumber parties, at sleepovers, and elsewhere. They would befriend their targets and show them a good time by introducing them to all the adult girl stuff, drugs, alcohol, and sex with sleazy adult men, who would soon turn out to be their pimps. The groomers and pimps preyed on girls in that tender age bracket who also had problems at home. A rebellious streak in any girl at that age was as good as a written invitation to the groomers.

Yet, despite having comprehensive information about the criminals and their crimes, little of it was good enough for prosecutors to make a case that would stand up in court. There were a few minor cases in progress before the courts right now, but the statistics showed about sixty percent of those cases would end in acquittals.

Rex summed it up very accurately. "The government's efforts to end sex trafficking is clearly a miserable failure. And they won't turn the tide until they get out of their own way and abandon some of their stupid rules of engagement with these animals."

"Precisely," said John.

The team was not disheartened by Harris's lamentations about how frustrating it was to catch the bad guys while being obstructed by crippling rules and regulations. Rex and his team had more than enough evidence to act upon.

They operated differently from the police and prosecutors, who relied on witnesses to come forward to testify against the scum. Rex and the team were planning to use the same strategy they'd been using for years to bring justice to terrorists, their financiers, illicit arms dealers, and drug lords. Find them, question them, and shoot them in the head. It worked. They never did evil again.

Greg's queries returned names, lots of photos, personal

details, and addresses of family, friends, associates, and adversaries of the crime bosses and their henchmen. Among them would be the miscreants involved in Courtney's abduction.

As much as the team felt like wiping out all the lowlifes shown in those files, they had to restrain themselves. To stand a remote chance of escaping a lengthy prison sentence for taking the law into their own hands, the mission had to be limited to only those who were involved in Courtney's abduction. Therefore, they started with Marc Martinez, the man who lured Rex's daughter away from her dying mother's house.

Chapter Sixteen

YOU CAN RUN BUT YOU CAN'T HIDE

From Reece's statement to the police, it was clear that soon after Courtney received the news about her mother's inevitable death from cancer, she suffered an emotional breakdown; she had abandoned her regular friends and joined the rebels and troublemakers at school, many of them older than she was.

"I'm wondering why the police haven't taken statements from her friends?" said John softly and then bumped his forehead with an open palm. "Ah, of course, they reckon no crime was committed. Courtney went with Mr. Sleazeball out of her own free will. She told her mother so in her own handwriting."

"Precisely what Harris admitted to me in a round-about way," said Rex. "Okay, let's start with Reece's USB drive. We should be able to extract a list of names and phone numbers coupled with text and Signal chat messages."

When Rex finished, Rehka pointed at the TV. "There's the list of names and phone numbers. There are four hundred and sixty-one records. I've sorted the list on the telephone number column from most used to least used."

"Any of those names in the Harris files?" asked Catia.

Greg shook his head. "Nope."

"Okay, let's start at the top. Each of us takes a name and reads the text and chats."

"Before we do that," interjected Greg, "give me all the keywords you can think of. Maybe I can save us a lot of time."

Greg was right.

It was the keyword 'weed' that led them to a chat with one of Courtney's new friends who had invited her to a twenty-first birthday party. The contents of the chat told them that was where she'd smoked marijuana for the first time. There she also met another of the older girls, Marion Cooper, twenty-four, with a stinking-rich dad.

The next hit led to a chat, starting with Marion inviting Courtney to what she promised to be a wild house party the next week when her dad and what she described as his courtesan were in New York for the weekend.

MC: There's someone who wants to meet you.

CL: Who?

MC: It's a surprise. I won't spoil it. But be prepared to be pleasantly surprised.

CL: Okay, I guess I can wait 2 days.

MC: Btw are you still a virgin?

CL: Yes, and ashamed to admit it.

MC: Nothing to be ashamed of. You can solve that problem on Saturday night with the Romeo I'm going to introduce to you.

CL: Why me?

MC: He asked me to introduce you to him.

CL: How does he know me?

MC: Why don't you ask him on Saturday night. Maybe he listened closely when I told him what a nice girl you are.

CL: What does he look like?

MC: Breathtaking. Like a movie star.

In the chats between Courtney and her new friends in the aftermath of that spectacular party, a picture emerged. It was at this party that she was introduced to Marc Martinez, snorted cocaine for the first time, and lost her virginity to a man who, she told everyone, was on the verge of becoming a famous actor with the stage name Duane Cruz. "Famous actors have stage names, you know. Did you know Whoopi Goldberg's real name is Caryn Johnson? Vin Diesel is Mark Sinclair." After sending them a few pictures of her beau, Courtney's 'friends' agreed Martinez definitely had the looks of a movie star. They wanted to see more photos, but she said he was camera-shy. She explained he didn't want some indiscreet photos published on social media to spoil his chances of being the next big hit on the silver screen. Despite that, Courtney had covertly taken a few photos. She'd only send them to her friends on Signal; she'd never post them on social media.

One thing was crystal clear; Courtney was infatuated with Marc Martinez.

They didn't find it strange that there was very little Signal chat traffic between Martinez and Courtney. Obviously, Martinez was careful not to give law enforcement a hold on him. The reason he kept his cellphone off most of the time was not, as he told Courtney, because he was not allowed to have a phone on him at work; it was so that no one could track his movements. Rehka quickly established that it was a burner phone bought at a supermarket for cash two days before the party at Marion's.

It took Greg and Rehka less than fifteen minutes to ruin

the reputation of Courtney's hero. The closest he came to acting was when he worked as a stagehand on the set of the 2016 remake of Ben Hur. He was tasked with picking up the horse manure after each scene. His name didn't even appear in the credentials at the end of the movie. Horse shit collectors apparently didn't get recognition.

"Well, Duane Cruz, your acting career that has never been is about to end abruptly," said John.

Josh nodded. "Marion Cooper will tell us where we can get hold of Mr. Lowlife Martinez."

"Right," said Rex.

Rex turned to Greg and Rehka to ask them to find photos and addresses, but Rehka pointed at the TV screen. "That's Marion Cooper," she said. "We have photos, names, addresses, and believe it or not, cellphone numbers of everyone mentioned in Reece's statement plus their friends."

"Where did you get—?" started John.

"Social media," said Rehka. "These girls like to keep the world in the know about what they did yesterday, what they're doing right now, and what they're going to do tomorrow. They like to talk about their lives and their parties and their friends. They gossip, too. And not only do they tell the world, they show the world, with photos and videos and audio recordings."

"Generation Alpha. The Zoomers or Generation Z, Gen Z as they call themselves," murmured Catia. "The first generation of the twenty-first century. The first one was born on the first day of January 2000. They're connected to technology; they're integrated with it. They've never been without it. And they can't live without it."

"They sound like cyborgs," said Josh.

Catia smiled. "In a few years, they could very well be part human, part machine. Computer chips in their brains so they can be constantly connected to the Internet of Things, IoT. The interconnection of computing devices embedded in everyday objects, including humans, enabling them to send and receive data between them."

They were still talking about the group characteristics of the various generations when Greg brought up a new screen on the big screen. It was a map of Los Angeles with several little red dots flickering on and off in various locations across the city. "The locations of the mobile phones of all those girls on our list."

Everyone was staring at Greg and Rehka. This was one of the rare occasions when they were in the presence of CRC's computer prodigies as they were performing their magic. CRC's IT team had few rivals when it came to hacking. With a few keystrokes, they could create havoc, blackout a city, take control of its traffic lights, enter government and corporate databases, access the bank records of any individual and organization, penetrate firewalls, break encryption, track down people through their cellphones, and much more.

There was no red light for Martinez's phone. It was obviously off, or more likely, he had destroyed it as soon as he had Courtney in his claws.

"You can run but you can't hide, Martinez," said Rex softly as he got up to get another espresso. "It's only a matter of time now."

Digger must have sensed the change in mood. He got to his feet, sat down, and stared at Rex for a while before a smile broke across his face. He had been on so many missions with this pack he knew when they were about to kick off a new one. He yelped once as if to say, "Let's get this show on the road."

The next day, for their covert transport requirements, John and Christelle had gone out and bought two old cars, a 2007 Toyota Corolla and a 2009 Hyundai, which would not look out of place in crummy neighborhoods. Greg and Rehka obscured the ownership and registrations so that it would be impossible to link the vehicles to them. The vehicles were thoroughly checked by a reputable mechanic who fixed and replaced what was necessary before they were parked in long-term parking garages ten miles apart. For their overt transport requirements, John had rented two identical white Toyota Hybrid RAV4s with tinted windows, one of America's most popular SUVs.

Chapter Seventeen

UNFORTUNATELY, WE'LL HAVE TO LET HER LIVE

The Pegasus Spyware App was originally developed by the Israeli cyber-arms firm, NSO Group. It was an application that could be covertly installed on mobile phones, laptops, tablet PCs, etcetera. It was named after the mythical winged divine horse, one of the most recognized creatures in Greek mythology. IT gurus described it as a Trojan horse that could be sent 'flying through the air' to infect communications devices. And unless the phone was examined by an expert with special software, it was impossible to detect the spyware.

The version operating on Marion Cooper's cellphone was the CRC version of Pegasus—enhanced by Greg and his team. To Marion, being part of Gen Z, her iPhone was the control panel of her life.

Installing the app on her phone was a walk in the park for Rehka when she, Catia, and Marissa disguised themselves with wigs, glasses, and a bit of clever makeup and went 'shopping' in the same mall where Marion was, according to her iPhone's GPS signal. They found her in a posh coffee shop. All they had to do was to get within ten yards of her for at least forty-five seconds. That was as long as it took Greg's version of Pegasus to 'fly' from Rehka's phone to Marion's, hack into her phone, and clone itself onto the hard drive.

They got a table a few paces away from Marion and her two young starry-eyed admirers. To any casual observer, Marion Cooper would've been stunningly beautiful. Almost six feet tall, blonde, and a shapely figure. Her demeanor made it evident that she knew she was a looker. Therefore, she dressed to impress and made the heads turn.

No wonder the young girls were star-struck. The young-sters' faces were unfamiliar. But it was the age gap and the manifest hero-worshipping of Cooper that set klaxons off for all three observers at once. The tragedy was that it was impossible to identify a psychopath by their looks.

Within minutes, Marissa had taken photos of the young girls and passed them on to Greg to find names and other biographical information.

From the moment the Pegasus software had been acti-vated on Marion's phone, Rex's team had become her constant though invisible companion. They could now read her text messages, listen to her calls, collect her passwords, track her location, and harvest information from the apps on her phone. They could switch the phone on and off remotely and could do the same with the microphone and camera. In short, they 'owned' her phone. The first thing Greg did was to switch the microphone on Marion's phone on remotely, and when he could hear the voices, he put it on speaker in the Comms Room and also connected to Catia, Marissa, and Rehka through their molar mics.

The Molar Mic was a relatively new communications technology for covert operators. The device consisted of a mouthpiece equipped with a waterproof microphone, custom-built to fit the molar teeth right at the back of the operator's mouth. The device converted incoming audio into vibrations on the teeth that traveled through the bones in the jaw and skull to the inner ear. The gadget was invisible unless one forced the operator's mouth wide open.

They came in at the tail end of the conversation but quickly picked up the gist of it.

"You're human, not some subspecies. When I was your age, it always pissed me off big time when so-called adults referred to my friends as children, kids, youngsters, and adolescents as if we were less than human. Insulting, isn't it?"

"Of course, it's insulting. Degrading," said the girl with the out-of-a-bottle pitch-black hair, matching eyebrows, inch-long artificial eyelashes, and impossibly blue contact lenses. She had what could've been a beautiful face if it wasn't marred by the unnatural hairdo and unsightly piercings in almost every part of her face: ears, tongue, lower lip, eyebrows, and nose. Her clothes were undoubtedly hiding more piercings, including in the unmentionable parts.

Catia couldn't help but wonder if the poor girl was aware of the perils of coming near strong magnets.

"Well, next time anyone insults you like that," Marion continued, "no matter who, parents, teachers, anyone, don't take it. Tell them they're out of line; you're as human as they are. You're not of a lower social order just because you're younger. Believe me, they're making the distinction only because they know they're not as sexy and alluring as you are. The two of you are more mature than most of the self-proclaimed adults I know," said Marion.

The receptive young girls were bathing in the praises, totally heedless of the deceit, not to mention the danger they were in. Soon that very youthfulness they so despised now would fetch their idol obscene amounts of money from a bunch of perverted people bidding for them as if they were stud cows at a livestock auction.

Marion's face displayed a self-satisfied smile that pleased the young girls but nauseated Catia and her companions.

Before any of them could voice their feelings, a text message with attachments arrived from Greg for Rehka. The girls with Marion were Karen Clark, the one with black hair and piercings, age sixteen, and Shirley Smith, age fifteen; she had shoulder-length bottle-blond hair with red streaks, a stud in her tongue, and a multi-colored tattoo of a rose on her left upper arm. The next message contained background information about them, their parents, and friends.

"Okay, let's finish up and go shopping for clothes that befit mature, sensual, seductive women such as you," said Marion as she winked. "Believe me, after your makeover today, men will be drooling over you."

The girls were giggling.

By the time Marion and the girls left the coffee shop, Greg's version of Pegasus had made itself at home on the iPhones of Mses. Smith and Clark as well.

Catia and her team kept out of sight of Marion's group while listening intently to the conversations and reading the flurry of vain and often vulgar text messages, photos, and videos broadcasted to their friends to get their opinions about every piece of clothing they considered and how they would drive men crazy with lust.

All the while, Marion Cooper was laughing and encouraging them to be more daring, more revealing. "C'mon Karen, that dress looks like a nun's habit. No man will look at you. You've been blessed with a great body; it's your biggest asset. Get something that accentuates your curves."

It didn't take long before Marissa verbalized what everyone in her group was thinking. "I don't know about you, but I am sick to my stomach. Those poor girls don't know that she's entangled them in a web from which it would be near impossible to escape."

Catia shook her head. "Over my dead body. We're going to save them. How many innocent young lives has this enchantress already destroyed? I can't help but wonder how many are dead because of this evil bitch... Why don't I just walk over and shoot her in the head right now?"

Rehka nodded. She didn't trust herself to speak. The bile was rising in her throat. Her ordeal, although more than a decade ago, had returned to haunt her the last few days since Rex told them about his daughter. Rex had killed her tormentor, the Saudi prince, Mutaib bin Faisal bin Saud, and she'd never batted an eye over that. She felt the same about Marion Cooper. The world would be a better place without her.

"I have the same sentiments," said Marissa. "But, for now, at least until we've throttled some information out of her, unfortunately, we'll have to let her live."

"I agree," said Catia. "But very reluctantly. Let's go back to the yacht and work out a plan to get our hands on this witch and save the two girls."

"I won't be surprised if she's got more young girls in her snares than only those two," said Rehka.

Chapter Eighteen

BEGGING TO BE THE EXCEPTION

The moment their better halves stepped into the Comms Room on the *TOMATS*; Rex, Josh, and Greg realized the ladies were on the warpath.

Marion Cooper's life was appraised as the market value of seven grams of lead—the weight of a nine-millimeter round.

While the ladies were at the mall, Greg copied Marion's address book from her phone and all social media and chat messages and gave the information to Rex and Josh to search for Martinez's details while he used a contact at the NSA to extract the historical GPS data of Marion's phone going back twenty-four months.

Between the NSA's GPS location data, the data on her phone, and on social media, the life of the spoiled brat Marion Cooper became an open book to them. She was the daughter and only child of what the media called one of LA's foremost investment bankers and multimillionaire, Robert Dorset. Marion had chosen her mother's surname when her parents got divorced when she was ten. She grew up with her mother in San Francisco, but since leaving school and finishing a one-year diploma in sales and marketing, she'd been working for her dad.

They didn't delve into the details of her job mainly because the GPS data suggested that she almost never visited her dad's posh offices in the city center, and they assumed it was just a front for her illicit activities. Nevertheless, every Friday, like clockwork, Dorset Investments International transferred three-thousand dollars into her personal account. It could've been her salary or her allowance. On paper, Robert Dorset was worth a little over three-quarters of a billion dollars. Paying his daughter an annual salary or allowance of a hundred and fifty thousand dollars and the full use of a red sports model company Mercedes-Benz Coupé plus free board and lodging in the two-bedroom guest cottage was an exorbitant remuneration package for a junior salesperson but would've been peanuts for Dorset.

Something about that scenario was bothering Rex; he just couldn't put his finger on it.

Greg and Rehka started searching for evidence of offshore bank accounts in the usual tax havens where bankers promised discretion and secrecy. It was a farce; the bankers would open their books with little protest when the likes of the CIA, FBI, and other security and law enforcement agencies of the world's most powerful countries came knocking on their doors. But Greg and his team were not sanctioned by any of those agencies now. So, they had to get the information the old-fashioned way—they'd hack into the banks' computer systems. However, when Greg got ready to hunker down for some serious hacking, Rehka stopped him. "You're the one who told me that oftentimes when the only tool you have is a hammer, everything looks like a nail."

A deep frown creased Greg's eyes and forehead. "Once more, with clarity, Ms. Gyan. Please."

Everyone stopped working and smiled while watching the exchange between the two.

Rehka had a beautiful little smile playing on her face; it didn't often happen that she could out-think her husband-to-be when it came to technology matters. To be sure, Rehka was brilliant, but Greg was a genius. "I found a text file with the password to her LastPass app, where she stores the login credentials of all her online accounts. I've found two offshore bank accounts so far. There are about two and a half million in total in those accounts. No need to go on a hacking spree." She brought the two accounts up on screen while she was talking. One in the Bahamas and the other in Vanuatu, an island about three hours by Boeing off the east coast of Australia, a former French colony.

LastPass was a password manager that stored encrypted passwords online. A very handy tool as long as no one else gets hold of the master password like Rehka did.

Greg was smiling from ear to ear. He got up from his chair, walked around the table, pulled Rehka to her feet and gently into his arms, and started kissing her with abandon under the raucous applause of their friends and Digger's excited yelping.

Rehka was blushing, but she made no move to get out of the wonderful embrace.

When order finally returned, Greg and Rehka set out on a tour of the contents of Cooper's LastPass account, while Rex and the others studied Cooper's life patterns.

She went to a gym near her dad's house religiously every week on Tuesdays and Thursdays at 7:00 a.m. She met with friends there, and after their workouts, they'd take saunas and massages before having breakfast together.

Having openly proclaimed herself to be bisexual, she frequented lesbian bars and clubs as often as she visited straight bars and clubs. All the same, Rex was the one who noticed that there was roughly one mention on her phone, with accompanying photos and videos, of her with her gay and lesbian friends for every nine of her with her straight friends. "I wonder why that would be?"

"Maybe she's only ten percent gay?" ventured Josh. "You know, like being ten percent pregnant."

"Or maybe she's not bisexual at all but labels herself only to get close to troubled homosexual kids that she could recruit? I'm sure there's a market for them as well," said Catia.

"I wouldn't put that beyond her," said Marissa. "The only thing anyone can trust about her is that she's a master cheat. Scum of the Earth. Ruthless. Heartless."

"A typical psychopath, callous, unemotional, and morally depraved," added Rehka.

Like a typical psychopath, Cooper loved excitement. She wanted constant action in her life. She wanted to be in the 'fast lane' all the time. Hence, Cooper was a party animal. If she didn't get an invitation to a party at least twice a week, she would arrange her own. She just had to have the attention and admiration of others, especially the young ones. Very few things thrilled her as much as the hero-worshipping of the young girls.

She snorted cocaine whenever she felt the need for a high, which was at least once a day. Her suppliers were among her plentitude of sleeping partners. "Friends with benefits," she called them. Her 'friends' knew she didn't believe in monogamous relationships, and neither did they.

And, as Rehka had foretold, Marion had more teenagers than only Karen and Shirley in her web already and at least half a dozen more in her sights. They ranged in age from twelve to fourteen, all of them emotionally damaged because of problems at home. A stepfather sexually abused his adopted daughter while her mother turned a blind eye. An alcoholic single-parent mother who turned into a savage when inebriated. Parents who lived off welfare because they were too lazy to work and blamed their child for their financial woes because they didn't abort her when they had the chance to do so. Heartbreaking and gut-wrenching stories, all of them.

It was bizarre; Cooper had gathered the background information and kept it on her phone for every child she'd targeted in the past, everyone she was targeting now, and everyone she planned to target in the near future. The name of Courtney Lloyd was among them, photos and everything.

It was at once sickening and depressing to realize that there were people as evil as that out there hunting vulnerable children.

Marion Cooper was drawn to tragedy and misery like a shark to blood in the water.

Catia found evidence that Cooper was the one who 'supplied' Elizabeth Clayton to Marc Martinez, or Juan Garcia, as he would've been known to Beth and her family. Cooper knew Beth had been killed, but according to her phone, she didn't know anything about the circumstances of her death and didn't care about them either. It was bad practice to mix business with emotions, something psychopaths are in short supply of. When she heard about Beth's death, the seventy-five thousand was already safely in her Maltese bank account. Therefore, it was not Cooper's problem. It was not as if she guaranteed the good behavior of her merchandise. Doing business in this industry carried risks—the participants knew it.

"God knows I've never killed a woman, but this one is begging to be the first," said Rex softly. Only Catia and Digger heard him. Catia had no comment—she'd been thinking about killing the bitch longer than Rex had. Digger was staring at Catia with a look that could've meant, "So, why are we waiting?" Or was he trying to let her know it was time to stuff his Kong with peanut butter again?

Chapter Nineteen

BUSINESS ASSOCIATES

Rex knew they were onto something when Marissa and Catia found five fictional characters, Batman, Superman, Spiderman, Zorro, and Barbie in Cooper's iPhone address book.

"Those could be her business partners and associates if you ask me," said Rex. "Chats between them?"

Catia shook her head. "Not really. Just short messages on Signal. Meet me here or there, time, date, etcetera."

"Hmm, she's somewhat security conscious when dealing with the superheroes," murmured Rex. "How often do they meet?"

"Working on it," said Marissa. "Give me a sec." A few minutes later, she looked up from her screen. "Once or twice a month, but it's random. Hang on. Seems we're in luck. It looks like she and Batman are having a date at eight tonight, same place as last time, wherever 'the same place' was about three weeks ago."

"Who asked for this meeting?"

"He did. He said it's about an auction."

"An auction… Where?" murmured Rex.

By now, Greg had taken an interest in the conversation. "According to the GPS location data on Cooper's and Batman's phones, that's where the last meeting took place." He pointed to the big screen displaying a Google Street View of The Pink Poodle, a third-rate nightclub in downtown Los Angeles.

"Good location for devious meetings," said Rehka when she saw the street view.

"And all manner of criminal activities," added Marissa.

"Greg, I have a bad feeling about this auction thing," said Rex. "Can you—"

"Are you thinking what I'm thinking?" said Catia.

Rex started to shrug and stopped. "Taken?"

Catia nodded and started talking, but Josh interrupted. "What are you two talking about?"

"The Liam Neeson movie, Taken," said Catia.

"Haven't seen it," said Josh.

"He is an ex-CIA agent. His teenage daughter is abducted by child sex slave traders when on vacation in Paris. He goes after them and eventually rescues her. In the movie, the traders put their captives on auction. It's horrible."

The room had gone quiet. Everyone was looking at Rex. His right hand was clenched in a fist, his knuckles white.

Digger must have sensed the emotion in his alpha. He left his Kong, not something he'd do easily, ambled over to Rex, snuggled up to him, put his head on his lap, and whined softly as if to say, "Don't worry, buddy, I am here with you. You just point me to the trouble; I'll make it go away."

Rex said, "Thanks, buddy, I know. Let's just figure out a few more things before we go after the bastards."

Catia and the rest had long ago given up on trying to figure out how the two of them communicated. ESP, mind-reading, telepathy, alien technology, and other outlandish ideas were the closest to a logical explanation they ever came. To ask Rex and Digger was like talking to a rock. Maybe they didn't know themselves. Regardless, that they had some kind of communication system was indisputable. Their refusal to talk about it, though, was suspect.

Rex was deep in thought while scratching Digger's ears before he looked up and said, "Greg, can you get more information about the superheroes now that you have their mobile numbers?"

"Piece of cake, boss. Give me a few minutes."

"Rehka, can you check out everything about the Pink Poodle. From the parking lot to the building plans, every-thing. Owners and all. I bet there are few streetlights and security cameras in operation around that place."

"On it."

Rex busied himself again, scratching Digger's ears and back, thinking.

"Hmm, you're right," said Rehka after about ten minutes. She had tapped into the data feed of the city's surveillance system. "Less than twenty percent of the cameras in that street block or the adjacent ones are in operation." A few minutes later, she had more. "Surprise, surprise, about seventy percent of the streetlights in the neighborhood need fixing."

"Maybe the city council has given up trying to fix things that the residents clearly don't want in their neighborhood," said Josh.

"You're probably right," said Rex. "If you want privacy, or the streetlights keep you awake at night, just shoot them out."

"And that's a photo of Batman," said Greg as he pointed at the screen where a grainy driver's license photo of Batman was displayed. "His real name, according to his phone provider, is Harry Lewinsky."

Rex nodded. "Harry Lewinsky, aka Batman," he whispered as he committed the face and name to memory.

"I think you were right about these heroes being Cooper's business associates. According to their GPS location data, they spend their days and nights at nightclubs, strip clubs, and bars. If you ask me, the heroes own or manage those joints."

"You could be right," said Rex.

Greg continued and showed them the details of the other four, one of them a woman who owned a budget motel that rented rooms out by the hour, about two miles from the Pink Poodle.

It never ceased to amaze Rex how Greg and his team could cut invisible holes through impenetrable firewalls like a hot knife through butter and jump over air gaps as if they were long jumpers at the Olympics. They collected secured information with as much effort as it would've required him to switch on a light.

"Keep digging," said Rex as he stood, stretched, and yawned. "Two teas, four espressos, and a gelato for Digger, right?"

A chorus of yeses followed. Digger yapped once. Rex left for the kitchen.

It wasn't really gelato, it was peanut butter, but Catia called it Digger's gelato because it always looked as if he enjoyed the peanut butter as much as she enjoyed the Italian version of ice cream.

Digger sat down with a big smile on his face, tail wagging, waiting for Rex to fulfill his promise.

Rex returned, pushing the trolley loaded with their drinks and snacks. He served everyone, including Digger. When he was done, he looked at his watch and said, "Okay, we've got about five hours to prepare for tonight's visit to the Pink Poodle."

Chapter Twenty

LOOKING IN FROM THE OUTSIDE

They were already criminals for conspiring to commit a crime. Actually, they were conspiring to commit a series of crimes and keep at it until they found and rescued Rex's daughter. If they were arrested and charged right there and then, their punishment would probably be a stiff prison sentence. If they were lucky, maybe a suspended sentence. But if they were caught after executing their plan, they were facing life in prison, and even though California had a moratorium on the death penalty, they hadn't abolished it yet, so that was a distinct possibility, too.

Between Google Maps and the city council's engineering department, Greg and Rehka collected a wealth of information about the Pink Poodle's layout and floor plans which included the electrical wiring schematics, wastewater ducts, and such. They collected the same information for the surrounding properties.

The Pink Poodle was on Cliffside Street. It was a short street lined with all manner of dodgy-looking enterprises, where visitors mingled with loitering drug pushers, and hookers tried to chat up passersby.

The two main architectural features and most popular businesses on Cliffside Street were the Pink Poodle and the Purple Pussycat nightclubs. The latter was closed for business while it was being renovated. The four-story Cloud Nine apartment block was between the nightclubs but was nowhere near as grandiose as the nightclubs. It looked like an apartment block.

What Rex's team needed to know now was what was going on inside those buildings. Greg and Rehka went to work to break into the computer systems and security cameras. Within an hour, they not only had unfettered access to every city council security camera for three blocks around the Pink Poodle and Purple Pussycat, but they were also looking at the video feeds from inside the buildings. Rehka showed them how the CCTV systems worked and the recordings. The data was uploaded to cloud storage in real time. Every week they made hard copies of the data onto DVDs, indexed them, and handed them to someone called Manza. They were using sophisticated, high-quality spy cameras—definitely not the stock standard CCTV system. The placement of the cameras and microphones was the work of professionals.

Every nook and cranny in both clubs was covered by high-quality video and audio equipment.

"That equipment is of much higher quality than is required for standard security," said Josh. "Why?"

Everyone agreed. Why the owners wanted to cover every inch of their buildings with such expensive equipment only for security reasons led to some speculations, but a logical explanation evaded them until Rex suggested,

"Maybe they want to get as many high-quality pictures of every visitor as they can to help them identify their guests?"

"Obviously, not just for the fun of it, but what…? Aha, bribery, blackmail, and such fun, right?" Josh changed his tone to that of a news reader. "Here is a video clip of Senator Jack Ass visiting his favorite strip joint, the disreputable Pink Poodle, in downtown LA in January this year."

"Exactly," said Rex. "But although a visit to a joint like that would raise some eyebrows and lose him a few votes at the next election, it wouldn't cost him his senate seat. There must be more to it."

"Okay," said Marissa. "So, what's the role of Cloud Nine? Surely, it's not just the wrong building at the wrong place?"

"That, my dear," said Josh, "is ten to one the brothel."

Rex leaned forward. "I think you're right. It's the only business that could possibly thrive between those two clubs."

"Why do I feel the three businesses are interconnected?" said Rehka.

"I think you're right. And in more ways than one," said Rex. "Let's start by checking if there are any physical connections, tunnels, drain pipes, etcetera below the buildings on the drawings. Rehka, you and Greg, see if you can find a way into the computers and CCTV system of Cloud Nine. And see what you can find out about the ownership of the three businesses.

The city engineers' drawings indicated Cloud Nine had four floors above ground and two below. It showed no interconnecting tunnels to the neighboring properties. But the team knew not to trust the city's schematics to be a true picture of the real layout of the building. It was easy to make structural changes, especially below ground, of which the authorities were not made aware.

Nevertheless, the official plans were a good starting point. The rest of the information they needed would come when Greg and Rehka got access to the computers and CCTV. And there was also the planned onsite reconnaissance by Rex and Josh.

About an hour later, they were looking at the high-quality still images of the inside of Cloud Nine and the staff. The ground floor consisted of a small reception area leading to a mock-Western saloon reminiscent of the Old West cowboy movies, complete with a bar, the big mirror behind the barman, and small tables, missing only the smoke and piano playing. An old-style flight of stairs leading up to the floors above obscured the modern elevator below it.

The three floors above were identical; eight rooms on each floor, each with its own en suite bathroom and toilet. The decor and furnishings screamed brothel. If anyone on the team were still in doubt, some rooms were occupied by couples, and their antics on the pink silk-sheet-covered king-size poster beds removed all uncertainty—this was a brothel.

What was said and done inside those rooms were captured in the minutest detail from every angle. The quality of the audiovisual recordings would match those of a professional recording studio.

"Shall we have a look at the underground?" said Catia. Everyone agreed—in the last ten minutes, they'd seen enough nauseating vulgarities for a lifetime.

Greg brought the CCTV feed from the first level below the ground up on the TV screen. The area was taken up by a large lounge with modern furnishings and a big-screen TV, a modern kitchen, and a dining area. There were a few people in the lounge watching TV. There were also four one-bedroom apartments with en suite bathrooms and toilets shown on the building plans, but they were not covered by CCTV cameras.

"More than likely, those are the quarters of some of the management staff on the premises," said Marissa.

"Quite possible," said Rex. "Okay, let's look at the next floor."

"There are no feeds for that floor," said Rehka. "It's strange, isn't it?

"Maybe they're hiding or storing something," said Catia.

"Whatever is happening on that floor, they don't want it recorded," said Greg.

Rex frowned. "Strange indeed. Every square inch in this building, even the bathrooms, and toilets, has wall-to-wall audiovisual coverage except this floor. No doubt this place is a den of iniquity, and I'll be surprised if that floor is not used for heinous purposes."

Another hour of research and hacking by Greg and Rehka revealed that in the early days of the Pink Poodle and Purple Pussycat, the owners of the clubs hated each other. They tried to buy or bully each other out. After a few years of intense hatred, numerous violent encounters, and finally, a shootout ending in three wounded and two dead, the owners met and declared a ceasefire. These days theirs was a thriving business, especially since the opening of Cloud Nine six months after the peace treaty went into effect.

And the gossip on social media was explicit about the carnal pleasures visitors could experience at those enterprises. Which, of course, begged the question of why the police were not aware or, if aware, why haven't they done anything about it?

According to the internet rumor mill, an anonymous person was the facilitator of the peace talks and the resultant truce. Shortly after, some extensive renovations were undertaken on the dilapidated apartment block, which would eventually become Cloud Nine. The strange thing about this mysterious character was that there was no information about him on social media. No photo or any personal information. Not in the places where Greg and Rehka expected to find it.

"We'll have to cast our nets wider," said Greg.

"Okay, let's park that for now and work on our plans for the visit tonight," said Rex.

Everyone agreed.

Rex continued. "Our main aim is to find out about this auction, see if we can get a word with Marion Cooper, and find out more about the Pink Poodle, Cloud Nine, and Purple Pussycat. I have a nasty feeling we're going to find a lot more than we saw on the spy cameras' footage."

In a few hours, they had photos of every staff member, pimp, and prostitute inside the Pink Poodle, Cloud Nine, and Purple Pussycat buildings. Greg and Rehka didn't have to search far and wide to get their pedigrees; they were in the LAPD's databases. Not a single one of them was without a criminal record. Their mugshots, DNA, and fingerprints were all on record. Their rap sheets contained details of crimes ranging from solicitation, prostitution, possession of drugs, dealing in the same, assault, theft, burglary, shoplifting, fraud, perjury, every sexually related crime under the sun, and every possible crime of violence, including two murders. The list went on and on. Except for the prostitutes, the rest of them were hardened and violent criminals who wouldn't hesitate to resort to extreme violence.

Chapter Twenty-One

MAKING ACQUAINTANCES

While disguising their husbands, Catia and Marissa expressed their indignation about their husbands' decision to leave them at home for this mission. But Rex and Josh were adamant that they'd never degrade their wives by taking them to a place of such ill repute.

The four of them were trained by CIA disguising experts to change their appearances so well they would defeat the best facial recognition systems on earth. Josh came out on the other side of the makeover with wavy red hair and matching eyebrows. He could've been in his early fifties. He was wearing large, square-framed, black hornbill glasses of which the lenses were slightly tinted. He was also wearing a knee guard on his left knee under his cargo pants to remind him to limp, which was why he was using a black metal walking stick. Blue contact lenses and a Dodgers base-ball cap fitted with a few of Greg's secret micro counter surveillance electronic devices would've befuddled even the facial recognition systems of China, the most sophisticated on the planet.

Rex, who was almost olive-skinned with black hair and dark eyes when he sat down for his makeover, came out looking as if he had aged about fifteen to twenty years, with a potbelly, gray hair, and all. The green contact lenses and Yankees baseball cap with the same electronics as Josh's completed his disguise.

Digger was a different story. It was only when Rex and Josh were about to walk out the door that he figured out he was not invited.

Rex would swear that he distinctly heard some choice canine words in Digger's yelps and barks, airing his dissatisfaction. He would not translate those words into English in front of the ladies. The look on Digger's face meant only one thing to Rex— "Traitor. How could you do this to me?"

"Hey, c'mon. How could you even think I'm a traitor."

Digger growled.

"Of course, I thought about it. It's part of my strategy."

Digger yawned. Rex knew that didn't mean what one would think—he wasn't tired; he was stressed. "Buddy, there's a very good reason I'm not taking you along. First, I don't want them to see you so early in the operation. You're my secret weapon. Second, when I bring you into the mix, you're going to be their worst nightmare come true. They're going to soil themselves when you show up."

Digger sat down. His head was turned at an angle, as if he was really baffled by Rex's logic. As if to say, "What are you on about?" But before Rex could respond, he yelped once, stood, walked over to Catia, sat down next to her, and smiled at Rex. As if he had a lightbulb moment, and everything was making sense to him now, he apologized for his irrational behavior.

"Apology accepted," said Rex. "But you and I need to

have a fatherly chat about your language in front of the ladies."

Digger made no reply.

The rest of the team was gawking at the exchange. They'd seen it a thousand times, but it still left them awestruck. There was no doubt about it; Rex and Digger were in each other's heads. No scientist would convince them otherwise. They gave up long ago trying to figure out how it worked. It had driven them to the fringes of madness —there was no sane explanation for it. Nonetheless, even though they couldn't explain it, they thanked God that it worked. That inexplicable magic had kept them alive since they'd become a team and earned them the eternal friendship and gratitude of some of the highest dignitaries in the world, including the presidents of the United States of America, France, China, and Namibia.

As always, Catia and Marissa provided operational support. Rehka and Greg were responsible for the technical side of the mission.

They didn't have enough information to work out any kind of detailed plan. They wanted to get a closer look at the inside of the three businesses, the buildings, the staff, and the clientele. And to see if they could get or create an opportunity to have a chat with Marion Cooper.

Shortly after 8.00 p.m., Rex and Josh arrived in their 2007 Toyota Corolla in the Pink Poodle's parking lot, about ten minutes ahead of Marion Cooper. The parking lot was half full. Strange, they thought. This place was supposed to be popular.

Rex and Josh played their parts as if they were old

friends, meeting up for a few drinks and some fun. They talked loudly as if they were quite excited to see each other after a long time.

On the *TOMATS*, Catia, Marissa, Greg, and Rehka were staring at the TV and their computer screens. Catia, the mission controller, kept Rex and Josh informed about their observations.

As Rex and Josh approached the front entrance and saw the lineup of taxis and Ubers, they understood why the parking lot was half empty. People visiting this establishment preferred to do so as anonymously as possible.

Josh shoved a twenty into the hostess's hand to move the reserved sign from the table they wanted where they could sit next to the wall with their backs to the wall and have a commanding view of the entire room, the bar, kitchen, and a dance floor. The dance floor was about thirty square feet, where people tried to move with the rhythm of the tortured music produced by the live band.

"They should outlaw bands like this," said Josh.

Rex smiled. "What did you expect to come out of a criminal enterprise."

"Speaking of which," said Josh, "if Whitey over there is not the lead criminal in this place, all the drinks are on me."

In one corner was a private lounge area where a tall, dark-haired guy with the physique of a linebacker in a white three-piece suit, a matching white long-sleeve shirt, and a red tie was the poster boy for stereotypical villains often seen in the movies. The macho display of flash and flair left little doubt that *he* was the VIP in this place. The only one.

"The LAPD records say that's Antonio Rubio," said Catia into their molar mics. "Cuban parents but born in the US. He has a rap sheet as long as my arm and a list of aliases to match.

He was released from the Los Angeles Twin Towers Correctional Facility five years ago, where he did time for possession of cocaine, assaulting a police officer, and resisting arrest. In jail, his alias was The Blade. But after serving his time, law enforcement lost interest in him. Maybe they thought he had rehabilitated or… maybe they just didn't care or… he had learned how to stay under the radar. Whatever the case, no one checked that he stayed on the straight and narrow."

"A pro," whispered Josh as he raised his beer in a mock toast.

"You should see the photo of the police officer. The poor guy has an ugly scar across his face, and his left eye is missing," said Greg.

"Thanks to Rubio's skills with a knife, I presume?" said Rex.

"Yep, he's an accomplished knife fighter, it seems. A brutal and utterly ruthless man," said Rehka.

"Pleased to make your acquaintance, asshole," whispered Rex. "I have a gut feeling our paths will cross somewhere in the not-too-distant future."

There was an unknown man with Rubio. He remained anonymous only for as long as it took Greg and Rehka to check him out, which was just short of ten minutes. Rehka told them he was Mark Dunn, also with many aliases, now going by the name of Rick. It seems he tried his hand at drug smuggling a few years ago. He got caught and served five years in the notorious Los Angeles County Sheriff's Men's Central Jail. He learned nothing from that; he was back to his old ways—dealing drugs.

"Dollars to donuts," said Josh. "Rick's pushers are also in attendance."

"You're probably right, but then, keep in mind, this

place is filled wall-to-wall with criminals, including us," said Rex with a wry grin.

Josh chuckled. "Well, when you put it that way…"

Although the band was nothing if not dreadful, the service was good. Thanks to an almost-sexy, friendly, young server in a cute pink poodle costume, they each had a beer in hand and two bowls of salted peanuts on their table less than two minutes after they sat down. A ten-dollar tip from Rex when she delivered their order might have played a role in her eagerness to please. Rex was wondering if a similar gesture, say twenty to thirty dollars, would persuade the band to call it a night.

Their friendly server told them all they had to do to get her attention was to raise a hand. And if they wanted other kinds of entertainment, the ladies over in Jake's private lounge would satisfy all their fantasies. They merely had to wander over and ask.

She pointed at the girls at the tables surrounding Rubio and his drug king partner.

They were all Cloud Nine residents. *More like inmates* thought Rex.

They already knew all the names and faces and backgrounds of the girls; they'd seen them on the CCTV footage earlier. Greg and Rehka extracted the information and criminal history from the police records. All of them were over eighteen, the Californian age of consent. And all of them had convictions for prostitution, soliciting, and possession of illicit drugs. Other than being held in pretrial facilities, none had served any prison time.

The brothel's clients were the patrons of the nightclubs. But not all visitors were interested in spending time between the sheets with the prostitutes. Some of them only wanted to stock up on their psychotropic supplies. Others were there for both.

The girls were sitting at small tables, deliberately leaving seats vacant as a tacit invitation to any of the patrons who felt like talking to the girls about purchasing the merchandise they had on offer—sex and drugs.

Josh was right; Rick's drug pushers *were* indeed present; the girls.

It was a clever way to keep the girls off the streets. They didn't have to harass passersby and risk being trapped by the vice squad. Here, on the inside, every visitor was a potential client—they didn't have to solicit them. Clients came to their tables and talked turkey. Anyone who wanted their wares had to approach them in the presence of many witnesses and ask for what they wanted. The price was negotiated with Rubio, not with them. A clever setup, no doubt.

Of course, it wasn't a foolproof system; undercover cops could still infiltrate them. But the thing was, the cops had better things to do than prevent the employees in the world's oldest profession from working. At least they were not out on the streets. Besides, prostitutes had been, and would always be, a good source of information for some law enforcement agents. It was amazing what secrets people were prepared to share with a total stranger when they were naked in the same bed. It was on par with people confessing their sins to a priest. And finally, some of their most influential clients were law enforcement officers.

As for the drugs they were selling, it was small quantities, meant for personal use—recreational purposes were the buzzwords these days—the cops let it pass. Victimless crimes, the politicians called it. The cops had bigger fish to fry; the growers, manufacturers, importers, and distributors of the hard-core drugs.

Rex and Josh watched as two young women entered Rubio's private lounge area through a side door and approached him. One went straight to him, plonked down on his lap, and whispered in his ear.

Rick was watching the women handing over cash to Rubio like a hawk. Some of that money was his.

There was more or less a constant stream of Cloud Nine prostitutes lining up to hand over their takings and then find an empty table where they awaited their next client. Over the course of the night, Rex and Josh saw the girls leave with male and female guests. Sometimes, the ladies returned without the guest within a few minutes, probably a drug deal, and sometimes they returned half an hour to an hour later, probably a sex deal, or both sex and drugs. They always returned alone, without the guests.

It was like dairy farming, except cows got milked only twice a day.

At this establishment, they catered to everyone—no racism, no sexism, and no ageism. The patrons were made up mostly of single men and single women, but there were four apparent heterosexual couples and several same-sex couples. They ranged in age from about twenty years old to what could've been a very optimistic octogenarian couple. There were no children, though.

Rex thought hell would have to freeze over before he'd ever bring Catia to a place like this.

"So, where are the children?" wondered Josh.

Rex shrugged. "I've been asking myself the same question, but I think we're soon to be enlightened by Cooper and Batman."

Chapter Twenty-Two

THE GIRL WHO LOOKED LIKE THE TV HOST

Cooper arrived about ten minutes after them and was escorted to a table with a reserved sign ten paces away from Rex and Josh. She ordered a drink. When it arrived, she looked at the time on her iPhone; it was 8:10 p.m. Batman was late. "Bastard is going to make me wait," she moaned under her breath.

Greg paired their molar mics with her iPhone. Despite the loud music, they could hear her.

She looked around, saw Rubio, and waved at him. He waved back and indicated to her to join his party. She took her drink and wandered over with a big smile on her face. She didn't like Rubio. Psychopaths don't like each other—they hate the competition. But Cooper was a consummate actor. Rubio worked for one of her wealthiest clients, Manza, whom she had never met but who had been the biggest contributor to her offshore stash.

She hugged and kissed him on the cheek and followed the same ritual with Rick, except that he shoved something into the back pocket of her jeans when they hugged.

"What do you reckon went into that pocket?" said Rex.

"Coke, it's her favorite."

Rex nodded.

When she took her seat, Rick handed her something, which she immediately swallowed with a sip of her drink.

"A party pill," said Josh.

"Probably ecstasy or something similar," said Rex.

Rex and Josh kept an unobtrusive eye on Rubio's corner while enjoying their beer, making conversation, and studying everything and everyone in sight. Unfortunately, when Cooper had gone over to Rubio's lair, she'd put her phone in her handbag—they could hear very little of what was said over the loud, terrible music.

"Don't worry," said Rehka. "Pegasus is already installing itself on Rubio's and Rick's phones. You should hear them shortly." Rehka was right; they could hear them five minutes later. The conversation was boring; it started with the long-time-no-see routine and moved to the how-have-you-been before it moved to weather and sports. About fifteen minutes later, Cooper finished her drink, excused herself, and returned to the table reserved for her and Batman.

She ordered another drink, took her cellphone out, checked the time, and swore under her breath. "Son of a bitch, why can't he be on time? I feel like a piece of meat being stared at by starving dogs."

She sighed, opened Signal on her phone, and started texting her friend whose party she was supposed to be at, letting her know she was running late.

Greg told them that Batman's cellphone GPS showed he was in the building. "On the second floor in the security observation room."

"What's his role here?" asked Rex.

"Rehka is working on that. I don't think he's the owner, but it's clear he's some kind of big shot. Maybe the manager."

"So, why is he not coming down to see Cooper? After all, he asked for the meeting," said Marissa.

"He could be checking to see if Cooper has a tail," said Catia.

"Or he's making sure she knows he's the boss," said Rehka.

While Batman made them wait, Cooper was getting more and more frustrated as she had to fend off wave after wave of drunk lustful men who had mistaken her for a *grande horizontale*.

She was swearing like a trooper. Rex and them could hear all of it and, in the process, expanded their vocabulary of profanities with several new words and concepts. Gone was the sophisticated role model performing for the two starry-eyed kids in the shopping mall that morning.

At the forty-five-minute mark, a seriously obese, potbellied, baldheaded man with an air of authority showed up at Cooper's table. He looked nothing like the photo on his driver's license.

"That, my friends, believe it or not, is Batman," said Rehka.

Josh groaned. "Even the fictitious Batman would be pissed off."

He hugged and kissed Cooper on both cheeks.

Rex caught the fleeting look on her face, which said she was tempted to rub her cheeks with a disinfectant wet wipe.

Pegasus was already busy installing itself on Batman's Samsung smartphone.

"Rehka, surely you mean Fatman?" Josh was struggling to get over this guy's unbefitting moniker.

"Shush! We want to listen," said Marissa.

"Lewinsky, promise you won't ever make me wait in this place again. Your customers give me the creeps," said Cooper without preamble.

He laughed. "What did you expect? How can any man of any age ignore a stunner like you in a place like this?"

She flipped him the bird.

For the next forty-five minutes, the discussion between Cooper and Harry Lewinsky, aka Batman, or as Josh preferred, Fatman, gave rise to the strongest emotions of anger, hate, and revulsion in Rex and the team as they listened to the details of the auction coming up in three days' time.

Catia was right; this was a human auction. Eight underage girls between twelve and sixteen years of age. Four black. Two white. One Asian. One Hispanic.

Cooper had two twelve-year-old girls in this auction. They were the youngest to come on auction for the past six months. She expected premium prices for them. But Cooper was not only a seller; she was also the joint owner of the auctioneering business with Lewinsky. They supplied and secured the venue. That and being the auctioneer were Lewinsky's responsibilities. Cooper had to assure as many potential buyers as possible were invited and screened beforehand, and she had to collect payment from them afterward. For their part in the transaction, Lewinsky and Cooper got a twenty percent cut off the final price. They estimated their commission for the upcoming auction to put between one hundred and one hundred and fifty thousand dollars in their pockets. Cooper stood to double dip at this auction, the profit on her two girls and a hefty commission on the sale prices of the others.

Rex was seriously tempted to walk over and shoot them in the head. The only thing holding him back was that he needed information from them first. The second reason was that their strategy was, once they went over to action, they'd descend upon all the vermin with speed, surprise, and over-whelming violence of action. Courtney would be rescued if she was still alive. The operation would be over, and anyone who had anything to do with her abduction would either be dead or grievously harmed or, if they were lucky, safely in police custody.

He was still fighting the bile pushing up in his throat when he noticed a new girl entering through the side door of Rubio's lounge. Rex hadn't seen her before. She whispered something in Rubio's ear and handed over the money with a kiss on the cheek.

"Look at the one with Rubio right now," said Rex.

"She looks very familiar," said Josh. "But I can't place her."

"She looks like Emma Beckett." Beckett was a famous and stunning host on the early breakfast show of one of the mainstream TV channels.

Josh nodded. "They could be identical twins, except this girl is much shorter than her famous double. And she looks worn out."

Rex's mind went into overdrive.

"Greg, Rehka, who's the Emma Beckett look-alike?" asked Rex.

"Street name, Abbie. Real name, Eva Hansen," said

Rehka a few minutes later. "Turned twenty a few weeks ago. From Orlando, Florida. Ran away from abusive parents at age thirteen. She's got a conviction for shoplifting and four for prostitution. But, for the past two years, she's kept her nose clean."

Chapter Twenty-Three

REMORSELESS

As soon as they heard what the meeting between Cooper and Lewinsky was about, Rex and Josh abandoned their plans to find a way into the areas of the three buildings that were not covered by CCTV. It was crucial to have a chat with Cooper as quickly as possible.

When they saw Cooper looking at her watch and heard her saying, "Thanks to you, I'm almost an hour late for a good friend's housewarming party. I *have* to leave now," it was time to get ready to put their plan into action. It was also Greg's cue to bamboozle the security cameras and start feeding them prerecorded footage of the parking lot.

Cooper was in a hurry. On her way to her car, she saw two older gentlemen, one of them with a walking stick, limping a few yards ahead of her. They were slow and conversing loudly about basketball, a sport she didn't care for at all.

The ecstasy, three vodka lime and sodas, walking and texting her friend, and her haste all contributed to her carelessness. She overtook them and never noticed that the men picked up their pace when she passed them.

Approaching her red Mercedes Coupé, she clicked the button on the remote. The car beeped once, loudly, the indicator lights flickered twice, and the doors unlocked.

There were no people in the parking lot. She was too preoccupied and intoxicated to notice that the old guy with gray hair was right behind her. When her hand touched the door handle, she felt the needle plunging into her neck. She tried to scream; no sounds came out. She tried to move, but the messages from her brain never reached her limbs. A sigh escaped from her mouth before her body went limp, and she lost consciousness.

When awareness returned, she had a throbbing headache, her mouth was dry, and her eyes felt as if sand had been rubbed into them. Slowly, she registered she was sitting in a chair at a large oval wooden table. She had no idea where she was or how she got there. It was a small room with no windows. A series of blocked prints of some unknown artists' impressions of some horrible realm hung on the wall. Cooper could see the pictures were related but had no idea what she was looking at, except that they were disturbing and sinister looking. When it came to art, she was an igno-ramus. She had no idea the images on the wall depicted the poet Dante's journey through hell. The place of torment for those who 'have rejected spiritual values by yielding to bestial appetites or violence, or by perverting their human intellect to fraud or malice against their fellowmen.' Therefore, she had no idea she was about to journey through the terrifying place portrayed in those images.

Gradually she regained enough sentience to make out a creature she thought would look less out of place in one of the disturbing pictures on the wall. She blinked and refocused; the creature turned out to be a big black dog. He sat across the table from her, in a chair, like a human. To his left was a man with black hair, tan skin, dark penetrating eyes, and a stern look. Frightening. To his right was a stunningly beautiful woman with shoulder-length auburn hair, Mediterranean-blue eyes, and light freckles across her nose.

The dark-eyed man and the big black dog, who looked as if he were smiling at her, immediately filled her with dread. The woman, on the other hand, filled her with irrepressible envy, much like Snow White's evil stepmother, who resorted to murder so that she could be the fairest in the land. The woman's superior elegance and beauty were gut-wrenching. So much so it cleared Cooper's head of the effects of the sedatives.

She was surprised to find that she was not restrained in any manner. Yet, she had the distinct feeling that she was not free to get up and walk out. Her hosts' forbidding countenances were what gave her pause.

And that damn dog's contemptuous smile.

They didn't look like cops, but she was about to find out that she would've been much better off if they were. Cops would've Marandized her and allowed her one phone call, even though they would've put handcuffs on her.

The man spoke in a soft voice. "Marion Cooper, my name is Rex Dalton. I want you to pay close attention. I promise you two things: One, I will be honest with you. Two, if you're not honest with me, I won't waste my time torturing you; I'll just shoot you in the head."

With that, Rex took his Glock 17 out of its holster,

checked that it was locked and loaded, fitted the silencer, and placed it on the table in front of him.

"This is my dog; his name is Digger. You might find it hard to believe, but he will know if you lie. Even if you are only thinking of lying, he will tell me right away. Believe me, you don't want to find out how upset he gets when people lie to me."

With that, Digger growled.

Cooper didn't bat an eye as her stomach roiled.

The pretty bitch spoke with an Italian accent. "I'm Catia. Rex is my husband. I have one promise to add to his; if he doesn't shoot you, I will. In the face."

With that, Catia pushed two headache tablets and a bottle of water across to Cooper.

She couldn't unscrew the top quick enough to gulp down half of the water with the tablets. All the while, she hadn't said a word. She wondered if it would be wise to remain silent. She was still toying with the idea when she got her answer.

"I am Courtney Lloyd's father. Is she alive?" Rex started.

Cooper was stunned. *Courtney's father.* Her blood ran cold. *How the hell did he know I knew Courtney?* "Who is Cour —" she started but shut her mouth when she noticed Catia shaking her head and pointing at the gun.

The dog growled.

The look in the man's dark eyes… She just about lost control of her bladder. "I… uh… honestly, I don't know."

"Who does?"

"Rigoberto." She tried her best to hide her fear. But she had no way of knowing that the three on the other side of the table were formidable interrogators; they were trained experts in body language and micro-expressions. She didn't believe what the man said about the dog's skillfulness with lie detection. Neither did she know the dog had more than three hundred million olfactory receptors in his nose, compared to her six million, nor that he could smell her fear, her lies, and her wickedness. The section in a dog's brain devoted to analyzing smells is forty times greater than in humans. That dog could smell drugs sealed in a water-proof bag inside a car's gas tank—Cooper didn't have a prayer.

"Rigoberto, aka Marc Martinez, aka Juan Garcia, aka Duane Cruz, the wannabe movie star, right?"

Cooper nodded. The blood was draining from her face.

"Martinez is the alias he used when you introduced him to my daughter, whom he seduced and abducted from her dying mother, right?"

Cooper's face was paper white. She made no reply. It was obvious that Rex's command of the facts was unsettling.

"You introduced Elizabeth Clayton to Rigoberto, who was using the alias Juan Garcia right?"

Cooper tried to keep up a fearless façade.

"You're an accomplice to Beth's murder." It was not a question.

"I didn't touch her!"

"Of course you didn't. But you delivered her to those who did."

She made no reply.

"Do you know how she died?"

She shook her head.

Rex nodded at Catia. She brought the coroner's images up on the big TV.

"Have a look at what your colleagues did to that sweet, innocent, underage child."

Cooper glanced at the screen and turned her head away immediately.

"What's the matter? Can't stomach your partners' handiwork?"

She made no reply and tried to stare Rex down. An exercise in futility.

"And now you're busy dragging two more innocent children out of their parent's homes into the hands of your murderous partners?"

"What are you talking about?"

Rex started to reach for the gun but stopped. Instead, he nodded at Catia.

She brought up photos of Cooper in the coffee shop that morning with the sixteen-year-old Karen Clark and the fifteen-year-old Shirley Smith. The quality of the accompanying sound file was exceptionally good.

"That's what I'm talking about."

Cooper was going to be sick.

Catia jumped up, grabbed the plastic wastebasket, and shoved it into her hands just in time to prevent her from throwing up all over the table and floor.

They knew Cooper's nausea was caused by fear, not the gruesomeness of the images on the screen. Psychopaths are egocentric. They lack remorse for their actions, have no empathy for others, and they often have criminal tendencies. Cooper had devoted her life, mind, body, and soul to doing evil. The nausea was caused by the knowledge that she'd reached the end of the road.

She wiped her mouth with the back of her hand and took a few sips of water. She was trembling, breathing heavily, and tears of frustration, not regret, started dribbling down her cheeks. Psychopaths are sore losers.

Neither Rex nor Catia felt any pity. This woman and her associates were evil incarnate. Without compunction. Remorseless.

Chapter Twenty-Four

NOT EVEN A MODICUM OF REGRET OR GUILT

Cooper was smart. Psychopaths often are. Throughout her life, eight times out of ten, she was the most beautiful and the smartest in the room. She knew it, and it gave her confidence and a sense of superiority.

But now her head had slumped to her chest. She refused to make eye contact. Her body language admitted defeat. She was no match for her hosts. She felt like a zombie in their presence. Even the damn dog made her feel inferior. And then there was the vomitus feeling that she looked like the wicked witch in children's picture books next to Catia. And Catia wasn't even wearing makeup—she didn't need any.

This situation had shaken her to the core. It had obliterated the last vestiges of bravado in her. In this room, she'd lost both the IQ and the beauty contests. The answers she gave had life-or-death consequences. She had no illusions—her captors were serious about shooting her in the head—or worse, in the face.

Digger was quiet throughout it all. It must have been

obvious to him that his storied prowess in the interrogation room was not going to be called upon tonight. Over the years, he and Rex had worked out a routine that made bad guys all over the world shake in their boots and got them talking without having to lay a finger on them.

But this subject, despite the evil scents emanating from her body, gave up after one soft growl. She was no fun. No bravado. No swearing and screaming. No threats. No action. What a boring interrogation this turned out to be. He yawned loudly.

This time the yawn meant, "I'm bored out of my mind. I'm going to take a nap, okay?" Rex looked at him and nodded.

Digger jumped off the chair and made himself comfortable in his preferred corner. He gave a big sigh which meant, "Wake me when you need me," as he closed his eyes.

"Enjoy," said Rex and turned to Cooper. "What's Rigoberto's real name?"

"Geraldo Gomez."

"And *he* would know if she's alive?"

"I can't say with certainty he would know, but he knows who bought her. I don't. She never went on auction."

"Why not?"

"She got scooped up before auction. The most beautiful ones always do."

"Who?"

She shrugged. "I honestly don't know. I got thirty thousand dollars for her, and that's where my involvement ended."

"Paid into your Cayman Islands account, right?"

Cooper nodded as she reached for the wastebasket again.

Rex continued when she let the wastebasket out of her

embrace. "What happened at the party at your house that night when you introduced Courtney to Gomez?"

Rex noticed the strange look in Cooper's eyes when she looked up and started talking. It was as if she'd regained her confidence. As if she was in charge.

She had a grin on her face, enjoying every bit of the shock and pain she knew she was inflicting on Rex and Catia. She didn't spare them any of the details as she told them cold-heartedly how she'd led Courtney astray. Invited her to a house party and introduced her to a man fifteen years older with the exclusive goal to drug her and have sex with her.

She told them she was well aware of Courtney's age. She knew Courtney was too young to drink alcohol, not to mention take drugs or consent to sex. And that was the precise reason she wanted her. "The younger I can get them, the better."

She told them that Gomez first introduced Courtney to marijuana when he persuaded her to take a few deep puffs from his bong. A week or two later, he introduced her to cocaine. Gomez was the oldest male at the party but by far the sexiest of them all. And as the supplier of the drugs, he was the life of the party. Courtney was smitten with him even before she'd taken one puff from the bong.

"That's where it started," said Cooper, grinning. "Courtney lost her virginity to him that night. What happened to her after that, I don't know. Gomez paid me the thirty grand a few days after Courtney eloped with him."

Catia couldn't help but think of her new friend, Jessie, on her deathbed, clinging to life, hoping and praying God would be merciful and let her see her daughter just one more time before she died. Catia had to fight the urge to grab the gun and execute this terrible monster. If they couldn't rescue Courtney, maybe Jessie would find solace because the villain who poisoned her daughter's mind was dead.

As if he'd read his wife's mind, Rex took the gun, removed the silencer, returned the gun to its holster, and the silencer to a pocket of his cargo pants.

Rex had come to the realization that Cooper was psychotic; she'd lost contact with reality. She was sick in her head—not even a modicum of regret or guilt. Remorseless. He'd decided not to shoot her.

However, his reality was if his daughter was still alive, she was in grave danger. He had to get to her as fast as humanly possible. And may God have mercy on the souls who tried to stop him. Therefore, he had no more time to listen to Cooper's abominable stories.

He spoke softly and measuredly. "Cooper, you have one opportunity to convince me not to shoot you in the head and feed you to the fish."

The shudder running through Cooper's body was visible. She looked bewildered, as if she'd come out of a trance. All the arrogance from earlier was gone.

"I am going to leave you in this room with a pen and writing pad. You're going to write out your confession. First, I want to know everything about the auction. Precise and detailed. Where will it be held, how will it work, when does it start, where are the girls held, who are your buyers, names, phone numbers. Detail Cooper, detail is what *might* save your life. But note the emphasis on the word might.

"Start at the beginning of your life and don't stop until you come to where you found yourself in this room. I want names, addresses, dates, where, when, how, what, all of it."

She nodded.

"Where are the two children you're putting on auction?"

She whispered, "At my house, I live——"

Rex interjected. "I know where you live. Who's looking after them in your absence?"

Cooper shook her head slowly.

"So, you've sedated them?"

Cooper nodded once, almost imperceptibly.

"For how long?"

"They'll come around between six and seven in the morning."

It was a quarter to midnight.

"Now take that pen and paper and write this down," hissed Rex.

Cooper pulled the writing pad closer, picked up the pen, and waited.

"Write down your full name, date of birth, social security number, driver's license number, and physical address. Then write down both your parents' names, addresses, and telephone numbers."

She did as she was told and looked at Rex when she was done.

"Okay, now write this down." Rex dictated slowly. "I don't want him to find out I left something out or lied. Because if I do, he *will* shoot me in the head and feed me to the fish."

She wrote it down and looked up.

"Good. Now, which of your five heroes is Gomez?"

"Spiderman."

In the Ops Room, Greg and Rehka went to work, starting with looking up his phone number in Cooper's iPhone address book so that they could track his whereabouts through his cellphone's GPS locator.

"Where is he right now?" said Rex.

"At his apartment."

"How do you know?"

She made no reply. Only stared at the table in front of her.

"He's with a girl, isn't he?"

She nodded.

"Underage?"

She nodded again.

"Of course, what a stupid question."

"One you introduced to him?" said Catia. "That's how you know, right?"

Cooper nodded.

"What's her name and age?"

"Diana Sweeney, fourteen."

Catia retrieved a gun from her handbag. A Glock 19, one of the most popular ladies' handguns on the market. She fitted a suppressor and checked that the gun was loaded and ready to fire.

Just as she finished and raised the gun, Rehka told her over the molar mic that she found Diana's picture, home address, and other personal details on Cooper's phone.

Catia lowered the gun. Rehka had just saved this bitch's life.

Cooper drew a sudden, sharp breath as she lost control of her bladder. She begged to go to the toilet.

Catia ignored her. "Where does Gomez live, and under what name? Write it down," she demanded.

Cooper tore a piece off the page, scribbled something on it, and handed it to Catia with a shaking hand.

Catia read it and nodded to Rex.

"Just in case you think there's something we don't know," said Rex as he stood, "we've got your handbag, car keys, iPhone, and access to your LastPass vault. We have access to your Signal, Facebook, Instagram, Twitter, WhatsApp, email, and everything else. Including complete access to your onshore and offshore bank accounts and your Dropbox account in the Cloud with all your files, videos, and photos. We know the names and details of your victims, your associates, everyone and everything."

Cooper's eyes shot wide. As if she'd received a kick in the guts. She grabbed the wastebasket and heaved. Her entire life was on her iPhone. There'd be nothing about her they wouldn't know. The smell of her own urine mixing with the sour odor of vomit was sickening.

Catia had already decided Cooper was going to scrub, clean, and disinfect this room as if it were an operating theater in a hospital before she would be moved elsewhere. Be that to be shot and thrown overboard, or handed over to the police, or, Catia's favorite, to be handed over to her victims and their families.

"If you need anything, food, water, toilet—don't ask because you're not getting any until you're done," said Rex. "Need I remind you to not tell any lies?"

Cooper shook her head and started sobbing again.

"Quit that and start writing—your life depends on it," said Catia.

Cooper grabbed the pad and pen and started writing.

"Use the wastebasket as a toilet," whispered Catia behind her hand in passing.

Digger looked relieved. The scents of fear and deceit and hate and vomit and urine emanating from this evil human must've been nauseating. It had its benefits to have only six million olfactory receptors.

Chapter Twenty-Five

THE MEANING OF A SOFT WHINE

They locked the door to the small lounge where they'd left Cooper to write and went to the Ops Room where Josh, Marissa, Greg, and Rehka had followed the interrogation on the big screen TV. Rex and Catia stopped Cooper's questioning so that they could get to Gomez's apartment to save that poor child and, while they were at it, extract information out of him.

Soon after they started on this mission, they knew they were dealing with the scum of society. Cooper was vulgar, ruthless, and certifiably insane. But she was like an angel compared to the animals they expected to encounter from now on.

After listening to Cooper, none of them was in a forgiving mood. Vermin were meant to be eradicated.

It was approaching midnight.

Greg and Rehka had located Gomez's phone via its GPS signal. If he and his phone were together, he was at his apartment, as Cooper said. Diana's phone was offline. No surprise there.

Greg and Rehka were in the Ops Room, while Rex, Catia, and Digger jumped into one of the Toyota Hybrid RAV4 SUVs after loading their equipment in the back.

Digger couldn't have been much happier when he got invited to jump into the back passenger seat. Rex was driving, and Catia navigated. Josh and Marissa were in the other SUV about one mile behind them.

The two vehicles and the Ops Room were in conference.

"Get everything about the apartment block and his apartment," said Rex to Greg and Rehka. "Check out their security. How to get us in and through all doors, including his apartment. Start recording CCTV footage to use when we enter. See if you can get control of the main power switch of his apartment and the building. Check out the security cameras for at least two blocks around his apartment block."

"Already on it, Rex," said Rehka.

"Excellent."

"When Cooper doesn't turn up for the gym session with her buddies later this morning, they'll ask questions," said Josh. "Before long, every scumbag and associate will be looking for her."

"Easy," said Catia. "Shoot her in the face, tie weights to her feet, and dump her in the harbor."

Rex was surprised. This was the fourth time in less than twenty-four hours he heard Catia say she wanted to kill Cooper. And he realized she'd not been joking; she'd do it in a heartbeat. He started to wonder what had made his loving and caring wife so aggressive. Then it struck him—mother's instinct. She promised him and Jessica she'd treat the children as if they were her own. She was serious when she said that. Rex couldn't help but wonder what she'd be like when they had children of their own. A mother grizzly bear would be hard-pressed to match her ferocity.

"Well," said Rex, "after talking to Gomez, we won't have much time to find Courtney before the culprits get suspicious and go into hiding."

"So, what's your plan for grabbing the snake?" asked Josh.

"Digger and I'll do it. The rest of you are our eyes, ears, and backup."

"Hey buddy, I'm not crazy about that plan. I didn't come along only for my extraordinary good looks."

"No point in getting us all in trouble if things go south," said Rex

"Hey, when I volunteered for this mission, I accepted getting into trouble as a distinct possibility."

"And I appreciate it very much, but it's still not reason enough to be stupid and taunt fate. Digger and I will handle it, and if we can't, you'll be the first one to know. Besides, I want you to be close by to evacuate the child as soon as I have Gomez under control."

Greg and Rehka virtually rolled out the red carpet for the SUVs as they created a safe passage by switching cameras off and on along the route so that there would be no record of the two white Toyota Hybrid RAV4s traveling through the streets of LA shortly after midnight. Neither would there be a record of the same vehicles parked two blocks apart from each other but less than two hundred yards away from Gomez's apartment.

Rex dropped Catia off at the Farleys' SUV. They were all connected through their molar mics.

Catia and Marissa assembled four mini-drones, known as Personal Reconnaissance Systems (PRS), which had become an essential part of their operational equipment during the last few missions. Each drone had four batteries, which could be recharged within fifteen minutes. They launched two. One to check out Gomez's apartment and one flying much higher to keep a watch on the surroundings, including pedestrians, vehicles, and police patrols.

These drones were mini-helicopters and measured a little over six inches in length and an inch wide. They weighed less than thirty-three grams, a little over one ounce, without batteries. The three onboard cameras: one looking forward, one looking straight down, and one pointing downward at forty-five degrees, had night vision and thermal imaging capabilities. They were also equipped with long-wave infrared and day video sensors that transmitted video streams or high-resolution still images to their base station, which could be up to three miles away. The drones could reach speeds of up to thirty miles per hour and stay in the air for half an hour before the battery ran out.

Josh was looking over Marissa's shoulder at her laptop screen. The night vision equipment was functioning properly, and the images that came back from the drones' cameras were of excellent quality.

Greg and Rehka had hacked into the apartment's CCTV system, located all cameras, and taken control of not only the CCTV but also the entire computer system.

Gomez lived in an old but decent apartment block in a middle-income neighborhood in a twenty-five-story building with little security and an unmanned lobby. The building supervisors were a couple in their seventies, living on the ground floor. Residents had their own FOB keys, which gave them access to the basement parking, the front door, the three elevators, and the doors leading to the fire escape stairs and the service elevator. There were CCTV cameras all around the building, inside and out. But Greg and Rehka were now in charge of those.

Gomez rented the apartment in the name of Joseph Nunez, yet another alias.

Marissa switched on the thermal imaging feature on the drone and lowered it to level ten, hovering it at the level of the balcony of 1006.

"This is weird," she said. "There's only one body on what I presume is the bed. Asleep by the looks of it."

"Must be Gomez," said Josh.

Catia spoke in a rush. "That means Cooper lied, or the child has gone home or—"

"Let's not borrow trouble," interjected Rex. "I'm sure Gomez would be more than happy to tell us where she is."

Rex was busy fitting Digger's tactical harness. The mini video camera on the top of his head, between his ears, mini earphones fitted in his ears, and mini microphone on the harness between his front legs were all activated and wirelessly connected to an iPad mini, which Rex had strapped to his forearm.

Both Rex and Digger were wearing night-vision goggles.

Digger yelped softly when Rex was done putting on his battle gear.

Rex ruffled his ears and pressed his nose against Digger's. "Who's a clever boy?"

Digger yelped again softly and licked Rex's face.

"Okay, buddy, scout and hide." Rex pointed to the apartment block.

Within seconds, he disappeared among the shadows.

Rex pulled the ski mask over his face and followed Digger in the shadows.

On their way to apartment 1006, Greg and Rehka switched off lights and cameras, opened and closed doors, hijacked elevators, and stopped others for them right up to the tenth floor, where they told Rex the coast was clear.

"Unfortunately, we can't help you with this door," said Rehka. "It's a manual lock."

Rex smiled. "Let's hope I haven't lost my touch." He hadn't. The lock surrendered to his ministrations with his lock pick tool in less than ten seconds. An eternity in a high-stress environment and at least nine seconds slower than when his IT team was opening doors for him and Digger. Nevertheless, most important, they were in the apartment without being noticed. It was dark inside. Rex flipped Digger's and his own night vision goggles over their eyes.

It was too dark inside for the video cam between Digger's ears to pick up anything.

Rex sent Digger ahead; he moved much quieter than Rex. He felt like kicking himself for not fitting Digger's night vision video camera.

Digger's soft whine would've been inaudible to others, but in the absolute silence inside the apartment, Rex picked it up. It meant Digger was upset about what he saw.

Ten seconds later, Rex stood next to the double bed, looking down at the half-naked body of the fourteen-year-old Diana Sweeney.

Chapter Twenty-Six

NO POLICE

Rex switched the bed light on and discovered the child was alive but unconscious. Checking her pulse and pupil reflexes, he concluded she'd been drugged.

"Ten to one without her knowledge or consent," Catia hissed.

"So, where the hell is that son of a bitch?" said Josh.

"He won't leave her here alone for too long. She's too valuable. Josh, I want you to come and take her to your SUV so that you can keep an eye on her while Digger and I wait for Gomez."

Josh arrived via the same route with the IT team's assistance within five minutes. He carried the unconscious young girl to their vehicle in his arms like a baby. Both Catia and Marissa had received advanced battlefield first aid training, just like Josh and Rex had. They examined Diana and concurred with Rex; she was in good health, in no danger, but drugged and unconscious. They thought it was actually better that way. If she was awake, it could've been much more difficult and riskier to move her out of the

140

apartment to the SUV. Not to mention how scared and perhaps unruly the poor kid would've been in the company of three strangers.

Rex collected Gomez's phone from the drawer of the bedside table and sent Pegasus to make itself at home on it. In the meantime, he looked around, found Gomez's laptop, and put it in his backpack. Then he and Digger had a chat.

"Buddy, have you any idea where this slimeball went?"

Digger moved around so that he was facing Rex and sat down, looking up at him.

"What do you mean which slimeball? The one who lives here. The one who was doing a lot of harm to that poor kid." Rex pointed at the bed.

Digger whined softly.

"Aha! Wait right there." Rex looked around and found a heap of dirty clothes in the washing machine waiting to be washed. He grabbed the t-shirt on the top, walked back to Digger, and held it out for him to sniff. "That slimeball. Where did he go?"

Digger growled as if to say, "Come, I'll show you." He got to his feet and headed for the door.

Rex, short on his heels, told the team, "I'm going out with Digger. He wants to show me where Gomez went."

"O-k-a-y," said Marissa, "but why can't he just tell you?" She wasn't joking; she honestly believed Digger could do it.

"I don't know, I'm just following his orders. Watch this space."

Rex opened the door when Rehka told him it was safe to do so and followed Digger to the elevator.

When the doors on the ground level opened, Digger growled softly and refused to get out.

"He says Gomez didn't get out on the ground floor."

The same happened at level one basement.

At basement level two, Digger got out and led Rex straight to Gomez's empty motorcycle parking space.

"Digger reckons Gomez left on his bike."

Just then, Digger whined softly. Something was troubling him.

Rex was about to ask when Catia said, "There's a person on a motorcycle heading in your direction. He's still too far away for the drone to read the registration number."

Half a minute later, Catia said, "Okay, it's the same type of bike in the pictures Reece took. Hang on… Bingo! It's the same registration number. That's Gomez's bike, okay. He's about three minutes out."

Rex acknowledged, turned, and looked at Digger. "Now, that was impressive. You'll have to tell me how you did that. How did you know he was on his way before the drone even saw him?"

Digger was smiling at him.

"C'mon, man, we're two levels below ground."

"One minute out," said Catia.

"But first, we've got to hide," said Rex.

Gomez arrived and parked. He switched the engine off, got off, and took his gloves and helmet off before he became aware of a figure behind him to his right. He twisted around, and in the ambient light, he saw the pistol with the silencer in the masked man's hand. Somewhere to the man's right was a creature who was growling ominously.

His courage deserted him. He turned and ran. He zigzagged and ducked. He stumbled, fell, jumped to his feet like a rubber ball, and ran toward the staircase door, fully expecting a bullet to penetrate his skull or back any moment.

Rex was smiling at Gomez's feeble attempt to get away.

Digger looked amused, too, while waiting for Rex's command.

The bullet never came, but a big black dog did.

Gomez never saw the dog coming. Not even halfway to the staircase, he went down, face first, into the concrete floor, which scraped away much skin and his vaunted looks in an instant.

He turned on his back. He was dizzy, disoriented, scared witless, and silent. The growling dog's enormous fangs were only inches away from his throat.

The black-clad man with the black ski mask stood a few feet away, pointing the black silenced gun at him.

"Geraldo Gomez?" The man spoke softly.

His street name was Rigoberto, many people knew him by that name, but only a handful of people knew him as Geraldo Gomez. This gun-toting masked man was not one of them. *Cop? Gangster? Rival? What does he want? If he's here to kill me, he could've done so already.*

Obviously, he wanted to talk, not shoot, at least for now.

He didn't resist when Rex shoved a foul-smelling cloth into his mouth and secured it with duct tape before he pulled a ski mask back to front over his face and zip-tied his hands behind his back.

His screaming came out as dull moans when Rex pulled him to his feet by his hair and shoved him toward the elevators.

Greg switched the lights off and took control of the elevators and fire doors on each floor so that Rex and company had one elevator dedicated to themselves.

Greg and the others were watching the drones' thermal imaging.

Josh was in the back seat of the SUV, keeping an eye on Diana, who was in the seat next to him with the back lowered so that she could be in a horizontal position. Josh had folded his jacket and placed it under her head as a pillow. The marks on her arms indicated she'd been getting injections for a while already. He kept an eye on her vital signs: oxygen levels, blood pressure, and heart rate while listening to Rex talking to Gomez and watching Catia's laptop screen displaying the feeds coming from the drones.

Greg and Rehka were on the *TOMATS*, also watching and listening while keeping an eye on Cooper at the same time.

Greg reported, "Cooper will soon need more paper and another pen."

Chapter Twenty-Seven

FROM THE TOP DOWN

Rex could've employed several harsh interrogation techniques on the miscreant—sleep deprivation, stress postures, starvation, extreme cold, extreme pain, etcetera—but those required time and patience. Rex had neither.

Instead, he and Digger took Gomez to the rooftop of his twenty-five-story apartment building and made him stand on the waist-high wall, right on the edge, before removing the ski mask so that he could see where he was.

Terrified of heights, he began shaking uncontrollably.

Rex removed the gag and zip-ties and told him to take off his shoes.

"Sh... Sh... Shoes?"

"You heard me."

"Please, please, I'll cooperate. If you want information, if I have it, it's yours. If it's money, all I have is yours."

"I don't need information. I need all your money and a confession."

"Con... Conf... Con... fes...sion?"

Digger growled.

"Yes. About all the children you've raped, drugged, and sold to child sex traffickers. Now, take your damn shoes off. Or do you prefer the dog to take them off for you? He will rip your feet off."

Seconds later, Gomez stood barefoot.

"Apparently, people who want to commit suicide by jumping off tall buildings always take their shoes off before they jump. Well, that's what I've heard," said Rex.

Gomez was shivering and stuttering and begging and sobbing instead of doing the right thing and jumping off the building. But, besides being a pedophile, and various other psychiatric deviations, he was nothing if not a coward.

Gomez started protesting.

Digger barked once, softly and menacingly.

"Okay, now about the confession; no lies, omissions, delays, misspeaking, misremembering, or anything of the sort. Understood?"

"Yes! You can trust me. I won't lie."

"You mean trust you like the children you misled and sold to the sex traders?"

Gomez didn't reply.

Rex made no promises about letting the scumbag live in exchange for the confession, because he didn't ask for it. Just as well; the answer would've been no.

Gomez required no further encouragement; he loved his own voice. After all, he was a budding actor.

"Is Courtney Lloyd alive?"

Gomez was stunned. His mouth opened and closed as he tried to speak, but no sound came out.

Digger's snarl got the desired effect.

"I don't know. TJ took her from me. He will know." Gomez talked fast, like a livestock auctioneer.

"Do you have a death wish, asshole?"

"No! Please don't—"

"You're lying. You sold her to TJ, you snake."

"Sorry, sorry, I promise it won't happen again. Yes, I sold her to TJ."

"TJ is the Pimp in Chief at Cloud Nine, right?"

"Yes. I don't know his real name."

"Doesn't matter. What did he do with her?"

"I honestly don't know. I delivered her to him. I know she didn't go on auction. TJ paid me a hundred and fifty thousand for her two days after delivery, and that was the end of my involvement."

Rex looked at his watch. "Start your confession. Begin with your real name and your background. Then all the aliases you've ever used and all the details of every child you'd ever molested. Just a tip, I have the names. I just want to compare notes."

His real name was indeed Geraldo Gomez, born in the US to Columbian immigrant parents. His siblings, two older brothers, made the most of their opportunities in the US. One was a high school teacher in mathematics, the other a chartered accountant.

They took care of him after their parents' tragic deaths in a car accident. The older brothers wanted to take him under their wings and help him get qualifications and a job, but the sixteen-year-old Gomez was not impressed with the effort his brothers had to put in to get qualifications just to get a low-paying job and start working their way up the corporate ladder by licking boots, scratching backs, greasing palms, and kissing asses. He decided there was an easier and quicker way.

When he finished school, he borrowed money from his brothers and headed west to California in search of his fortune, much like the legendary gold diggers of the 1848 gold rush known as the Forty-Niners. He told his brothers he was going to find work so that he could pay for his studies at the University of California - Los Angeles, one of the best schools for drama and theater arts in the country. He believed he possessed the looks Hollywood was looking for in their next film star, his moral values which were lower than a snake's anus notwithstanding.

Gomez's stinking vainglory didn't prevent him from telling Rex the truth; whether it was embarrassing, incriminating, painful, or degrading didn't matter. He was betting on the notion that the truth might save his life. *How could it not? The man had kept his ski mask on. That was a good sign, was it not? It meant the man didn't want to be identified later.*

"But the film industry is a cutthroat quagmire in which I made no headway," said Gomez. "So, when my rags to riches dreams didn't come true, I started looking for other opportunities where my notable good looks would be appreciated. I found it in the 'minor-attracted persons' niche."

Rex had a hard time not pushing him off the wall. But Gomez was just verbalizing the ideas of certain academics who insisted they should not be called child molesters or pedophiles anymore. According to them, it was just a different kind of love that some adults had for minors. Hence, the term minor attracted person. They advocated that it was the politically correct term to use instead of the narrow-minded and insulting pedophile or child molester.

"TJ is the one who recognized my potential as a recruiter and introduced me to Marion Cooper, who coached and helped me establish a lucrative business in this niche." Rex thought Cooper was insufferable, but this guy was orders of magnitude worse.

His modus operandi was to work with talent scouts and groomers such as Cooper to provide him with underage girls who he would 'break in' meaning seducing or raping them, hook them on drugs, and sell them to pimps such as TJ or Jake or put them on auction.

"The younger they are, the more I get for them. My most lucrative job so far put four hundred and fifty thousand in my pocket, after expenses. It was a twelve-year-old blonde-haired, blue-eyed girl, deserted by her parents when they divorced. They blamed her for the divorce because she was unplanned and unwelcome. They regretted not aborting her.

"When they reach the age of consent, they lose their attraction for me. Their shelf life is too short," he told Rex.

"But if they're the right age, there is no shortage of very rich buyers.

"The kids are gold mines. Their owners take good care of them. They have their own rooms, TVs, play stations, dolls, you name it. They get free board and lodging and drugs and job security in the form of a constant stream of clients, sometimes ten a day. And a free doctor's checkups, mainly for STDs, once a fortnight."

Rex started toward Gomez, but Digger stopped him with a growl and a short yelp, which meant, "Don't do it!"

Gomez continued. It took him between two and six weeks to complete a recruitment. He was always working on two to three prospects at the same time. He paid talent scouts, such as Cooper, ten to twenty percent of the sale price. Some scouts were senior and popular girls at schools. Others were young adults, such as Cooper, role models for the ten to sixteen-year-olds.

He had been at this for almost five years now and had accumulated a tidy sum of almost five million. Of course, Rex was more than welcome to all of it.

He remembered some names, but when his memory

failed him, he was quick to point out he had everyone's names and photos and details on his phone, like the notches on an assassin's gun.

"Tell me about Manza."

He had never met Manza; he always dealt with his henchman, TJ. Gomez wasn't sure of the facts but told Rex that he'd heard Manza was the head honcho of one of the major drug and sex traffic gangs in LA with ties to other powerful gangsters around the country.

He gave up the names and addresses of two more joints, just like Cloud Nine, owned by other gangs whom he dealt with.

He also told Rex about TJ, Johnny, and Sammy, the pimps at Cloud Nine. He had neither photos nor last names. The latter would've been bogus. But he could describe them in much detail, including their distinctive tattoos. TJ, besides the tattoos, also had a scar stretching from below his left eye halfway down his cheek. He liked to tell people how he had killed the man who did that to him. He was lying. That scar was the work of a sixteen-year-old girl with a broken beer bottle. The fate that befell the girl was nothing but diabolical.

Rex had seen all three pimps in the footage that Greg and Rehka found.

"Tell me about Elizabeth Clayton."

"I had nothing to do with her death."

"Of course not. You only drugged, raped, abducted, and sold her to the killers, right?"

He didn't answer that. "You know why she's dead? She tried to escape. She almost made it." He didn't explain how he knew that. "I don't know who killed her, but I'm sure TJ would've been involved. He's a barbaric, ruthless, soulless beast."

"Right, and you're the angel of mercy who abducts children and sells them to that barbaric, ruthless, soulless beast."

In that moment, Rex had a vivid vision of Beth Clayton's battered body, except her face was that of his beautiful daughter, Courtney.

He gave Gomez a slight push.

The sound of a human body hitting a solid concrete sidewalk at a hundred and twenty miles per hour is sickening. The mess was stomach-churning.

Digger threw his head back and howled like a wolf. It was spine-chilling and sent every dog within earshot into a cacophonous frenzy of barking, howling, yelping, yapping, and whining, unnerving their owners.

Rex didn't look down at the body; he turned and walked away with Digger next to him.

Chapter Twenty-Eight

THEY LIKED TO DO IT UNINTERRUPTED

Gomez's twenty-five-floor descent went unnoticed by everyone in the neighborhood until around 6:30 a.m. when he was discovered by a young man living in the neighboring apartment block on his way to work. A 911 call was made shortly after.

The police cordoned the area off with the standard yellow crime scene tape and started knocking on doors to question people in search of witnesses. There were none.

The supervisor and his wife recognized the deceased and told the homicide detective his name was Joseph Nunez. He had moved in about six months ago. He was the friendly but quiet type who kept to himself. No one there had ever socialized with him, so they couldn't say if he was depressed, worried, or suicidal. His circle of friends obviously lived somewhere else.

A young woman among the curious crowd lamented about what a pity it was that she would never again have the pleasure of beholding Joseph's striking features.

"Why did he have to jump off the building?" wondered another of the onlookers.

"It's hard to believe that a man with those looks and so much going for him would throw himself off a building," speculated another. "He must've been extremely troubled by something."

The supervisor took the detective to Nunez's apartment and unlocked the door for them with his master key. The detective took one look at the unmade double bed and knew Nunez had been living there with someone else. The clothes in the closet and the toiletries in the bathroom left little doubt it was a woman. Although these days, one can't be sure. At first, he didn't want to believe the supervisor's denial that he knew about Nunez's sleeping partner. But after questioning his wife and other residents and getting the same result, he changed his mind. It was bizarre.

How did he manage to hide the cohabitation from everyone, even the neighbors?

Things got even more perplexing when he couldn't find anything in the apartment to tell him more about the deceased or his companion. No mobile phone, no computer, no bills, no next of kin. Within half an hour, he was told by his head office that not only was the registration of the motorcycle fake, but so was the name Joseph Nunez.

Gomez's body went to the morgue. The detective had seen these types of cases. Without the deceased's identity, his investigation was DIW, dead in the water.

Back on the *TOMATS*, Rex bubble-wrapped Gomez's phone after Greg had loaded it with the recording of Gomez's confession and Rex's voice computerized. He wiped the phone clean with an alcohol cloth before putting it in an envelope with a typed note and addressing it to Lieutenant Harris. He paid a twenty-four-seven courier to drop it at Harris's front door. Rex had to pay extra for the anonymous or, as the driver called it, a drop-and-run delivery.

After handing the packet to the courier, Rex and Digger returned to the yacht and visited Cooper.

The room smelled worse than repugnant. She had written one and a half notebooks full and was still going strong. Greg had made sure she had enough stationery and pens to last for a few days.

She was tired, hungry, thirsty, emotionally exhausted, and morally bankrupt. Defeated.

"I beg you, please give me something to eat and drink."

Rex ignored her.

Digger jumped on his chair and smiled at her.

Rex took the first notebook and read the auction information. It was at once sickening and depressing. He was struggling not to give in to the intense desire to choke the life out of this heartless creature.

When he was done, he looked at her and said, "You better keep on writing, Cooper. Your life is balancing on the edge of the precipice."

With that, Rex took the notebook and left with Digger short on his heels. He had to rescue eight children before they were pushed through the gates of hell.

He stopped at the door and spoke over his shoulder. "Oh, I almost forgot. It's all over the news; a former movie star who was also a pedophile had a bout of remorse. He confessed all his sins before he threw himself off the top of his apartment building." Rex made a scene of looking at his watch. "A few hours ago."

Cooper stopped writing. Her face was paper-white, her eyes wide, and her jaw slack.

The news about Rigoberto's death was shocking, but nothing compared to the shock when she looked into Rex's cold, dark eyes. They radiated death. It made her shiver.

In the lounge, while pouring coffee for him and Catia and stuffing Digger's Kong with beef jerky, Rex was wondering so loudly Catia could hear him. "I wonder what would happen if I told Cooper that Diana is here on the yacht and dying, so to speak, to see her again?"

Catia suppressed a smile. *My husband is finally catching my drift.* "What's stopping you?"

Rex didn't hear her. He was staring at Digger, who was staring back at him.

Catia saw the stares and remained quiet. She knew when Rex and Digger were working on a plan, they liked to do it uninterrupted.

Chapter Twenty-Nine

WHO HELPS THEM?

A minute or so before Josh and Marissa arrived on the *TOMATS*, Diana began to groan and stir. Josh carried her to one of the staterooms, where Catia, Marissa, and Simona took care of her as she slowly regained consciousness.

When her eyes finally opened and stayed open after the first sip of water, they helped her to sit up against the pillows, but before she could get comfortable, her hand flew to her mouth, and she pointed at the bathroom with the other hand.

"She's going to be sick," said Simona, grabbing the kid's hand, pulling her up, and hustling her to the bathroom with the help of Catia and Marissa. They almost didn't get her to the toilet in time. The child knelt on her knees for close to ten minutes, with Simona rubbing her back and talking softly to her as she emptied her stomach into the toilet bowl in waves.

Afterward, Marissa helped her to take a shower and put on pajamas provided by Catia. They were too big for the skinny fourteen-year-old, but to her, all that mattered was that they were cozy and smelled like roses.

It surprised them how calm and cooperative Diana was as if she knew she was in no danger.

"Maybe she sensed that our empathy was genuine," suggested Simona, who had been the girlfriend of an abusive Camorra clan leader who'd put her in the hospital with multiple bruises, lacerations, and broken bones. Was it not for Rex saving her and taking her to Rome, where Catia took care of her and became her best friend, she would've been dead.

Just then, Rex came in to check how Diana was doing. Simona motioned for him to follow her. "We should get her to a doctor," she said when they were outside.

Rex nodded. "Agreed. We don't have the knowledge to treat her. The poor child will need medication to counter the hellish withdrawal symptoms, which will surely kick in soon."

"Declan has many friends and family in these parts," said Simona. "Let's ask him."

They found her husband on the bridge and told him what they wanted. "Okay, give me a few. My cousin, Julie Williams, is a nurse practitioner. She'll help us herself or know someone who can."

A few minutes later, Declan ended the call with his cousin. "We're in luck; it's her week off. She said she'd be happy to do it for her favorite cousin and make a house call, or a yacht call in this case."

Declan and Rex were waiting for Julie when she arrived forty minutes later. She was professional and thorough. She had much experience in psychiatric wards in hospitals and clinics where drug addicts were often treated. She found

Diana to be in good health, except, of course, for the damage caused to her body by the drugs.

She spent two hours with the kid who told her a heart-rending but not uncommon tale of growing up in a single-parent home as an only child and being abused from the age of nine by her mother's live-in alcoholic boyfriend.

Two months ago, she genuinely believed her lucky fairy had touched her with her magic wand when she was befriended by a girl who was much older than her. Marion Cooper made her feel so special. Neither of them knew that said Marion Cooper was on the same yacht no more than forty yards from them, busy saving her life by writing a non-fiction book about all her transgressions in the minutest detail, and she, Diana Sweeney, featured in that book.

Two weeks after meeting Marion, she introduced Diana to this Adonis, John Costas. She couldn't believe that a man so good-looking, more than double her age, could be so much in love with her and make her so happy. He introduced her to cocaine and other drugs. She became hopelessly addicted within a few weeks. John's attitude started to change. Before long, he asked her to have sex with some of his friends. She refused in the beginning, but only for as long as she did not need drugs. Soon John stopped asking and started ordering her to do it with strangers whom he befriended in clubs and bars. She never saw him getting paid for it, but she was sure he did. She wanted out, but it was impossible. He held all the aces.

Diana was exhausted by the time she finished telling her story. The *lofexidine* Julie gave her to counter the effects of the cravings and withdrawal symptoms helped her to relax and fall asleep peacefully for the first time in years.

When Julie finally emerged from the room, she told them that Diana would be okay physically. Psychologically, she was facing a long uphill battle. She briefed everyone on how to take care of her but also cautioned them. "For the next few days to a week, you can't let her be on her own, not even for a short time. She's just not emotionally strong and stable enough to be left alone. When the cravings come, and believe me, they will, with a vengeance, the medication might not be enough to stop her from being irresponsible and irrational. She could try to run away or hurt herself."

"Shouldn't we rather find a place for her in a rehabilitation facility somewhere far away from here?" said Marissa.

"Yes, eventually. For now, she needs someone she can trust. Remember, she doesn't even understand the concept of trust simply because she's never experienced it. If you dump her at a clinic somewhere, she's got no one on the outside who she can look forward to going to when she gets out. Her rehabilitation would fail. You or someone else has to be that anchor for her first. Remember, she's only a child."

Simona was shaking her head. "It's horrible. How many girls like her are out there?"

"Too many, tens of thousands. I don't know the exact numbers."

"Who helps them?" asked Catia.

Julie was shaking her head. "Nobody. There are places and programs for drug addicts, sex addicts, alcoholics, kleptomaniacs, child molesters, you name it, there's a rehabilitation program for it, but for prostitutes, there is nothing. Nobody wants to help outcasts like these girls except some church groups."

Her audience listened in stunned silence.

"They die early. Some die at the hands of a pimp or client who got too rough or an infected needle transmitting hepatitis, AIDS, and so forth. But the bulk of deaths are caused by drug overdosing, accidental or deliberate; who knows? Fentanyl is the drug of choice for the overdosers. A Hundred thousand Americans a year die from Chinese-manufactured fentanyl overdoses. The 'experts' who are predicting war with China make me laugh. They must've been sleeping for the past decade. China is already at war with us.

"Just think about it, we went to war in Afghanistan and Iraq when three thousand Americans got killed on Nine Eleven. Our military lost a little more than seven thousand souls over twenty years in the War on Terror. Yet, the Chinese are slaughtering us at the rate of a hundred thousand per year with impunity."

Listening to Julie made Rex nervous. His daughter was in even more danger than he thought.

Chapter Thirty

THE AUCTIONS

When Diana fell asleep, after talking to Julie, Simona took over the nursing duty while Rex and the team met in the Ops Room. John and Christelle had arrived half an hour earlier. Marissa had called and updated them about everything that happened since Josh and Rex arrived at the Pink Poodle the night before. When John heard about Cooper's and Gomez's fate, he knew war was about to break out. That was only the first skirmish. His place was in the Ops Room on the *TOMATS*, directing the operations. Less than an hour later, he and Christelle were in the air on the way to Los Angeles, where all hell was about to break loose.

The chef prepared a sumptuous breakfast for them, which he brought in on a large trolley. He checked that there were enough pods for the espresso machine to get them started. If there was one thing he learned since Rex and company had set foot on the *TOMATS*, they went through gallons of coffee faster than a 1980s twelve-cylinder Chevy through gasoline.

He left them with a, "Let me know if there's anything

else you need. I'll come around later to replenish the coffee pods."

Except for Rehka, who had never acquired a taste for it, the rest of them were coffee aficionados. John had quoted Dave Barry to a lackadaisical barista in D.C. one morning in a crowded coffee shop. "Son, it is inhumane to force people who have a genuine medical need for coffee to wait in line behind people who apparently view it as some kind of recreational activity." A minute later, he and Christelle took the first sips of their coffee and relaxed.

There were no discussions about Gomez's departure. There was nothing to discuss. Everyone in that room, if given a chance, would've pushed Gomez off that building. The children of this planet were safer without him around. They had only one gripe, though, with Rex and Digger; why didn't they make him suffer even just a little like his victims did? But no one brought the topic up as it would've been a waste of valuable time on something they couldn't undo.

Declan was on the bridge, busy with various administrative tasks while keeping an eye on Cooper on one of the TV screens patched into the surveillance cameras in the small lounge.

She'd been writing ferociously; it was her only hope to avoid a bullet in the head or die from starvation or thirst. Access to a toilet and shower would've been nice, too. Not imperative, though.

Rehka scanned Cooper's auction notes and showed them on the big screen. Reading them had the same effect on everyone as on Rex earlier; it was at once infuriating and repulsive.

The auction was to be held on basement level two at Cloud Nine.

"Now we know why there're no security cameras on that floor," said Greg.

Little did he, or anyone else in the Ops Room, know what horrors awaited them on the subterranean levels of Cloud Nine.

Rehka continued scrolling down slowly. Cooper's chronicle disclosed that the girls would be transported over to the Pink Poodle the day before the auction, where they'd receive makeovers and new clothes so they could look their best for the buyers.

On the night of the auction, they'd be moved to the auction room at Cloud Nine via secret tunnels connecting the three buildings. Clearly, Cooper was highly motivated to be diligent and detailed; hence, she provided rough drawings of the three buildings, including the secret tunnels and doors and the combinations of the locks. The latter corresponded with the information on her phone.

"There's your confirmation, Rehka," said Greg. "Those businesses *are* connected."

Buyers had to register a week before the auction and pay a refundable deposit of one hundred thousand dollars. At the auction, every potential buyer had a private soundproof booth to which they'd be escorted in absolute privacy. The food and drink were on the house. But no one could know who the buyers were. They weren't even allowed to know each other. The exception, of course, was Cooper and Lewinsky, who knew everyone at the auction, buyers, and sellers.

Those were part of the security arrangements, and anyone who didn't abide by them, or attempted to circumvent them, was summarily kicked out of the fraternity, followed by a visit from a few enforcers armed with rubber hoses, batons, and other tools of their trade. The rebel would be lucky to be alive afterward. And that was on top of being forbidden to ever do business in this industry in LA again.

It seemed, despite Cooper's dispirited state of mind, her memory was still functioning reasonably well, as she remembered almost seventy-five percent of the names of the buyers and sellers who ever attended her auctions.

For completeness' sake and to avoid ending up at the bottom of the harbor as fish food, she wrote down in which Dropbox folder all the information could be found: names, addresses, telephone numbers, photos, etcetera. She pointed out explicitly that in case some of her handwritten facts and figures contradicted what was in her Dropbox, the latter should always be regarded as the source of truth.

Greg and Rehka couldn't get their fingers on their keyboards fast enough. Within minutes the documents in the Dropbox started to appear on the TV screen. Not only had she kept detailed records of the buyers, but she'd also kept the same kind of details for all the sellers and the children they'd sold. For the children, however, she didn't have much more than an alias, age, and some sketchy background information. But she'd recorded high-quality videos of them at auction.

The purchase price was payable at the end of the auction, either in cash or drugs or wire transfer to an offshore bank account, before the merchandise was released to them. After that, the girls became the sole responsibility of the buyers.

She had a list of eleven buyers who'd participated in her auctions over the past few years. They'd all registered for this auction. She knew them all. They were stinking rich. She wasn't worried; for a successful auction, she only needed two buyers going for the same merchandise. But eleven of them going for the same girl made it so much more exciting. And lucrative.

"Why on earth would she want to keep such damning information?" said Rehka.

Rex held up two fingers. "To protect herself against her clients and for blackmail."

Rehka nodded. "Of course, a my-lawyer-has-a-copy-just-in-case-I-die-of-unnatural-causes type of thing, right?"

"Precisely."

Chapter Thirty-One

JOHN DOE

The coroner had finished the autopsy. The cause of death was no mystery. This guy plummeted face-first into a concrete pathway from the top of a twenty-five-level apartment building. It always caused death. Almost every facial bone was fractured, the jaw in several places, only a few small patches of undamaged skin were left, the front teeth were missing, and there were lots of deep cuts. This cadaver's face was too damaged to restore. It was impossible to figure out what the man's face was even supposed to look like, to start with. Unlike the cause of death, his identity was going to be a mystery. The coroner took some photos of what was left of the man's face, more to show the damage than for ID purposes. No facial recognition system would find a match for that mess.

After Harris had discovered the courier package, he went to the kitchen, poured himself a coffee, and unwrapped it. Inside, he found the latest model iPhone. There was a typed note, and it said this was the phone of the late Geraldo Gomez, his real name, aka Marc Martinez aka Rigoberto aka Juan Garcia, and a long list of other aliases. According to the note, the owner of the phone committed suicide in the wee hours of the morning by throwing himself off the top of the apartment building where he lived.

His body was kept at the morgue.

The note also said that there was an important recorded message to be found under the audio files on the phone titled, 'I Confess,' and the recipient was encouraged to listen to it.

He did so.

Even though Gomez's testimony was coerced, Harris believed it to be truthful. Unfortunately, it was what was known in the legal world as the fruit of the poisonous tree. It meant evidence obtained through illegal methods, i.e., an unauthorized search or seizure or the use of illegal interrogation techniques, was inadmissible as evidence in a court of law. It meant Harris could not get warrants to arrest the criminals named by Gomez. But it didn't frustrate him as much as it always did.

As he got closer to retirement, he couldn't help but look in the rear-view mirror at his career, so to speak. On paper, officially, he had reason to be proud of his achievements and more than just a few commendations from his superiors. After a lifetime of service, he had good reason to look forward to a peaceful retirement with his wife of forty years, the cabin by the lake, the trout lined up just waiting for him to cast the line, and four grandchildren to spoil.

But emotionally, something was amiss. Over the years in the vice squad, he'd been instrumental in bringing quite a few child molesters and drug dealers to justice. He'd enjoyed it when the prison doors slammed shut behind them for ten to thirty years. But to this day, he'd not experienced the satisfaction of seeing the prison doors slam shut behind the leaders of those sex trafficking gangs. He had accepted that he would never experience that. But then the Courtney Lloyd case landed on his desk. And then he got the visit from her dad, Mr. Rex Dalton, and his dog, a few days ago.

A little smile was playing on his face when he powered off Gomez's smartphone after listening to his rooftop confession for a second time. The voice of the interrogator was scrambled, but Harris had no doubt who it belonged to. "And this is only the beginning, scum. My money is on the US Marshal and his smirking black dog to put several more of *you* out of *my* misery."

Compared to Beth Clayton and other innocent kids like her, Gomez had an abrupt and merciful ending. He didn't deserve it.

At the office, Harris searched the databases for Geraldo Gomez and found no match. The coroner's fingerprints and DNA found no matches either. That was puzzling. It meant Gomez had never crossed paths with law enforcement. He wasn't even mentioned in passing in any police database.

"Highly bloody unlikely for the drug pusher, pedophile, unscrupulous scumbag I heard on the recording earlier." He knew it *was* indeed possible that Gomez never had a run-in with law enforcement—it was just highly unlikely.

"That means his details have been scrubbed from the system." Harris shook his head. "Nah, hang on right there, we're not going there; too frightful to even consider."

He got into his car and drove over to the morgue.

The coroner told him everything pointed to suicide. He couldn't find any signs of a struggle or anything to hint at foul play.

Harris concurred. After all, the evidence he had that contradicted the coroner's conclusion was the fruit of the poisonous tree. Every word of that confession was obtained illegally and was inadmissible. Hence, when he got home that night, he went to the workbench in his garage, retrieved a hammer from the shelf, and went to work on the iPhone.

John Doe was the name on Gomez's toe tag. If no one identified and claimed the body, it would eventually be cremated and the ashes buried in a collective grave with other unidentified people.

Good riddance.

Chapter Thirty-Two

MARION'S FRIENDS?

"We know the ins and outs of the auctions now," said John. Our dilemma is what to do about the two kids at Cooper's house and the six being kept elsewhere. And Courtney."

Everyone was looking at Rex. All the adages, such as charity begins at home and blood is thicker than water, were flashing through his brain. He ignored them all. The choice was difficult, but there was only one right thing to do. "It's the lives of eight children versus one. We *must* get those children out. By any means."

Everyone agreed.

"Do we want the auction to proceed?" said John.

"Yes, but without Cooper's captives," said Rex.

"Maybe Rehka and I could send messages to Cooper's friends and business associates, especially Batman, creating the illusion that she's come down with a very contagious strain of COVID and won't make it to the auction but persuade them the auction should go ahead without her and her merchandise," said Marissa.

Josh nodded. "Uh-huh. That way, we can rescue the two

kids at Cooper's house today and the remaining six tomorrow night at the auction. And there is a chance that one of them has Courtney or knows where she is."

According to Cooper, the buyers came from across the country. She had no idea how many children they owned, but just the number that went through her auctions since she started a few years ago added up to fifty-five. There could be hundreds, if not thousands, across the country.

It was close to 5 a.m. The sun was almost up. The children at Cooper's house would start to wake up within the next hour or two.

Thanks to the IT whiz kids, Rex and Josh had aerial photos of the property, plans of both dwellings, and diagrams for the plumbing, drainage, and electric circuits. They also knew the make, model, and vulnerabilities of the alarm systems.

The Dorset estate was in Bel Air. The security at the estate was all about image—rich people had security guards and bodyguards. Eight-foot walls bordered the property. There were security cameras, sensor lights, and alarms in the main house and cottage. The three guards in Dorset's employ worked eight-hour shifts each. They had no weapons or dogs.

The rescue mission followed the team's tried and tested battle formation. However, the operators had swapped roles. Rex was the mission controller instead of Catia. Josh was the drone pilot instead of Marissa. Greg and Rehka were in control of the communications and responsible for removing any obstacles that could hamper the operators in the field. If required, they'd remotely open and close doors, switch security cameras on and off, switch power and lights on and off, hold elevators, take over traffic lights, and so forth. Oh, and listen to the police radio frequencies.

Catia and Marissa were augmented by Digger, who would be fitted with his tactical harness and leading the way. Military dog handlers and any soldier who ever had the privilege of having a trained military dog in their unit would tell you that the dogs were force multipliers. With the IT team's technology behind them and Digger in front of them, Catia and Marissa were probably the equivalent of six to eight trained soldiers.

Greg and Rehka sent the guard at the Dorset estate's front gate a deepfake voice message on his cellphone mimicking Cooper's voice and told him that she'd been feeling unwell, took a COVID test, and got a positive result. She had to quarantine for the next seven days. Two of her friends were on the way to pick up some of her stuff and bring it over to her. She didn't say where she was, and the guard knew better than to ask. Marion Cooper was a TB— terrible bitch. Finally, she also told him she'd be sending through pictures of her friends and the car's registration. The pictures of her friends and details of the car's registration arrived less than two minutes later.

Deepfake voice, also called voice cloning or synthetic voice, uses Artificial Intelligence (AI) to generate a clone of a person's voice. The technology has advanced to the stage where it can closely replicate any human voice with great accuracy in tone and likeness. As always, with these things, the bad guys quickly found nefarious purposes for it. There was a time they could get around voice recognition systems about thirty-four percent of the time. Lately, the good guys had been catching up, and their success rate had dwindled to only six percent. But for that kind of accuracy, one required powerful computers and sophisticated voice recognition software. Robert Dorset's security system had neither.

Long before Catia, Marissa, and Digger pulled up at the

front gate, Greg was in control of the estate's electronic security systems, internet routers, and electrical switches.

Rex and Josh were a hundred yards down the street, ready to step in if the guard became obstinate. If the guard knew what was good and healthy for him, he would treat the ladies and their dog with the utmost respect.

They were wearing clothes and makeup in the same style as Cooper, nauseating as it was, gym shorts, halter neck t-shirts, layers of cosmetics plastered on their faces, spray-on tans, false eyelashes, and all. Facial features were covered by sunglasses and Greg's counter-surveillance baseball caps.

Marissa was driving. She lowered her window so the guard could look inside and recognize them.

He approached, looked inside, and struggled to keep his eyes in their sockets and focus on their faces instead of their other assets on display. "Good morning, ladies. Marion's friends?"

"Yeah, and you must be the guard she sent the message to, right?"

"I am."

Digger was in the baggage area. His eyes were closed, but they knew there was no way he was asleep. He was on a mission.

Could it be that he was acting? Dogs were known to do that.

They weren't sure if the guard had seen Digger or not. If he did, he was not bothered by his presence.

"All good. You can drive through." He took a step back and waved them through.

"Getting into the house shouldn't be much of a problem," said Rex to Marissa and Catia. "But there's a little hiccup on the inside. There are three bodies showing up on the thermal images. One is on a bed in the main bedroom. Two bodies are in the same room but on different beds."

"Could be the children," said Catia.

"Possibly. All three seem to be asleep."

"Cooper either lied or forgot about the third person. Either way, she's going to be fish food," said Catia.

The cottage hid in the lush bushes and trees on the five-acre estate. With the near-silent Hybrid engine of their SUV, they could get close to the cottage, out of sight of the guard, and rig Digger up with his tactical harness. They both gave him a hug and a 'clever boy' and sent him off to inspect the outside of the house. The video camera, the size of the back end of a pencil, between his ears enabled everyone to see what he was seeing.

Catia and Marissa were about ten yards behind him, Glock 19s in hand.

Although Rex had been coaching his team to work with Digger on missions, this was the first time they were doing it for real. Rex was watching and listening closely so that he could help Catia if necessary. But, within minutes, he knew his input was going to be minimal, if at all. Digger couldn't be bothered by PCness, Catia was his favorite female in his pack, and he made no secret of that and, apparently, didn't care what anyone else thought of it. Sexism, racism, ageism, bias, discrimination, and others were concepts Digger paid no mind to.

Digger stayed in the shadows among the shrubs and trees while circling the cottage. They weren't expecting an open door with a red welcome mat. All doors were closed, probably locked. But Digger went around and 'pointed out' all the windows to them. Some blinds and curtains were open or partially open. Catia asked him to go closer so that she could take a peek inside with him. Through a slither of an open curtain of the main bedroom, Digger gave them a glimpse of a person asleep on a double bed.

"Then the bodies in the other room must be the kids," said Rex. A few minutes later, he was proven right; the kids were on single beds in the other room.

"Okay, let's get inside and introduce ourselves," said Marissa.

Digger led the way to the back door. Marissa picked the lock, and Catia let Digger in. The main bedroom was closest, and the door was open. He sneaked forward slowly and quietly and sat down next to the sleeping man. He looked at Catia as if to say, "All yours. Or do you want me to wake him up?"

Marissa took a few steps and shook the man by the shoulder while holding the gun against his head. He stirred only slightly.

Catia whispered, "I think he drugged himself. She pointed to the bedside table where there was a needle, syringe, and a glass bottle with a label indicating it was Propofol, a powerful intravenous narcotic agent that would bring on sedation and unconsciousness within forty to sixty seconds. As Michael Jackson's physician could tell anyone, Propofol was also very easy to accidentally overdose.

Marissa felt for a pulse in his neck. His heartbeat was weak, and his breathing shallow. "I'm no expert, but this guy is not well. He could croak any moment. Rex, Josh, what do you want us to do? I have nothing here that I can use to resuscitate him."

In the meantime, Catia took photos on her mobile phone and sent them to Greg and Rehka.

"Easy," said Rex. "An adult who injected himself with drugs versus two innocent twelve-year-old children drugged involuntarily and on their way to a short and horrifying life as child sex slaves."

Everyone agreed.

They zip-tied his hands and feet, left him, and went to the children's room.

In the meantime, Greg and Rehka didn't waste time searching in their usual places. Greg took his Glock 17, fixed the silencer, and went straight to Cooper.

He was not a skilled interrogator, but he'd seen Rex et al. in action enough times to know what had to be done. When he walked into the room with Dante's Inferno paintings on the walls, he already had the gun pointed at Cooper's head.

She looked shocked. "Wait... I... I'm not finished. There's a lot more to write."

"That might be so, but the deal was you wouldn't lie or forget things."

"But... but... I haven't. l swear to God... I..."

"You don't believe in God."

"If that's what you want, I'll believe in God. But what did I lie about?"

Greg pulled his cellphone out and showed her the photos of the man on her bed. "Who's that?"

Cooper started breathing heavily. She was hungry, thirsty, tired, and dirty, and she would've forgone everything if she could just get a nice big snort of cocaine. The withdrawal symptoms were driving her crazy. And now this.

"Bob Jordan," she said. "He's one of my suppliers. He brought the two girls in the other room to me."

"And he has unfettered access to your house and your bed?"

Cooper nodded.

"You knew he was there. You hoped he would surprise our operators, right?"

Cooper's head was hanging. She said nothing.

Greg turned and left.

Catia picked the lock of the children's room and found Vanessa Marcos and Jinny Lee inside. Comatose. Two more missing children who could be removed from Lieutenant Harris's missing children's list.

Marissa examined them and found their vital signs to be good. They'd probably stay unconscious for a few more hours.

It was 7:30 a.m. The guards would change at 8:00 a.m.

Catia stayed with the children while Marissa and Digger fetched the SUV and parked it in the empty garage. They lowered the back seats and laid the two kids on folded blankets with pillows under their heads in the recovery position. On their sides, heads tilted back to keep their airways open. In this position, the tongue falls forward, and vomit can drain out instead of choking them. They collected bundles of Cooper's clothes and spread them over the children to hide them.

They checked on Jordan. He had no heartbeat. Lucky bastard. He was another candidate for leaping off a tall building in a single bound. The only conciliation was that his mobile phone might provide important information and more leads.

The guard waved them through without checking a thing.

Marissa blew him a tarty kiss as they drove past.

He smiled and waved.

Not long after, Greg and Rehka sent out deepfake audio messages to Cooper's favorite contacts. Not friends, because it was unimaginable that a human being like her could have any friends. They kept to the same story as with the guard; she had contracted COVID and had to be in quarantine for at least five days. Please don't bother me. I will be in touch when I am over it.

Understandably, Fatman was bitterly disappointed. He suggested that he could collect Cooper's girls wherever they were and go ahead with the auction on his own. She told him that was not going to happen. She wanted to be present to protect her investment. Psychopaths always have trust issues. Fatman didn't argue further; he probably realized he wouldn't have trusted her if the roles were reversed.

Chapter Thirty-Three

WHEN HER NEW LIFE STARTED

Rex and Josh arrived at the Pink Poodle that night at seven in the Hyundai. Rex's hair was a salt-and-pepper color tonight. He was dressed in black cargo pants, hiking boots, a white t-shirt, a dark denim jacket, and large blackout dark glasses often worn by the blind. His headdress was a Dodgers baseball cap enhanced by Greg's modifications to confuse any facial recognition systems not under his and Rehka's control. He held a long white stick in one hand, and with the other, he held the handle on the harness attached to a big black dog with a service dog sticker and a prominent warning, DON'T PET ME. I AM WORKING. Josh was the older man tonight, with gray hair, gray mustache, gray beard, Dodgers cap, and all.

If anyone wanted to check, Rex had the necessary papers to prove that Digger was indeed a service dog. All of it was legal and genuine, and necessary according to the vet and the physician who issued the certificates.

Antonio Rubio, Jake, Rick, and Marc Dunn were in the same private lounge as the night before.

There was a different band on stage. "Not much better than the cat stranglers from last night." In Josh's judgment.

They got the same almost-cute server in her Pink Poodle outfit. A twenty-dollar tip bought them the same excellent service as before. Yet she didn't recognize either of her clients from the night before.

They'd finished about half of their beer when Josh touched his blind friend's arm and said, "She's here."

Shortly after, Josh walked over to Abbie's table. She was with a coworker.

He greeted them politely and stood until Abbie invited him to sit down. He sat opposite her and looked at her when he spoke. "I'm here for my unfortunate friend over there." He motioned toward Rex and Digger. "He lost almost all of his sight a few years ago in the war. He's a good guy and a good friend but extremely shy. He's still ah… ah well… oh dear, how shall I put it? He's never been… you know… with a woman… he's never had —"

Abbie smiled and held her hand up. "Say no more; everybody has shy friends."

On the *TOMATS*, Marissa and the others were laughing. It was rare that her husband was at a loss for words. She was going to needle him about this when he got home.

Josh looked at the other girl apologetically. "No offense intended, ma'am, but when my friend could still see, there was only one woman he obsessed about, Emma Beckett, the—"

"TVN Twenty-Four-Seven morning show host, the former Miss USA," interjected the girl. She upped and left without saying goodbye.

"I hear that often," said Abbie.

"So, will you? … please… I mean, are you… ah—"

"Yes, I will. You don't have to charm me; I'm a sure thing. Now take me to your friend."

"Ah... sorry... just one more question. Money... I... I... mean... payment... ah, how much for the night?"

Abbie smiled. She knew the type who fancied themselves Olympic-level performers. They usually fell asleep from exhaustion within an hour. But it was this one's first time. She was not going to dissuade his friend from what would be an easy night for her. "All night is fine by me, but you see the man in the white suit; he takes care of the financial side of things."

Josh didn't bat an eye. "Thank you. It's his thirty-first tomorrow. This is a present from all his friends who can't stand his innocence anymore."

"I promise I will do my best to make your friend happy."

"Thank you. I appreciate that." With that, Josh stood and walked over to Rubio's table. The chat with Rubio lasted less than a minute. Josh felt like disinfecting himself afterward.

Josh went back to Abbie's table and told her he was ready to introduce her to his hapless friend.

The dog was sitting next to the blind man. His friend left after he'd introduced them. She said her name was Abbie. She didn't ask for his name, and he didn't offer a name.

"What about him?" she asked when they were alone.

"Who?"

"Your dog."

"What *about* him?"

"I don't do bestiality. You'll have to go somewhere else for—"

Rex held his hand up. "Neither do I."

"So, he's going to watch?"

"I don't mind. I can't see him," said Rex.

Abbie giggled. It was the first time she was going to entertain a blind man. It felt weird. Not to mention having a dog watch. But, somehow, this man had put her at ease. She didn't even notice that he didn't sound nearly as shy as his friend made him out to be. She escorted him to her room on the first level above ground in Cloud Nine. On the way, she offered him some drugs, but he assured her that he didn't do drugs.

Chapter Thirty-Four

PLEASE HOLD ME

She laid down the rules when she closed the door. "No kissing on the mouth, and I keep my shoes on." It worked only sometimes with some types. This one seemed to be *that* type.

But then this guy turned into one of the weirdos. At least for the first few minutes, until he took her breath away, that's what she thought. She had many weird requests from customers during her seven years in the profession. This was one of them.

The blind guy didn't want to touch her. He had no interest in getting her naked. Though she put that down to his vision impairment, she still didn't know whether to feel insulted or relieved. What his eyes couldn't see, his hands could feel, but he had no interest in that either. He told her he only wanted them to sit in the easy chairs, have drinks, and chat.

The whole night.

Bizarre.

Her clientele paid a lot of money to have sex with her.

But this guy took the cake; he paid an obscene amount of money just so he could chat with her for the rest of the night. An easy night indeed.

Abbie had a few self-imposed rules taught to her by one of the older ladies. Two of the most important were: Never trust your clients and never get emotionally involved. But she had to admit, if she ever broke those rules, it would be for a man like this. Courteous, soft-spoken, confident but not arrogant, and regardless of being blind, he had a calming effect on her.

Although she didn't grow up with dogs or any pets, she loved animals. This big black dog had crept into her heart quickly when he looked at her with what she was sure was a smile. It made her smile, too.

"Whatever you want. I've been paid for. If you want to talk instead of enjoying your birthday present, I'm good with that. I'm also a good listener. Just don't expect me to explain to your friends that their money went into an all-night chat instead of ending your abstinence."

Greg had disabled every bit of surveillance equipment in Abbie's room, except for Rex's cellphone, the molar mic, and the microphones in Digger's studded collar. They knew there was no one dedicated to watching video feeds in real-time. There were two security guards in a room watching a bank of monitors twenty-four-seven, but it was an exercise in futility. The guards must've realized that before the end of the first day on the job. That's why they played cards, read books, watched TV, and glanced at the bank of monitors whenever they remembered. Why bother? Everything was recorded anyway.

If this room's videos were eventually watched, all they'd see would be a black screen with an error message that the room's surveillance had malfunctioned and that it took about twelve hours before the problem was discovered and resolved. However, on the guards' screen, they would be broadcasting a medley of the past weeks' recordings.

"Great, I want to talk about my daughter, Courtney Lloyd," said Rex.

"How old is she?"

"Sixteen."

Abbie remained quiet, waiting for Rex to continue and tell her about his daughter.

But Rex was waiting for her to tell him about Courtney. Then it hit him; *Of course, she wouldn't know Courtney by that name. In this world, people try to be incognito. But Rex had heard no one mention Courtney's alias.*

He took his dark glasses off, pulled his mobile phone out, clicked and scrolled a few times, and showed her the photos he got from Reece and Lieutenant Harris. It was impossible to miss the shock on her face. A double shock, first when she realized he wasn't blind, and second when she recognized the girl in the photos.

That put an end to what she thought was going to be an easy night. Her heart had skipped more than just a few beats. She struggled to breathe and to find her voice. When she finally did, she stammered, "I... I don't... I don't know... any... anyone by that name."

Abbie was scared to death. Rex had sympathy; he knew she was deeply worried. Things had become life-threatening for her. Because she, like every girl in that place, knew all too well that every room was bugged with video and audio surveillance equipment. Every word she uttered and every movement she made would be recorded. By now, she was fully expecting one or more of the pimps or the guards to storm into her room momentarily. Her heart was palpitating wildly. Her palms were sweating profusely.

Later during the night, Rex would find out that this brought back the brutal beating she'd received from TJ not too long ago. Every punch, every lash, and every kick were still edged in her memory. The bruises were no longer visible, and the broken ribs had healed, but the scars on her back and legs were for life. She'd feared another beating like that more than death itself. That was if she wasn't tortured to death like Chrissy in front of a bloodthirsty audience of sociopathic savages.

Rex nodded slightly, imperceptibly to Digger, who got up and sauntered over to her chair. He sat down next to her and made soft, comforting sounds while resting his head on her lap. As if to say, "Don't worry, everything is going to work out just fine. You're safe with us."

Instinctively, she started stroking his head and ears gently. She began relaxing a little.

"Abbie, I want you to take a few deep breaths and try to relax," said Rex. "Believe me; you're in no danger. I'm not with the police. I'm not here to harm you. I'm only looking for my daughter, and I'm also going to help you get out of this hellhole, if that's what you want."

She just stared at him wide-eyed.

"I have friends who are helping me. We are trained special operators. For instance, every camera and microphone in this room has been disabled by them. Nobody is watching or listening to us. My friends are in control of all security cameras and microphones in this building and that next door. No one except you, me, and my friends know about it. No one will find out about it either."

She just stared at Rex, the fear and disbelief written all over her face. She saw Digger was looking up at her.

He yelped once, softly, as if to say, "You can trust him.

He's my best friend." She kept stroking his head and ears softly and relaxed a little more.

"Just think about it; if they could hear and see us, they would've broken your door down by now, don't you think? Even if they come through that door, Digger and I will protect you."

She nodded slowly.

"Will you please listen to me now?"

She nodded and whispered, "I will try, but I'm scared to death. I fear death."

"I understand, but you have my word; my friends and I can protect you as long as you work with us and do exactly as we say. We need information about this place and the people who live and work here. We know about the pimps TJ, Johnny, and Sammy. But hopefully, you can tell us more."

Every fiber in her body wanted to believe him. The little flame of hope she thought had died a long time ago was, to her surprise, still flickering and had been rekindled.

When Rex took off his disguise and Digger came over to comfort her, she realized she'd not reached the end of hope yet. When he told her he was part of a team of special operators who were planning to rescue her, the flame of hope in her was burning higher and brighter than she believed possible.

Trust was a commodity so rare for her that she couldn't remember the last time she trusted anyone. What she remembered well, though, was how she got hurt every time she did. However, this gentle and compassionate man and his empathetic dog made her feel safe and secure for the first time in her life.

"I will try my best."

"Okay, let's start with my daughter. I saw when you

looked at the photos you recognized her. Is she alive? Where can I find her?"

Abbie nodded. "I knew her as Rosie. She..." but she couldn't continue; the dam wall had collapsed. She started crying and babbling and laughing all at once.

Everyone watching and listening, including Rex, were worried; it appeared Abbie was hysterical.

If they'd looked at Digger like Rex did, they would've seen that he had relaxed.

"Rex, this is the part in the movie where you put your arm around her." That was Catia, reaching him through his molar mic.

Rex walked over to her, took a knee next to her chair, and put his arms around the young girl's shaking shoulders. He was a little lost for words, so he just repeated the same thing in different words. "Don't worry, Eva, everything is going to be fine. Don't be afraid; all is okay. Nobody is going to hurt you, Eva, I promise. Believe me, no one—"

Catia was smiling. Men. She'd never understand them, but she loved this one with her whole being, regardless.

Eva suddenly stopped crying, sniffed noisily, and wiped her eyes with the back of her hands, smudging her mascara. "How do you know my real name?"

Rex smiled at her. "We've done our homework, Eva. I told you we've got special skills. We—"

Rex couldn't finish his sentence. Eva had thrown her arms around his neck and wept on his shoulder. "Please hold me. Just for a little while. I'll be okay."

Digger yapped softly. Eva was going to be okay. He was happy.

Chapter Thirty-Five

THE HOUSE OF HORRORS

She told Rex there were four floors below ground, not just two, as he thought. The first was the kitchen and recreational area for the staff and girls living and working on the floors above ground. "Level two below is the studio and—"

"Studio?"

Eva nodded.

"For...?"

"Making porn movies. What else?"

Rex wondered how much worse it could get.

"It's their best money spinner," continued Eva. "Sammy told me one night when he was having his way with me that he was planning to go into business for himself, selling child porn online. 'Little overheads,' he said. 'Could be managed from anywhere in the world with an internet connection.' According to him, Cloud Nine generates millions a year from that studio."

"What's on the third and fourth levels below?"

"Basement three is the kitchen and entertainment area for the children whose quarters are on level four—"

"Children?"

"Yes, children. Six of them, between twelve and fifteen years old."

"Six... teenage... girls—?"

"Yes, the stars in the kiddie porn movies."

Rex took a deep breath, held it for ten counts, and let it out slowly.

On the *TOMATS*, Christine was shaking her head. "Six more children? How's it possible that law enforcement is unaware of this? You've been at this for only a few days, and you've found fifteen missing children. All of them are chained to their pimps with drugs. Like a dog on a leash."

John put his hand on his wife's arm.

Rex stared at Digger. *Six more kids in the dungeon, just a few floors down.*

Digger whined softly. He was upset.

"Is Courtney down there?"

Eva shook her head.

"Where is she?"

"She was brought into the residential area on basement level four by TJ and Sammy a few months ago, stupefied by the drugs they injected into her."

Despite the effect of the staple of mind-numbing drugs fed to her every day, on top of alcohol and nicotine, and living in these conditions day in and day out, there was much less havoc wreaked on Eva's brain than Rex would've expected.

"Rosie was a beautiful child, not yet ravaged by the life of a sex slave. But she was in a state of shock."

Eva didn't have the papers to claim a higher education, but she had an above-average IQ, and she was well-read and well-spoken. The state Courtney was in, as Eva described it to Rex, was known as catatonia. It meant she had little or no reaction to her surroundings.

"I was worried she might commit suicide. I've seen it happen in this place more times than any human being of any age should. But to be honest, sometimes I envy those who have the guts to do it."

Rex put his hand on her arm. "It's almost over, Eva."

She nodded and wiped more tears away. "She stayed only a few days before she was moved to some unknown location. I was there when TJ sedated her to be transported to her new home if that's what one can call these hellholes. TJ told Johnny that Courtney had been selected by the boss himself for his special harem. He said, for the next two to three years, she's going to live the good life. She'll be entertaining only the rich and influential. Maybe once or twice a week. Paradise compared to this place."

"Who transported her to the new place?"

"TJ. I loaded her suitcase into the trunk of his car while he and Johnny loaded her into the back seat."

"Who's this boss he was talking about?"

"His name is Manza. I have never heard his last name. I've never seen him, not even a photo of him. I've heard rumors that he owns Cloud Nine, Pink Poodle, and Purple Pussycat. And he owns many more similar businesses across the city and the country. I can't vouch for the truth of it, but that's what I've heard."

Rex nodded.

"So, unfortunately, I have no idea where Rosie could be. But I am sure she's alive."

"How can you be—?"

"No, I can't be a hundred percent sure; it's just a gut feeling and the fact that TJ always uses the death of one of us as part of their scare tactics to keep us in check. They would've told us if she was dead."

"Is there someone who supervises the children?"

Eva pointed to herself. "I have to report any issues with the children immediately. I'm supposed to keep discipline and punish them severely for the smallest transgressions. 'They have to respect you. And respect you will get only when they are shit scared of you,' TJ always tells me. But I never discipline them. These children have been abused for all of their lives before they even landed here. And when they get here, they're abused every day. They don't need more of it.

"They do what I ask, not because I scare them, but because they know I try to protect them. I'm one of the longest inhabitants here. I know all the dos and don'ts to stay out of reach of the studded belts of TJ and his sidekicks."

Rex took another sip of his beer. He saw Digger was fast asleep next to Eva's chair. He'd done his bit. Eva had shared a small biscuit with him when Rex had forbidden her to give him chocolates. Rex almost smiled when he thought about what must've gone through his best buddy's mind before he fell asleep. *No chocolates? Some cockamamie about how unhealthy it is for dogs. What a heap of cow confetti.* Digger liked to show off his command of Aussie slang whenever he got the chance.

"I am also responsible for administering their daily drug quota," said Eva. "And then, for the rest of the time, I entertain clients. Sometimes five to six per night."

Rex didn't know what to say to this wretched woman. Empathy and tender-heartedness went only so far. Anything he said would ring hollow. Was it not for his daughter he had to find, he would've called Josh and asked him to bring all the weapons and ammunition he could lay his hands on and meet him at the front door. From there, they'd come down on these lowlifes with speed and overwhelming violence of action.

"Tell me about Antonio Rubio and Marc Dunn."

Eva frowned. "Who?"

"The guy in the white suit and his buddy, the drug supplier."

"How do you know their—?" She stopped talking. Rex had already answered that question; they'd done their homework. It was comforting to know.

"The one in the white suit is Jake. In jail, he was known as The Blade. The other is Rick. I think they have some business deal with Manza, but I don't know the details."

"Do they have anything to do with the children?"

"Of course, they do. This is not an old-fashioned brothel. This is a house of horrors. A division of hell. The older girls are only a smoke screen for the evil that is going on below."

Rex nodded. *A division of hell indeed.*

"During the day, TJ, Johnny, and Sammy keep us locked up. They're ex-bouncers. Ex-convicts. Bullies. Murderers. Drug pushers. Rapists. Child molesters. Women beaters. At night they're supported by the security guards who are just as bad as they are."

How is this even possible in America? We're fighting the wrong wars in the wrong countries. The war is here. How is it possible that the police, the FBI, DEA, and others don't know? Or don't they want to know? Or perhaps they know but don't take action.

Whatever was going on, the silence from law enforcement was deafening. Infuriating.

Rex realized he might never get answers to his questions, but one thing he didn't have to speculate about was that he and his team were in over their heads. They were up against more than a few pimps and drug pushers.

Regardless, four levels below his feet in this shithole were six missing children who were abused day-by-day several times a day by unscrupulous and deviant sadists. And then there were the older girls, above the age of consent, such as Eva, fifteen of them, 'handcuffed' to their pimps with drugs.

He couldn't believe the police didn't know or even suspect what was going on. That there was not enough probable cause and suspicion to get a search warrant defied logic. But until Rex could locate and rescue his daughter, he couldn't dare point the police at this place.

And this was only one of Manza's many outlets.

Drugs, prostitution, and pedophilia would've made him a very rich man and ruined countless lives in the process. Not to mention how many were killed by his drugs and his pimps.

What Eva wasn't telling him because she had no knowledge thereof, was the blackmail, extortion, and payola. The territory of the wealthy, influential, and powerful. That would certainly explain the expensive high-quality surveillance equipment with which someone was collecting extortion information.

That's where you'll find your daughter. A cold chill ran down Rex's spine when the thought flashed through his mind. He looked at Digger for his opinion.

Digger was awake, or at least half awake; he was staring at him, kind of lazily, with only one eye open, as if to say, "And how does that change anything? We still have to rescue Courtney. Whose asses we kick in the process doesn't matter. Right?"

Right.

Chapter Thirty-Six

YOU'RE NEXT

"Has anyone ever escaped?" asked Rex. And a few minutes later, he regretted asking.

Eva's voice went cold as ice. She shivered. "No, but Chrissy tried. A few months ago. They killed her. It was terrible, and they made us watch. Rosie was there too."

"Do you know Chrissy's real name?"

She nodded slowly. "Elizabeth Clayton."

Rex took a deep breath. It was as if there was some kind of connection between Beth and Courtney. Lieutenant Harris discovered the link when he recognized that the man who lured Beth into a trap did the same to Courtney.

"TJ almost beat me to death when he discovered that she'd spoken to me before she ran away. She told me her real name and where she was going. TJ beat it out of me." Eva's body started shaking as she sobbed. "I betrayed her. I killed her."

"No, Eva, don't do that. You didn't kill her."

"She almost made it," whispered Eva. "TJ and Sammy found her less than a mile from her mother's house." The tears were streaming down Eva's face. She didn't even bother to wipe them away anymore.

Rex put his arm around her again.

"Eighteen hours later, we were put through another kind of hell when they made us watch the show."

"Show?"

"Yes, people paid thousands of dollars to watch these animals torture Elizabeth to death. Some paid a lot more to participate in the show. Raping, hitting, and sodomizing her. They performed the most despicable, unthinkable, unspeakable sexual perversions - you can't even imagine. Each paid for a five-ten- or fifteen-minute slot to live their deviant fantasies.

"Apart from the money, which must have been close to a quarter of a million dollars, the show also served as a lesson to us—don't ever try to escape."

It must've been a sight no human being of any age is supposed to behold, ever.

"I wanted to scream, but the pain from my swollen face, cracked jaw, broken ribs, and bruised buttocks kept me quiet. Yet the pain I endured was nothing compared to what Elizabeth was going through. All I could do was hope that she'd die quickly."

"TJ, Johnny, and Sammy were there. The show lasted two hours. TJ gave her the fatal jab, an overdose of fentanyl."

Rex was fighting a towering rage by the time Eva stopped talking. He not only wanted to kill them, he also wanted to burn the place down. Then he'd dump radioactive material on the ruins so that no one would dream of coming near it for the next hundred years. A monument to all pedophiles and child sex slave masters with a message; "You're next."

I'm going to kill them, Digger. Do you hear me? I'm going to kill all of them.

Digger growled as if to say, "Absolutely. We've got to put a stop to this."

Rex asked her about the auctions. She knew all about them. She was one of the two hostesses who welcomed the bidders, escorted them to their booths in privacy, served drinks and snacks, and saw to their carnal whims, which they often had after the excitement of the auction.

She drew pictures and diagrams of the four floors below ground, including the second floor, the studio.

Rex was impressed with the detail she'd put into the drawings. Not only that, but the scale was also very accurate. When he commented on it, he was surprised when she told him she'd never received any training.

Chapter Thirty-Seven

I WANT TO TELL YOU ABOUT ME

"What now?" Said Eva.

"Okay, I know you're worried. But it's unnecessary. Just carry on as you always do. Remember, everything the guards and pimps can see, we can see and hear, too. We're watching you and everyone else in this place. If they so much as raise a finger against you, we will come for you.

"Eva, it's most important that no one knows about our conversation. Please don't talk to anyone. Don't trust anyone in this place. No one. Okay?"

"Yes. I promise."

"And I trust you, Eva. You're a brave woman."

"How do you know you can trust me? You don't even know me. You don't know my history."

Rex took a deep breath. "I know you're an honorable person."

"Yeah, right, an honorable whore."

"Was that your career choice, or did someone else decide for you?"

"It was not my choice. But that doesn't matter; you still

don't know me. I want to tell you about me. After you've heard it, we can talk about trust."

"Eva, you don't have to do it. I made up my mind hours ago."

"I must, because I've never told anyone. I want you to know."

Rex knew this was important to her. He nodded.

She told him she was twenty years old. The first thirteen years of her life were spent in a loveless home. Her mother was not only a drunk, but she also had a severe problem with her eyesight; she never saw her third husband, a pedophile, raping her daughter since the age of ten.

The day Eva turned thirteen, she did some serious damage to stepdaddy's privates with a meat cleaver, then shouldered her dilapidated backpack with some of her clothes, six paper-wrapped peanut butter and jelly sandwiches, a plastic coke bottle filled with water, and two hundred dollars stolen from her mother over four months. She appropriated another hundred and fifty from stepdaddy's wallet on the way out. He didn't object because he was too busy being unconscious on the bathroom floor from the pain and blood loss. As far as she knew, he was still alive, but his manhood was irreparably damaged. The children of Orlando, Florida, were a little safer.

It took almost two full days on the Greyhound buses to get to LA. Within hours after her arrival, she came to the attention of a talent scout who hung around bus stations on the lookout for runaways like her. He followed her until he was sure she was a runaway before he approached. That night she smoked marijuana and slept with the man who insisted on paying for her dinner earlier. And to think she was worried she had nowhere to go when she arrived in LA.

On the third day, Mr. Good Samaritan told her he was

going to visit family in Austin, Texas, for two to three months. But he had a friend who was kind enough to offer her a room that she didn't have to pay for upfront, but once she had a job, she'd have to start paying him back.

Two days later, she and her handsome landlord were sleeping together.

She was hooked on crack cocaine within two weeks.

Within three weeks, the boyfriend's painful slap across her face made the thirteen-year-old climb into bed with an unknown man they'd met in a bar.

A week and four more sexual encounters with total strangers later, she discovered a bottle of what she thought were painkillers in the drawer of her boyfriend's bedside table. She emptied the contents into her mouth and chased them down with a glass of milk. She threw up for two days, and when she finally recovered, she got a savage beating for trying to escape. That's when she realized her body belonged to someone else.

For the last seven years, her pimps had been selling her body to anyone willing to pay. She used to be a money spinner in her young days, six, seven years ago, during her early teens. Pedophiles paid dramatically more for their fads than anyone else.

So far as she could determine, her mother had never even reported her as missing. Her stepfather would never report it lest someone made a connection between her disappearance and his antalgic gait caused by his mutilated genitalia.

Then one day, TJ turned up, roughed up her handsome boyfriend for trying to go into business for himself, and took her to Cloud Nine, where she was supposed to have been living the dream—happily ever after.

She had a wry sense of humor which Rex found to be something special, given her circumstances.

"Now you know what I am. You still want to trust me?"

"Yes, Eva, I know a little more about you now, and I have the greatest respect for you. You're just about the most courageous woman I've ever met. If we were in uniform, I would pin a medal for bravery on you right now and salute you."

Eva didn't reply; she was just shaking her head in disbelief. No one had ever said anything as nice as that to her. It brought tears to her eyes.

Over the years, the beatings, sexual abuse, and drugs had depressed her to a nearly catatonic state. Lately, she'd been spending inordinate amounts of time thinking about the easiest, least painful way to end it.

Drug overdose was her eventual choice. Fentanyl the drug of choice.

But to collect a lethal quantity of it required time and shrewdness. The pimps were monitoring their drug consumption closely. They had to swallow or inject the drugs in front of them. They were not allowed to carry drugs other than what they wanted to sell to clients, and to try and steal from that carried the death penalty. Same as Elizabeth.

And now this man and his dog were sitting here in her room, telling her they could save her from this place. Not only that, but this man was also praising her. No one ever had a nice word for Eva Hansen. She had already broken one of her critical rules; she trusted him. And his dog. But she couldn't just leave it at that.

"How do you know I haven't lied to you?"

"I am a specialist in body language and lie detection.

And you haven't lied to me once tonight. But even if you did, and I didn't catch it, you wouldn't get past my dog."

"He knows when people lie?"

"Yes. I can assure you there's not a lie detector on this planet that can beat him. He can smell a lie from miles away."

Her mouth was agape while Rex regaled her with a few stories about Digger's lie detection aptitudes. "And, if you were a bad person, he wouldn't come near you. He would be between us at all times so that he could protect me."

She smiled and gave Digger another biscuit.

Eva wasn't able to give Rex much information about the computers on the levels below ground except that she knew they had a little room with computers on the second floor where the studio was. She had no idea if they were linked to the other computers upstairs. But she knew one day, after some storms, there was some kind of glitch, and TJ and Sammy went out to the rooftop to fix or replace the satellite dish or something.

Another visit from Greg with his Glock 17 pointed at Cooper's forehead helped to put the last pieces of that puzzle together.

It was almost five in the morning. By six, the meter would run out. There was a lot more to talk about. But for now, Rex had what he wanted.

He left Eva with the promise to return with his friends to set her and the children and the others free. He didn't commit to a specific day or time but promised it would be soon.

He could only hope and pray that Eva wouldn't have second thoughts.

By the time Rex and Josh were back on the *TOMATS*, Greg and Rehka had unimpeded access to every computer and server and surveillance equipment on the network of the lower levels of Cloud Nine. And they also had the layouts of each floor and the diagrams of the electrical circuits, switches, elevators, and the main switchboard. Marissa and Catia had almost finished the construction of a rudimentary scale model of Cloud Nine on the table in the Ops Room.

On request from Rex, Greg tried various queries to find out if there were any well-known people in the client database. That's when he discovered the blacklist. His query returned not only a list of famous people who were pedophiles and clients of Cloud Nine, but also every one of their clients who were in the public service. There were City Council members, mayors, police officers of all ranks, military personnel of all ranks, politicians of all stripes, pastors, priests, rabbis, and teachers, from the classrooms to the principals, and many more. There was no specific physical profile. They were young and old, blond and dark, tall and short, ugly and sexy, fat and lean.

They made up part of the four percent of the populace believed to have pedophilic urges. Some psychologists categorized pedophilia as a sexual orientation in a similar way that heterosexuality and homosexuality were orientations. Their reasoning? The sexual attraction to children appeared to be involuntary and remained stable. It was in their DNA; they couldn't help that they were sexually attracted to children.

Bedamn the children.

Someone in Cloud Nine had made sure that every pedophilic client was identified and photographed and entered into the database together with the video clips of their trysts with the children.

Rex would bet serious money that someone was using this list to get things done their way and to become very rich.

There are about 780,000 people in the US sex offender registry. Every state has its own sex offender registry. California has 60,000 registered sex offenders, the second highest in the USA after Texas, with a list of 100,000. New York, with 43,000, came in at a distant third.

The blacklist had five-hundred and fifty-six names on it. All of them were compromised and extremely likely to be highly susceptible to blackmail and extortion. All of them were rich or famous or influential or all of the above.

Chapter Thirty-Eight

HOW TO GET THE GIRLS TO SAFETY

With the two girls tended to by Julie in the stateroom next to the Daltons' the team gathered to plan what was next.

John was chairing.

"Let's look at what we have." In his legendary elegant handwriting, he listed two topics with a black felt pen on a whiteboard. John went to school in an era when teachers wrote with white chalk on blackboards and didn't spare the rod, especially not for bad handwriting. "Your handwriting shows people that you respect them," the teachers told them.

In short order, he'd listed the two major topics: Save the girls going on auction tomorrow night. Invade the facilities. Capture TJ alive. Save the other girls.

He wrote down a single word. How?

Josh answered, "Ideally, we would have enough troops to do it in one big bang. But now we'll have to get creative."

"Is that going to be a problem?" said John.

"What?"

"Getting creative."

"Of course not. We're all geniuses, and Digger is many levels above that."

"Hmm, two gunslingers and a clever dog," mumbled Rex.

"What do you mean two gunslingers?" said Christelle.

"Josh and me."

"At last count, we were eight, including Declan, who knows which end of a gun gets pointed at the vermin. Simona will look after the children, and Rehka will provide communications and IT support.

When joining CRC on a full-time basis after working as Rex's IT guru and administrator for a few years, her friends, Catia and Marissa, had dedicated significant time to train Rehka to protect herself, including the use of weapons ranging from long guns to a paperclip. But despite Rehka's self-defense skills, she'd never experienced being shot at or had someone intending to kill her. The team needed at least one IT sage to ensure they didn't have to kick doors down, run upstairs when they could use elevators reserved for their exclusive use, or blow electricity boxes up or shoot out security lights and cameras when switches could be flipped on and off remotely, and so forth.

Simona had fired a few shots, but not enough to put her in the field and expect her to shoot bad people.

Rex almost smiled. This was why this beautiful former French spy was like a mother to him. He'd met Christelle years ago when she was instrumental in getting John rescued from the clutches of a New York-based drug cartel from the deck of a container ship in the Mediterranean. Just like his mother, her way of putting her foot down was to push her chin forward ever so slightly. And just like his mother, he knew what a good choice it always was to do precisely what she wanted after that chin had moved forward. Unless, of course, you were a sucker for suffering and wished to second-guess her.

Rex looked around the table slowly. His eyes rested momentarily on each of them. One by one, in absolute silence, everyone nodded.

Rex and Catia looked at each other, then at Digger, who had a smile plastered over his face. They realized their friends had been caucusing prior to this meeting.

Rex had a lump in his throat. Catia had something in her eye. Digger whined softly.

Rex cleared his throat. He thought about thanking them but couldn't find the words. He cleared his throat again, more forceful, louder.

Digger came to the rescue when he yapped once, drawing the attention away from Rex, or maybe he just wanted to remind Catia or Rex that with this lull in the conversation, it was an ideal time for his jerky Kong.

"Thanks, but... Ouch!" That was caused by Catia's elbow striking her husband's ribcage. He started to turn to her to enquire, but his eye caught sight of Christelle's protruding chin. He changed his mind. "Thank you all very much. So, what's your plan?"

John answered. "TJ knows where Manza is. So, we'll go over to his place and ask him."

"Right."

"Manza is an enigma, to be sure, like a phantom; nobody we know has ever seen him—neither in the flesh nor in a photo—yet he owns everything we've seen so far. Maybe we can ask TJ about him, too."

"Right. What about Jake and Rick?"

"They've only been seen with the adult girls. But Eva told us that's not where their involvement in this perversity ends. So, we need to have a chat with them, too. At least with Rubio."

"Johnny and Sammy?"

"They're just evil. And they work for people far worse than themselves."

Declan added, "Our problem is not about taking down the pimps and security staff; it's how to get the girls to safety."

Chapter Thirty-Nine

WHY THE VIOLENT ENTRY?

The mission had grown far beyond their capacity. It was no longer just a matter of shooting their way through the crowd of criminals to get to Courtney, even though they had the desire, weapons, and skills to do it. They knew they might not come out of it unscathed, but all child molesters known to them would be captured, indisposed, or dead. The world would be rid of a lot of terrible monsters, worse than terrorists. The problem was every lowlife they came across held the lives of several innocent young children in their hands. Courtney Lloyd was one of them.

"We'll have to get the police involved," said Josh.

"As in inviting them over?" said Rex.

"Yeah, but not in the beginning."

Rex frowned.

Josh continued. "In broad strokes, here's what I propose. We go in just before the auction starts. The buyers, sellers, and the girls will all be there. Team One gets rid of the pimps and captures TJ. Team Two goes for the merchants. Team Three tells the girls to be calm; help is on the way.

"We go in with John's credo on our lips: Speed, Surprise, and Overwhelming Violence of Action."

"Also known as a full-frontal assault," mumbled Rex. "Otherwise known as, I don't have a plan."

"Yeah, something like that. So, we burst through three doors at once. Guns blazing. A few minutes later, we phone the police and tell them there was a massacre at their favorite whoopee parlor. They will be there in less than five minutes. We will be gone, and the girls will be safe. The world will be a better place."

Josh had a way with words that could make Rex laugh sometimes. But this was not one of those times. He'd been thinking about it as well, and what Josh explained so eloquently was that there was no other way.

Rex nodded slowly. He was wondering when his friends had the time to come up with this plan. He liked it, but there was something that bothered him.

Digger's whining pulled him out of his reverie. He was standing next to Rex. "Give us a minute," said Rex to everyone around the table.

Everyone knew what Digger's whining meant. It was the ideal time to take a coffee break.

Rex and Digger went to the upper deck. At the back was an open space covered with synthetic grass where Declan could practice his putting. It was also one of Digger's favorite places to get away from it all and think about new ways to save the world, especially when the morning sun was as nice as it was today. Rex made sure that he cleaned up after Digger's visits. That way, he and Declan remained friends. Declan and Digger that is.

Digger went straight for his favorite corner. Rex turned his back and looked out over the calm water. Digger always insisted on privacy.

What can go wrong with this plan?

Nothing. It's not a plan.

What don't you like?

The violent entry. You're making too much noise too early.

We don't have the time for other options. We must get in and out quickly.

How violent were you last night?

Rex turned halfway towards Digger.

He yapped once.

Rex turned back. "Sorry, buddy, I thought you were done. But that was a good idea. That might just work."

A minute later, Digger yapped twice.

Rex turned back and went to clean up.

The uh-huh preceding the moving of Christelle's lower jaw forward by a tiny bit of an inch was to make sure Rex understood that there would be no more discussion of them getting in serious trouble for helping him.

Rex replied, "I understand, but do *you* all understand we could cross swords with law enforcement?"

"Yes, we do. Next question." She didn't have to add the word stupid to the last sentence; she and Rex understood each other's manner of speaking.

"Okay, what about the kids?"

"Call and run," said Josh.

"Huh?"

"Didn't you get it the first time? We go in, do our thing, call the police, and run. The police will be there in minutes, and the kids will be okay. And then we let the media know."

"O-k-a-y. But why the violent entry?"

Josh stared at him slack-jawed. "You don't want to do violence to these douchebags?"

"I absolutely want to and have all the intentions to visit an inordinate amount of violence on them. But I don't want to start it too early."

"Sounds like you've got an idea?" said John.

"Maybe. How violent did I have to get last night?"

In the silence that followed, an almost imperceptible smile started playing on John's face as he realized the implications of Rex's suggestion.

And then, as if they got it all, they all started speaking at once.

In summary: The men were okay with it. The women? Not so much.

Christelle said, "So, you go as men, and we go as …?"

"Lesbians or transvestites," said John. He was out of arm's reach of his wife. "Or you can be my partner."

Christelle smiled. John was off the hook.

Another silent spell descended as everyone contemplated what Rex's suggestion meant for them.

Digger growled, meaning to say, "I can't be bothered by who goes as what and with whom. I want to know who you want me to go with, you or Catia?"

"Of course, you go with Catia," said Rex.

"What are you talking about?" said Catia.

Rex shrugged. "Just Digger wanting to know who he's going with. I told him he goes with you."

"Unless we're going together," she said.

"Be warned," said Josh. "I know you've heard the band over your speakers and earphones, but believe me, in person, it's much worse—they are criminally incompetent."

Rex, Catia, and Digger went to the kitchen and collected some sandwiches, a few bottles of water, a bucket with hot water, a plastic bag with brushes, and various cleaning products.

They found Cooper in a state of delirium from lack of food, water, and drugs, curled up in the fetal position on the table. The withdrawal symptoms had turned her into a babbling idiot with violent spells in between. She'd chewed her fingernails to the quick. She'd been scratching and kicking at the door for hours, to no avail.

The odor in the room was stomach-churning. No wonder Digger refused to follow Rex and Catia inside.

Rex and Catia put the food and water and the cleaning stuff on the table in front of Cooper's face. "We'll be back in an hour, and then this place better be as clean and fresh as when you arrived."

Cooper had a wild look in her eyes when she climbed off the table and started swearing. She told Rex and Catia what they should do to themselves. It was obvious she had a lot to learn about human anatomy. Then she launched into an extensive tirade about what unsavory characters their ancestors were before she got to insulting Rex and Catia.

The straw that broke the camel's back and drove her over the edge was when neither Rex nor Catia reacted to her ranting. They only smiled at her, turned, and left.

When they locked the door, they could hear a chair crashing into the door. Shortly after, she was kicking it while howling like a wolf.

Marion Cooper had lost her mind.

Then Cooper's eyes caught sight of the big TV. She walked up to it, examined the dark screen closely, stepped away, threw a middle finger at the screen, turned her back to it, pulled her jeans and panties down, and bent forward. She thought the camera spying on her was built into the TV. It wasn't. There were cameras hidden behind the prints depicting hell on the walls.

Chapter Forty

THE SECOND DROP-AND-RUN PACKET

It was Saturday morning, almost 10 a.m. Lieutenant Harris was off duty for the weekend. He had just finished the lawn when he received the second drop-and-run packet in two days from an unknown courier service and a secret sender.

It was a big envelope. The same as before. It was addressed to him, but no sender details were visible. Same as before.

Then a smile broke across his face. He'd seen one of these before. The previous one was to inform him that an unidentified man who had sexually abused several minor girls over a long time had confessed his sins and, in a state of guilt and repentance, threw himself off the roof of a twenty-five-story building.

"What will this one hold?"

He went inside, took a shower, put the espresso machine on, and opened the envelope with a kitchen knife. His wife was out shopping with friends.

The envelope contained two thick A4 writing pads,

which were filled with handwriting in blue ink. The author must've been of the younger generations, those that grew up with computers and had no idea how to write with a pen on paper. It looked as if an inebriated fly had fallen into an inkpot and crawled all over the pages. Although it was tough on the eyes, with a bit of effort, the writing was decipherable.

It was a confession—but the words at the very top of the first page gave him pause. It read, *'Reminder: I don't want him to find out I've left something out or lied. Because, if I do, he will shoot me in the head and feed me to the fish.'*

This confession was the fruit of the poisonous tree.

Harris knew who 'him' was. He also knew the confession would be true but inadmissible in a court of law. He sighed. "Story of my life."

He took a sip of his coffee. "But I was right; this US Marshal and his dog are not to be trifled with." He took another sip. "Unless, of course, you have a desire to see what all the fuss about the afterlife is."

He put the notepads aside and removed the remaining two items from the envelope. A USB thumb drive and one sheet of paper with typed instructions.

1. *Plug the USB stick into your computer.* He did it.
2. *Listen to Marion Cooper's recorded confession, which she made before she wrote it down.* He listened to Cooper's confession interrogated by a man and woman whose voices were computerized.
3. *Look at the photos and videos in the Media folder. You can't use them in court, but they are 100% real and true.* He spent a long time studying the folders containing the information about the children.

4. *The photos of the children in the cages are real and true. All of them are on your list of missing children. Put them through your facial recognition systems if you don't believe me. That's where I found their details.*

5. *Now listen to the audio file marked 'Instructions.'* He listened to the instructions.

He was ready to go on a shooting spree by the time he finished. The only thing that prevented him from doing so was that he didn't know where the children and their captors were. For that information, the instructions said he'd have to wait until midnight.

Harris got up from his desk, picked up his empty coffee mug, and headed for the kitchen. He started the espresso machine again, and while he waited, he walked out into the garden and rolled his neck and shoulders to get rid of the tension.

Marissa's mini drone was hovering silently about four hundred yards up in the air. He couldn't see or hear it, even if he knew it was there.

He was excited. The kind of excitement that was a mixture of anxiety and eagerness. He'd been waiting for this day for a very long time. He promised his wife dinner and a movie tonight, but he was not going to miss *this* opportunity to retire as an accomplished man.

He'll propose to the missus that they go to the matinee and then to their favorite seafood restaurant. Then they'd have the whole night free to do whatever they fancied.

"All that accompanied by a wink ought to do it." He smiled complacently.

When Harris went back into the house, Marissa brought her drone back to base about two miles away while Josh phoned Rex on his secured satellite phone. "Harris did his neck stretches."

"Great. Thanks."

On the *TOMATS*, Rex turned to Catia and Digger. "Harris has agreed to cooperate as we've requested."

"Excellent. That'll solve a lot of problems for us."

Chapter Forty-One

NOT WITHOUT TRUTH SERUM

John knew a few influential reporters whom he had worked with over the years. There was no special relationship with them, but he'd run background checks on the few that he'd dealt with. So, this was not the typical situation where one of them owed him a favor. John had a good story he wanted to be publicized. The journalist's job was to chase good stories and print them.

If there was anything untoward, such as bribery, it was the coffee and the slice of cheesecake the journalist had, which John paid for.

John started. "Dan, I've got a strange request. So, shut up until I'm finished, okay?"

Dan Curtis smiled and nodded. He and John had been exchanging information long enough that they knew the nuances of each other's manner of speaking. He took no offense.

John said, "It comes in two parts. You can listen to part one and decide if you want to stay or go.

"Here's part one. There's something big brewing in the

child sex slave industry. Names are going to be published this time. Not just some of them, all of them." John couldn't help but throw in a few clichés. "It goes to the top, Dan. Eggs will land on faces. Heads will roll."

John stopped and looked at Dan.

"And?"

"That was part one. In or out?"

Dan shook his head and laughed. "John, I feel insulted that you don't trust me."

"I know enough about the concept of trust to know that I should trust no one."

"O-k-a-y, I am in."

John told him that the police had a sting operation going for a few days and were planning a raid. "Here's what they're going to find: Twelve kids in cages, child sex slaves. Fifteen adults, sex slaves. They're all hopelessly addicted to the drugs their pimps administer to them. They'll find a sophisticated studio producing child pornography. They'll find computers and servers and storage devices loaded not only with the pornography but also names of clients complete with photos, videos, address details, and so forth."

"And you want me to make sure they do indeed discover all of those and to publish all the information?"

"Yes, that's precisely what I expect from you."

"I can't make any commitment; I need to know more. I need a few names to start with. When is the police raid? You know, the usual stuff, who did what, where, and when? That's what I need."

"In due time, Danny Boy. Keep your phone charged, switched on, and with you."

"For how long?"

"Until further notice."

He'd had better briefings in his twenty-five years in the media industry. "C'mon, John, you can do better than that."

John said nothing; he just scooped a piece of carrot cake from his plate with a dainty little cake fork that looked ridiculous in his big hand and ate it while Dan stared at him in anticipation.

When Dan realized he might as well be waiting for the wall to answer, he turned his gaze to Christelle.

"How about another coffee or more cheesecake? It is commendable, don't you think?"

He was not going to get anything more out of them—not without thumbscrews and truth serum.

Chapter Forty-Two

NOT IN THEIR WILDEST NIGHTMARES

Rex, Catia, and Digger arrived at the Pink Poodle in one of their rented RAV4s shortly after 7:00 p.m. John and his entourage arrived in a white rented Mercedes Benz SUV a few minutes later. Josh and Marissa parked a few spaces away from John and walked through the doors of the Pink Poodle a few steps behind his group. None of them were in disguises.

The Daltons sat at their own table. To their left, five tables away, sat Josh and Marissa. To their right, four tables away, was John and company.

They'd left Greg with Rehka and Simona on the *TOMATS*. Not that Greg wanted to stay. The argument with him was fierce. He was adamant that the team needed his gun in that fight. He was going to do his bit to help them clean the weeds off the public lawn. And if getting his ass kicked by Rex was what it cost, then so be it.

It took John's authority to convince him that the mission was doomed if both he and Rehka were not in the Ops Room operating those computers for the duration. "Something you apparently haven't grasped yet is that you and Rehka are the new special forces. We don't win battles by just kicking down doors and shooting people anymore; we win by outsmarting them first. Just think about it, son; how many of the missions of the past ten years could we've pulled off without you?"

And with that, the matter was settled.

John, Christelle, and Declan also went without disguises unless their 1970s outfits counted. After being shown to their table, Declan didn't let the grass grow under his feet; he went over to the business girls' tables and 'procured' four hours of one of the ladies' time. She could've been somewhere between twenty and forty years old, by his estimation. She said her name was Suzie, and she was quite content to dance away a few hours before they'd be heading to her room. After agreeing on the time and price, Rubio was happy for Declan to do whatever he wanted over the next four hours.

He didn't give a name; it didn't bother her. Clients seldom gave their real names, and she never remembered them anyway.

Understandably, she was more than just a little apprehensive when he led her to the table where his companions were waiting. Usually, her encounters with clients were private one-on-one affairs. And her pimps had beaten enough social skills into her to handle that, but for a foursome with three seventy-odd-year-olds, she'd received neither training nor had she any experience.

When the band took a break, and the two old men excused themselves to make a 'pit stop,' as they called it, the beautiful lady with the French accent told her that their friend had been wifeless for almost ten years. They persuaded him that it was time to hit the dating circuit of LA to find a new companion.

"Man was not created to be alone," said the French lady. "So, we brought him here tonight just to help him regain his confidence. If you know what I mean." She winked.

"I do, and I think he's doing very well so far," said Suzie. "I'll do my best to help him with that." She also winked.

Despite their age, Suzie's companions obviously had a lot more energy than most of the younger people, just sitting there drinking and staring at their cellphones and grunting and snorting cocaine. The rest of the crew were hard-pressed not to laugh too much when they saw CRC's golden oldies doing some Grease and Saturday Night Fever moves on the dance floor.

"John Travolta, eat your heart out," mumbled Rex in near disbelief when he saw the old men's antics.

It earned him a kick under the table from Catia, who was also giggling, albeit only a little. "Rex, you're not supposed to know them; stop staring."

Christelle and Suzie were a bit more modest; they didn't try to mimic Travolta's female counterparts in those movies.

Rex and Catia had to wait for Eva to make her appearance. According to Rehka, she was with a client, but she didn't know for how long.

It was early, and there were only four things one could do in this place: drink, drugs, dance, sex, or a combination of two or more of them. Rex was probably the world's worst dancer. Catia was as Italian as they came, and Italians liked to dance—but not to music as bad as this. So, they drank slowly and talked a lot.

John's group was the oldest group in the club, no doubt. Everyone was aware of them and, openly staring at them and maybe thought there was hope for themselves in their own old age. And that was precisely what John's group had in mind. They wanted everyone to remember them. Because then, in the aftermath, no one would even think of accusing the three old people with the adventurous spirits of the mayhem later that night.

Suzie soon relaxed. Her companions were down-to-earth, fun-loving, adventurous people and excellent conversationalists who helped her to relax, even though she was constantly aware of the watchful eyes of Antonio Rubio, the Blade, aka Jake, and Mark Dunn, aka Rick, and the ever-present concealed spy cameras.

She had no way of knowing the cameras were malfunctioning tonight. Well, not exactly malfunctioning, as in not operational, but displaying weeks-old footage to anyone who might be watching. Greg assured them no one was watching.

Josh and Marissa stayed until eight before they approached one of the girls. They had a lot to do. The auction was at midnight. The kids were in their cages. The buyers and sellers would arrive at regular intervals from ten thirty onward in order to maintain their anonymity. The last one was scheduled to arrive at a quarter to midnight. Rex and the team didn't believe for one moment that the child traffickers didn't know each other. In the dark world of drug- and sex trafficking, you survived by knowing, among others, who your rivals were. Besides, psychopaths never trust each other.

Rex's way into Cloud Nine was not without risks, though. However, if they pulled it off, the surprise factor was infinitely better than kicking down doors, as Josh had suggested.

Everything was going according to plan.

Although they didn't expect their encounter with the

bad guys to turn into a protracted gun battle, they came prepared for one. They wore no body armor under their loose-fitting clothes but carried .22 Glock pistols. The G44, as the compact but lethal pistols were known, was one of the quietest handguns on the market. With a silencer fitted, shots made less noise than opening a can of Coke. No wonder it was one of the favorite guns of assassins.

Each of them had five 22LR 25-round spare magazines fitting neatly into small pockets around their belts, hidden by loose hanging tops. The sixth magazine was in the gun. Locked and loaded. Between the Magnificent Eight, as John called them, there were one thousand rounds of .22 ammunition, three stun grenades, aka flashbangs, needles, syringes, sedatives, tranquilizer guns with many ketamine-loaded darts, zip-ties, duct tape, penlights, and more, all hidden under their loose-fitting clothes and in the ladies' oversized handbags. They were also wearing molar mics and were in communication with each other and the Ops Room on the *TOMATS*.

In short, they were loaded for bear.

Not in their wildest nightmares had the pimps of Cloud Nine ever met anyone like Rex Dalton and his band of vigilantes, including his dog.

———————

From the *TOMATS*, Greg and Rehka kept the team up to date with short reports about Cooper's escapades.

She'd broken a few more chairs against the walls and door. Futile. There was a small round window, but she knew it was armored glass, even stronger than the walls and door. The label on the window said so. She yelled at the TV. Defeated, she sank to the ground.

It was about an hour later when she got up from the floor and walked to the nearest picture on the wall, and started talking to the tormented souls depicted in the paintings. She moved from picture to picture, talking endlessly, sometimes crying, screaming, and yelling. Other times it sounded as if she was praying.

The praying gave all of them pause. As Christians, they believed in a merciful and loving God who would forgive and forget even the worst of sins if one repented, but Marion Cooper was an unrepentant, remorseless seductress and killer of defenseless children.

When Cooper reached the TV and looked behind it, she started giggling incessantly as she ripped the cables out of the back of the TV and the wall. Still babbling on incomprehensibly, she sat down on the floor and tied the ends of the cables together to make one long cable.

"Uh-oh, she's planning suicide," said Rehka to Greg.

"You're right! Good catch," said Greg and unmuted the audio link to the field team.

By the time Rehka told them what Cooper was up to, she'd wrapped one end of the cable around her neck and was looking around to find something high enough to tie the other end too.

"What do you want me to do, Rex?"

Rex didn't hesitate. "Let her be. She might just succeed. It will save me the trouble of shooting her."

Catia nodded slowly.

Rex was somewhat disappointed when he heard Cooper screaming at the top of her lungs in frustration when she couldn't find something suitable to tie the other end of the electric cord to.

Chapter Forty-Three

HIS HOURGLASS HAD RUN EMPTY

Without exception, they were still infuriated by the sickening child pornography they saw on the subterranean computers that morning. The poor kids locked up in cages. Kids drugged and abused. It was maddening just to think about it. It was frustrating to stick to the plan because they were ready to go immediately. The problem was if they did that, the auction wouldn't happen, and six kids would not be rescued.

Around ten o'clock, Greg and Rehka started keeping an eye on Eva's door. They needed to know when Eva was finished with her client so that they could warn Rex and Catia about her imminent arrival.

At ten thirty, Eva was still a no-show, and Rex started to worry that the client might have booked her past midnight or for the night like he did the night before. That would not ruin their plans, but it would complicate things somewhat.

Josh and Marissa had already struck out with their girl. They tried the same tactic as Rex the night before. They told her what their plans were. It was a disaster. She started crying and shaking, on the brink of hysteria. No matter how many times they hugged her and told her all was okay, that they were not police, there were no cameras, no microphones, no one was listening or watching, she didn't believe them.

Eventually, they managed to get her anxiety levels down to where she stopped crying and stopped threatening to push the panic button on her bedside table. The cup of tea spiked with a sedative given to her by Marissa helped to calm her down.

But that didn't mean she trusted them.

Just to be on the safe side, Greg disabled the power plug next to her bed, into which the panic system and her bed light were plugged.

Josh and Marissa weren't totally unprepared for this behavior. They knew the girls lived in fear and might not want to cooperate. For her own safety, it was best if they sedated her just before the pawpaw hit the fan. Their plan to ask this girl to take Marissa to the other girls' rooms when the shooting started, to round them up and take them to the bar area and tell them to stay there until someone came to fetch them, was canned. Hopefully, Declan's lady, Suzie, might step up to the plate. Failing her, Marissa and Christelle would work together to get the girls out of harm's way.

It wasn't a good start for tonight's mission. But there was no reason to call it off either. They were in the belly of the beast and didn't have to break down doors to get in when the time came.

They knew the odds. Twenty-two bad guys, most of whom were carrying guns, versus seven vigilantes with guns, two with computers, and one military-trained dog.

"Twenty-two?" said Declan.

Josh answered. "Well, it's TJ, Johnny and Sammy, Jake

and Rick, six buyers and four sellers, Fatman, plus four guards and two bouncers."

Rex had a plan he wanted to discuss with Digger, but they couldn't leave the room. He started scratching Digger's back and gave his mind free rein.

We've got heavy odds against us.

So, what's the problem? We've been outnumbered before. Divide and conquer. Napoleon Bonaparte.

You're into history now?

Digger sighed. *Discussion over.* He closed his eyes.

Rex smiled when Greg told him that Eva was on her way. If they could get to her room, there were several ways he could get over to the Purple Pussycat unnoticed. The manager of the guards and bouncers had an office there, and he was at his desk. His door was closed but not locked.

This was where Rex's plan to get inside Cloud Nine without firing a single shot was at its weakest.

"Eva could've changed her mind since this morning," said Rehka.

"I agree with her, Rex," said Marissa. "Drugs or the lack thereof do strange things to the human mind. As we've seen with Cooper."

"You could be walking into a trap," said Josh.

Rex spoke into his molar mic. "I'll take the risk because we have no choice, and I trust Digger to sniff out any duplicity; he always does."

With that, he and Catia stood and walked over to Eva's table. Rex saw the recognition in Eva's eyes as they sat down. The first good sign was that their presence didn't scare her. She would've been nervous if she had something up her sleeve. She acted as if they were strangers.

The moment of truth. He looked at Digger and nodded in Eva's direction.

Digger walked around the table to Eva, sat down next to her, and extended his right paw for her to shake.

That meant he hadn't detected any underhandedness in Eva. That was good enough for Rex and Catia.

Rex and Digger took the tunnel route to the Purple Pussycat and stepped out on the other side just a few yards from the manager's office door. Along the way, Greg and Rehka did their magic to guarantee no one saw them.

The manager was surprised and shocked when he looked up into the business end of a .22 Glock pistol. The hole where the bullet would come out, looking enormous from his viewpoint, captured his attention to the exclusion of everything else. He even stopped breathing. His stomach roiled, and his heart felt as if it wanted to break out of his chest. A lot of panic-inducing chemicals were pumped into his bloodstream.

He wanted to go for his gun, but his hand wouldn't move.

Maybe it was because his brain finally made him aware of the man holding a Glock pistol in one hand and an FBI badge in the other, standing on the other side of his desk. Just as well his hand hadn't obeyed the idiotic command it had received from his brain; he would've been dead if it did.

Cold shivers ran down his spine in ripples. And he became aware of a big black dog standing next to the FBI man with the gun. The dog had a snarl on his face, displaying fangs that conjured up images of a lion killing a buffalo he'd once seen on TV.

The manager comprehended his hourglass had run empty.

Chapter Forty-Four

EVERYONE IS GOING TO BE OKAY

It was about a quarter after eleven, forty minutes after entering the manager's office, when Rex and Digger left the office and returned to Eva's room with the help of Greg and Rehka.

Eva and Catia had become fast friends. Eva was scared but willing to help Marissa with the other girls. The thing was, Rex needed her to go with Catia and Declan to collect the children.

Eva told them one of the other adult girls had confided in her frequently in the past that she was looking for a way out, and if she couldn't escape, she'd get out with an overdose or cutting her wrists. "Lucy is her name, she'll help, but I'll have to talk to her first. So, can you get me to her room unseen?"

Rex had a better plan, less risky. "Let's first find out where she is." He pulled out his phone, showed Eva the photos of all the girls, and she identified Lucy.

"Where did you—? Don't worry, I remember now. You've done your homework. Right?"

Rex nodded. "Okay, Greg, Rehka, where's Lucy?"

"She's at a table with another girl waiting for fresh customers," said Rehka almost immediately.

"Okay, John and associates, a slight change of plan." He explained what he had in mind. Everyone agreed it could work. It was not without risks but still better than the alternative; to kick down doors and start shooting bad guys until they were all dead or neutralized.

Catia saw the confusion on Eva's face as Rex seemed to talk to someone with no phone, microphone, or earbuds in sight.

"Who's he talking to, and how?" she whispered to Catia.

Eva was a complete technophobe. They were not allowed to have mobile phones or any devices with internet access. Getting caught with any of those carried the same punishment as an attempt to escape—a horrific and protracted death.

Catia explained the technology in broad terms. She opened her mouth and showed Eva the molar mic. "We're all carrying one of these."

Eva was stunned. "So, last night, when he and Digger were here, you were listening?"

Catia smiled and nodded.

Eva giggled. "So, you know he was a good boy?"

Catia laughed. "I know."

"He's a good man, Catia."

Catia smiled proudly. "You won't get an argument from me about that. Okay. Now while he's busy talking, I'd like to show you a few things you're going to need later on; one of them is this molar mic." She took one out of her handbag, put a surgical glove on, and fitted it over one of Eva's molars right at the back of her mouth.

"Okay, Rehka, you can activate Eva's comms."

Eva grabbed her cheek when the mic activated with a vibration.

"Speak to me," said Rehka.

Eva almost fell off her chair. "Oh, my God! Who's this? It's as if you're talking right inside my head!"

"Amazing, isn't it?" said Rehka.

"Amazing? This is magic!"

"You're right," said Catia. "I felt the same the first few times. Now, let me show you a few more things you need to know before you report to the auction room."

It was not the ideal place to do it, but h-hour was approaching fast. The original plan was for Declan to go with Suzie to her room on the second floor and brief her about what was going to happen, and ask her to help when the time came to round up the girls on the second floor and escort them to the lounge area on level one below ground. If that plan was still in play and it turned out Suzie didn't want to take the chance, she would be in her room, and no one would be wiser. But now there was a real danger that she could get as emotional as Farley's subject out here in full sight of everyone and ruin everything.

Rex was scratching Digger's back when he said, "I suggest we go ahead with the Suzie-Lucy plan. Suzie doesn't have much of a choice. I reckon she will cooperate with us in the end."

"Whatever you say, boss," said Josh. "We either push ahead or call everything off and storm through the doors with blazing guns."

"Precisely," said Rex.

Not only did they have to brief Suzie right there at the table, but they also had to get Lucy on their side as well.

So, while Declan approached Lucy with a proposition, John and Christelle briefed Suzie.

While Declan made small talk with Lucy and took his time doing so, he was waiting for the signal from John to tell him if Suzie was on board or not. If she was, he'd make a deal with Jake for Lucy and go over to her room at Cloud Nine.

It was imperative that John and Christelle stayed at the Pink Poodle until the kickoff. Someone had to take care of Jake and Rick.

Christelle, who'd built a good rapport with Suzie over the course of the night, started the brief.

Suzie was furious from the get-go. She felt she'd been misled, and they'd placed her in mortal danger. Of course, she was right and justifiably upset.

Christelle and John apologized and explained why they had to do it. But that didn't placate her much.

Even after Christelle and John explained that their people were in charge of all cameras, microphones, and so forth, Suzie remained apprehensive. It was expected. Christelle explained to her that it was normal to experience fear.

"However, Suzie, what is important about fear is how you handle it. Some people allow fear to control them, others simply refuse to take delivery. You're a strong, brave, and intelligent woman, Suzie; you're not going to let it paralyze you, are you?"

Suzie wasn't listening. She was making calculations, umming and ahing as she did so. "There are about thirty of them. You're three old people."

"Seven," said Christelle. "The others are much younger than we are."

"And a dog," said John.

"Oh, and a dog," said Christelle.

Suzie was horrified. "Seven against thirty?"

"Eight," said John. "Don't forget the dog."

"Stuff the damn dog. Do you have any idea what you're dealing with here? They're the worst criminals imaginable. Gangsters, robbers, rapists, killers, child molesters, women beaters—" She had tears in her eyes. "They're animals, all of them. They'll kill you in a heartbeat,"

"We've handled much worse," said John softly.

"Let me guess. That would've been when you were a third of your current age, right?"

John was getting a little antsy. He spoke in a measured tone. "They have no idea who we are, how many we are, or how, where, and when we're going to hit them."

Suzie started shaking her head.

Christelle stepped in. "Suzie, we're not forcing you to do anything. We're here to rescue the children and anyone else who wants to be rescued. We're going in with or without you. The choice is yours. Whatever you decide, we're still committed to keeping you safe. You and everyone who is not part of this evil cabal."

Suzie managed to keep the tears at bay. She spoke softly. "You've got no idea what it's like. It's hell. There's no way out for us. We can't leave because we're hopelessly addicted to drugs. They pump it into us every day. Once we reach the age of consent, they keep us until we look old and ugly, and in this place, that doesn't take long, believe me. Then we get kicked out on the streets, and that's the end for us. We're dead within weeks because we don't know anyone outside this place.

"There's no hope, no future, no life, only sex with

strangers, day in and day out, drugs that numb the senses, and death.

"No one has ever escaped unless you regard suicide as an escape. Those who've tried are dead or would never try it again. There's not a single one of us who are not contemplating suicide, but they're watching our every move, and if they catch us trying... Well, let me put it this way, there are fates worse than death. They're not always successful at stopping all suicide attempts. Those of us who remain behind envy those who were successful and pity those who weren't.

"So, you want to know if I want to be rescued? Really? What do you think? Would *you* want to stay?"

Christelle shook her head in silence.

"Of course, I want out, but I also want to be alive when I get there. I don't know what you people are capable of. But I know what those monsters are capable of. I've seen them in action, and I've experienced them in action—I am scared to death—"

"We understand," John interjected. "I can't, and none of us can give you any guarantees, but we're the one and only chance you have."

Suzie took a sip of her cocktail. "I will help you get in, and I will help you with the girls on my floor, as you've asked. And I'll do whatever else you ask of me because either way, I could be dead before the night is over. And the only reason I'm doing it is that I'm desperate to believe some of what you told me, that you might get me out of here alive. Even if you can't, I get the impression death on your side of the fence would be less painful than on the animals' side."

Christelle nodded and placed her hand on Suzie's arm.

"We're going to do our best to keep you and all the other girls and children alive or die trying."

"I know very little about the children down in the dungeons. I've seen none of them. The furthest down I'm allowed to go is level two for the filming of porn movies two or three times a week, sometimes more."

"Don't worry; we've got the children covered. You help us with the other girls, and you've done your bit," said Christelle. "Everyone is going to be okay."

Chapter Forty-Five

PHASE ONE

Greg and Rheka kept them up to date with the whereabouts of the bad guys.

TJ was in the bar on the ground level of Cloud Nine. Johnny was patrolling the four floors above ground. Sammy patrolled everything below ground. They were all armed with guns and stilettos.

Fatman was at the Pink Poodle and about to waggle over to Cloud Nine. He was unarmed. He was the auctioneer tonight.

Jake and Rick were in their usual place in the private lounge in the corner of the bar in the Pink Poodle under the watchful eyes of John and Christelle. John detected the bulges under their clothes; they were carrying guns. Jake would certainly carry at least one knife, probably more, apart from the gun. He had to keep his reputation as a fearsome knife fighter up.

The two bouncers were at their usual spots at the front entrance of the Pink Poodle. The four guards were at various locations throughout the building and moving around. They all carried guns and were in contact with each other via small handheld two-way radios, aka walkie-talkies.

Rex checked his watch; it was 11:45 p.m. Fatman, six buyers, and four sellers were now all in the makeshift auction room on the second floor below ground, where temporary soundproof booths with one-way windows had been erected for each of them. They couldn't see or hear each other, but they could see the floor where the children would be paraded. They had big headsets covering their ears to block out all external noise so they could concentrate on the girls and the voice of the auctioneer. On the table in front of them was a big green button. Bids would be incremented by five-thousand dollars every time the button was pressed.

The six girls going on auction, in a state of abject misery, were locked in small, soundproof cells on the third floor from where they'd be brought to the arena by Sammy when it was their turn to be paraded on the catwalk in front of the lust-filled eyes attached to the sick minds of eleven child rapists and killers.

TJ was expected to arrive shortly after the last of the buyers and sellers were in their booths. His job was to make sure the auction happened in an orderly fashion, and the buyers and sellers didn't kill each other before, during, or after the event. That's why all of them had to report to TJ in the lounge on the first floor below ground upon arrival, where they were subjected to a physical search and scan from head to toe for weapons and communications devices. They all had 'contraband,' guns, knives, mobile phones, etcetera. He confiscated all of it and put it in plastic bags, and labeled each with a sticker with a number on it. He copied the number onto a separate piece of paper and handed it to each owner. "It's your receipt. After the auction, your property will be returned to you."

No one argued with TJ; that scar over his face was forbidding by itself. And then there were the rumors about his barbaric nature.

Rex and Digger were to take TJ down first.

Then Josh had to take care of Johnny and Sammy. After that, he had to help Rex and Digger secure the auction room. Eva and Lucy would be in the auction room with them.

John and Christelle would take care of Jake and Rick. Suzie would help them get the girls to the Cloud Nine lounge.

Catia, Declan, and Marissa would stay put in their respective rooms for Phase One as the backup for the others.

It started at precisely 11.50 p.m. when TJ glanced at his watch, finished the last of his whiskey in one gulp, put the glass down, and rose to his feet. At that moment, a masked man and a big black dog strode into the lounge.

Instinctively, TJ reached for his gun but froze when he realized the man was already pointing a gun at him. He could swear that gun wasn't there a split second before, or was it? The three double whiskeys could've diminished his observation skills.

He started to speak but stopped when he felt a short sharp jab in his chest. He looked down and saw the colorful tranquilizer dart protruding from his torso. Automatically his hand came up to remove it but didn't quite make it all the way there before a dizzying sensation overtook him, and he saw the floor rushing toward his face before darkness overwhelmed him.

Rex activated his molar mic and told everyone TJ had been neutralized and secured.

"We have five minutes to neutralize the pimps and other scum. Let's do it."

Digger stood by while Rex secured TJ's arms and legs with zip-ties. He ripped the stinking wife-beater vest off TJ's body and gagged him with it before he hauled the body into the walk-in refrigerator. He slipped the zip-ties, holding TJ's hands together behind his back, over the meat hook, and with the pulley system used to hang carcasses, he hoisted the body several feet above the floor. He didn't make any sound then, but when he regained consciousness in an hour, he was not only going to have a spectacular headache, but he was also going to experience new adventures in pain coming from his dislocated shoulders. And that was only going to be the preamble to his misery.

"We'll find out if you can take what you dish out," said Rex, as he closed and locked the fridge door.

Digger looked bored. He hadn't seen much action so far tonight. He probably had a hard time understanding why Rex hadn't set him loose on this evil-smelling human.

Josh and Marissa had put their girl to bed ten minutes earlier. They were reluctant to do it, but it was better than risking her being harmed in the turmoil that was about to start. They did everything they could to be as gentle as possible with the unsuspecting but nervous young girl. Josh was talking to her about her favorite movies to distract her. It worked; she almost didn't feel the needle entering her upper arm. For a moment or two, she looked at Marissa in shock, but before she could utter a word, her body went limp.

They carried her from the chair to her bed. Marissa made sure she was comfortable in the recovery position while Josh ran quietly up the stairs to the third floor and waited in the stairwell behind the door.

According to Rehka, Johnny was less than two yards away on the other side, sitting in an easy chair next to the elevator door having a cigarette and a beer while watching a replay of the highlights of the previous night's Dodgers game on his iPad.

When Josh got Rex's message that TJ had been neutralized, he opened the door, took one step, and shot Johnny with a tranquilizer dart in the neck at point-blank range. The lowlife had just enough time to look up, eyes wide. He tried to say something, but no sound left his mouth. His eyes rolled back in his head, and his body slumped back in the chair. Josh zip-tied his arms and legs and gagged him with duct tape.

He told Rehka to open the elevator door, and then he dragged Johnny in. Less than a minute later, the door opened on the first basement floor in the lounge. Johnny's unconscious body came flying out like a bag of rubbish and landed on the floor with a dull thud.

The door closed, and the elevator descended to the third floor below.

Greg told Josh, "Sammy is sitting in front of the cages of the girls he has to escort upstairs to be auctioned." He told Josh, next to Sammy, on a small table, was a half-empty bottle of tequila, a few limes, his stiletto, and a ramekin filled with coarse salt. His gun was in its shoulder holster.

On the wall in front of him was a big screen TV playing a horror movie on deafening volume.

Probably to scare the forlorn kids even more and keep them in check, thought Josh.

Sammy sat with his back to the elevator door. He didn't hear the door opening. Even if he did, it would've been too late. The tranquilizer dart hit him in the back of the neck. A minute later, he was trussed and gagged like a chicken ready for the slow cooker. Except, he got thrown into the elevator.

The poor, bewildered kids were watching in stunned silence. It was clear they had no idea that the masked man was their friend and liberator.

It pained Josh to leave the kids in their cages, but it was for their own good. With his index finger in front of his mouth, he whispered, "Nobody's going to hurt you. I'm here to help. Be quiet; someone will come for you in just a few minutes."

They just stared at him—benumbed, detached, dizzied by the drugs.

Greg closed the elevator door and moved it to the second basement floor, where the auction would take place. Upon arrival, he didn't open the door yet. Josh took the stairs up to the same floor.

With that, the last of the three pimps of Cloud Nine had reached the end of his career, just like his two colleagues, Johnny and TJ, a few minutes before.

Chapter Forty-Six

TIME TO WRAP UP PHASE ONE

After hanging TJ out to cool down in the refrigerator room, Rex and Digger took the stairs down to the auction room. They waited behind the door in the stairwell for Josh to arrive.

Eva had not quite gotten used to the molar mic in the back of her mouth, but she didn't give anyone of the slime-balls she was serving with drinks and snacks any reason to be suspicious, either. Rex and the others were listening as she kept up the charade. She and Lucy had barely served their last clients in their booths when Rex, Digger, and an unknown man, also wearing a black ski mask, stepped in through the stairway door. That was their signal to step back and let the two men and the dog take charge.

Rex and Josh started at opposite ends of the eleven auction booths arranged in a semicircle around the arena and worked their way to the middle, shooting a ketamine-filled tranquilizer dart into each of the vermin. They were all taken up by the drivel Fatman was spouting about the quality of the merchandise on auction tonight, isolated from any external noises by their noise-canceling headsets, hidden behind one-way mirror glass, they were oblivious of their surroundings until they felt the sharp pain from the darts entering their bodies. Too late. They were all comatose before they could make a sound.

Fatman was last. His booth was the middle one. He was still talking like a slimy second-hand car salesman when Josh's dart hit him between the shoulder blades. He slumped forward in his chair, and Josh removed the dart.

While Eva and Lucy zip-tied everyone's hands and feet and wrapped their mouths with duct tape, Rex and Josh dragged the comatose bodies to the elevator. They noticed how Eva and Lucy worked together to drag the last unconscious man by his hair into the waiting elevator.

"Lucky son of a bitch," mumbled Josh. "He should've been awake."

It was time to wrap up Phase One and get Phase Two going.

Rex took his satellite phone out and called the guard manager, who was in his office eagerly awaiting this call.

When he answered, Rex said, "Smith, it's Special Agent Donnelly here. Are we still good, or should my dog and I pay you another visit?"

"Not necessary, sir. We're good. My men are all on board, awaiting my orders to move, and I'm just waiting for yours."

"Smith, I still think I've made a terrible mistake. But I gave my word. So, you better make sure I don't regret doing so."

"I promise, sir, you won't regret it. You won't ever see me again. "

"We'll have to see about that. But make no mistake, if I see you or any of your men *ever* again, it will be too soon. Understood?"

"Yes, sir."

"Now, vamoose. *Ever* starts right now. "

"Yes, sir. We are vamoosing."

Rex ended the call and said to Greg and Rehka, "Time to create chaos."

"Here it comes," said Greg as he nodded to Rehka. She clicked the mouse twice. Thirty miles away, the lights in the Pink Poodle flickered a few times and returned to normal. However, in the Purple Pussycat, the lights flickered, went out, and didn't come back.

About thirty seconds later, a computerized voice blared over the speakers. "This is an emergency. This is not a drill. Evacuate now. This is an emergency. This is not a drill. Evacuate now. This is an emergency. This is not a drill. Evacuate now." Soon the voice was joined by the fire alarm. A minute and a half later, the fire sprinklers discharged water onto everyone and everything. Finally, to ensure absolute pandemonium, the lights flickered twice, and then all lights in the Pink Poodle went out and stayed out. Cloud Nine was the only building with lights on in the entire block.

Greg and Rehka had created a perfect storm. The place was filled with bedlam and panic, screaming and shouting, swearing and pushing, and shoving as everyone tried to get out.

Well, not everyone; Jake and Rick had to protect their merchandise. As the computerized voice bellowed over the intercom, John, Christelle, and Suzie moved to an empty table just a few feet away from Jake and Rick.

Jake and Rick screamed at the girls at the top of their lungs. "Assemble at the door, girls. Now! Don't make us come and get you. Move it! To the door! Right now. Move it, bitches! Move it!"

Said 'bitches' did as they were told, and all started moving toward the door. Suzie, John, and Christelle joined the queue.

By the time the alarm went off, the procession was at the door. Rick stood at the door and told them to form a single line. He was holding out his hand for the girls to hand over the drugs they were supposed to sell to the clients but hadn't yet.

Jake was next in line; he stood inside the hallway and told them to assemble in the lounge on level two below ground and wait for him. Seven of the fifteen adult girls were there, and the remaining eight were in their rooms with clients. Rehka had already passed their names, photos, and room numbers on to Marissa's team, including Lucy's room, where Declan was waiting for the signal. Lucy had gone to the auction room earlier when the child sex slave traders started arriving. They also locked the doors to all eight rooms remotely. They'd unlock them only on Josh's or Declan's request.

When the lights went out, it became evident that there were many smokers or drug users or both in the room as many little flames coming from butane lighters sprung up all over the place.

Christelle passed Rick, who was too heavily invested in collecting his cocaine from the girls, to notice the unknown woman in the group. He was disturbed when one of the girls bumped into him. He didn't feel the needle that Christelle plunged into his ass. He swore loudly at the girl. She protested that she was pushed from behind. Rick raised his hand and tried to say there was no one behind her, but not a single word escaped his mouth—he just collapsed to the floor.

"Romeo down," reported Christelle over her molar mic.

John kept walking past Christelle, who was on her knees next to Rick on the floor, busy zip-tying and gagging him.

John's eyes were fixed on Jake. At the five-step mark, Jake wasn't aware of him. The same at the four-step mark. At the three-step mark, Jake looked him straight in the eyes, and John saw the alert in his eyes. But Jake was stupid; he pulled a knife. This was a gunfight. The two .22 rounds from John's gun hit him an inch apart in the middle of his forehead.

No one heard the shots in that ear-splitting noise. "Juliet, KIA," he reported. Just then, the lights went out, and not long after, more cigarette lighters came to life. Nobody saw Jake's body propped up against the wall out of the way of the girls filing through the door.

In the light of the cigarette lighters and two powerful pen flashlights, Suzie waved her arms, got the attention of a few, and signaled that they should follow her. She turned and led the way through the tunnel over to Cloud Nine. Next to her was the tall gentleman they'd seen socializing with Suzie. His gracious partner was at the back of the line. They both had high-strength pocket flashlights, which helped the group see where they were going.

"How thoughtful of them to come and help us," said one of the girls.

Christelle smiled when she heard that. *We came prepared, my dear.*

Chapter Forty-Seven

RESCUING THE PRISONERS

"Where are the damn guards when you need them!" shouted one of the patrons who had gathered in front of the Pink Poodle.

"Guards! Guards! Guards!" The crowd started chanting from all directions.

They got no reply. Smith and his men were already miles away. They couldn't hear the alarm, let alone the shouting.

Smith had earned himself the eternal gratitude of his men. He'd made them an offer they couldn't refuse, just in time. All they had to do was walk out on their employer at Smith's command and never come back. "But you have to stay until I say you can go."

"What's in it for us?" one smug guard wanted to know.

"You'll avoid the FBI and jail."

"But I'm only a guard," he pushed on. "I can't be held responsible for what's going on here."

"Yeah, and how did that work out for the guards at the Nazi extermination camps?" said Smith.

"But—"

"Look, if you want to stay and plead your case with the FBI and the courts, I won't stand in your way. I'm going, and my advice is that you all do the same. Get as much distance as you can between yourself and this place."

In short order, they agreed this was a deal of a lifetime, and they all took it. Even the smug one had come to his senses. So, when Smith gave them the order, they were long ready. They grabbed their bags and ran for their cars.

Rex and the rest of the team didn't decide this easily. Letting the guards go meant seven criminals, guardians of the devil's disciples, no less, would be on the loose. The arguments that it was for the greater good didn't feed the bulldog, though. Those guards were every bit as bad as the pimps and the sex slave traders. They knew what was going on under their noses. They not only condoned it, but they also participated in it. The girls told them the guards were not much better than the pimps. The team's problem was the guards were armed. It was their job to shoot at people if they deemed it necessary. Any encounter with the guards would end in a shootout, and innocent people would die. And it would attract police attention too early, which would put their plan to save the girls in jeopardy.

"But may God have mercy on them if our paths ever cross again," said Rex in conclusion.

"Amen!" said Josh.

They were ready to kick off Phase Two—rescuing the prisoners.

Marissa and her team, Josh, Suzie, Lucy, and Declan had seven rooms with girls and clients to secure. Catia and her team, Rex, Digger, Eva, John, and Christelle, had twelve children and six pedophiles to take care of.

Marissa's team met in the bar on the ground floor. From there, they went to visit the rooms upstairs two at a time; Josh and Suzie were on one team, and Declan and Lucy were on the other. They didn't generate much excitement other than embarrassing the occupants of the rooms. There were no doors to kick down; Greg and Rehka had unlocked them on demand. There was no girl or client who was willing to upset a masked man holding a gun. It took all of seven minutes to get the seven girls to dress with modesty and assemble in the lounge room and convince the clients to stay in bed and follow the doctor's orders—a jab of ketamine and a two-hour nap.

In the meantime, Catia's team had met in the lounge on level one below. They didn't pay much attention to the thirteen unmoving bodies lined up against the one wall. They knew who the bodies were, and it would've been great to tie weights to their feet and drop them in the sea. Or… maybe shoot them in the head first, then tie weights to their feet, etcetera. Dying either way would be merciful compared to what they'd done to their victims over the years.

The first stop was on level three below, the location of the six girls who would not go on auction, ever. John and Christelle were tasked to take care of them and take them up to the lounge area. Eva spoke to the children first and then introduced them to John and Christelle before she left with Rex and Catia to the fourth floor below to rescue the six children there.

John and Christelle thought they'd seen and heard the worst of humanity until the moment the six desolate children stood before them, made up to look even younger than they were. Child sex slaves. Outcasts. Forsaken. Drug addicts. John and Christelle had tears in their eyes as they hugged the kids and led them out of their cages. None of the children said a word. They did everything Christelle and John asked them to do. They'd met Eva only a day or so ago, but she was nice to them, and she'd assured them that the old people would do them no harm. They were there to set them all free. The elevator took them up to the first basement floor, where the lounge and the kitchen, and the walk-in refrigerator were.

John and Christelle led them as far as possible away from the unconscious child sex traffickers. Christelle asked the children to sit down on the floor with her and move in close. She told them they were going to be okay. That no one would hurt them.

Christelle didn't have children, but there was nothing wrong with her motherly instincts. Or maybe it was grandmotherly instincts. The children started to relax and moved closer to her. Some started touching her and snuggling up.

John went to the kitchen to see if he could get together the ingredients for sandwiches and hot chocolate.

In the process of trying to find out where everything he needed for the sandwiches and hot chocolate was, John opened the walk-in refrigerator. He blinked a few times when the lights came on and another few more times when he recognized TJ hanging off one of the meat hooks.

"Tsk, tsk. TJ, if you can hear me, I suggest you listen carefully. When the guy who hung you here comes for you and asks you questions, it would be good for you to cooperate with him. Believe me, I've seen him and that dog of his take their time to make a man talk. I couldn't eat for a week, and I'm still getting nightmares."

John got no reply.

"Ah, well, suit yourself. I've done my Christian duty to

ease the pain and suffering of a fellow man." He closed the door and switched the lights off.

In the meantime, the rest of Catia's team had arrived at level four below. Digger and Rex led the way. Rex and Catia wore ski masks and carried their .22 Glocks in their hands, pointing to the ground.

One by one, Greg and Rehka unlocked the children's rooms at Rex's request. Rex and Digger went in first. Then followed Catia right on their heels. Eva only entered when Rex told her it was safe to do so. She and Catia helped the children to get dressed and escorted them out of the room, leaving Rex, Digger, and the pedophile behind.

The children were crying nervously when they were led out of their rooms. Four of the child molesters were so frightened by the big black dog and the masked man with the gun they meekly submitted to Rex's ministrations of zipties, gags, and a shot of ketamine each. The exceptions were a sheriff and a judge who loudly voiced their indignation at the intrusion on their privacy.

The sheriff became aggressive in his language and demeanor, but it ended abruptly when a .22 round smashed through his left kneecap. The high-pitched screaming was an indication that the pain must've been excruciating. The pain generated by the second round, which made a mess of his right knee, must've been indescribable—he passed out.

The egomaniacal scumbag judge thought he was above the law and claimed to have the right to have sex with anyone he damn well pleased. Whether his right derived from the constitution or some legislation, he didn't say. He started threatening with the law, and the courts, long prison sentences, and so forth. He worked himself up during this tirade so much he lost his marbles and stormed at Rex.

Digger did nothing to stop his honor; he just stepped

deftly out of the man's way as if to say, "Mate, if you want to charge at my alpha, I'm not going to stand in your way. It has never ended well for those who've tried it in the past. But maybe you'll have better luck." He didn't.

Rex hit him in the throat and crushed his windpipe. That was followed by a nut-crushing kick to the groin to assure that if the honorable justice survived the trauma to the throat, at least he wouldn't be able to sexually abuse children ever again.

But then air began to leak into the pedophilic judge's neck and chest due to his broken trachea. Within minutes, his honor had serious respiratory problems. Rex ignored his medical issues and cuffed him with cable ties but didn't jab or gag him. The man was supposed to be the exemplification of honor, uprightness, decency, integrity, honesty, righteousness, ethics, morals, morality, virtue, principle, right-mindedness, trustworthiness, incorruptibility, and so forth. He wasn't. He suffocated and died before Rex and Digger were out of the room. Rex didn't care at all. He'd just crossed out one of the five-hundred and fifty-six on the blacklist.

The principal, pastor, politician, and mayor were happy to stay in bed and take their medicine—a shot of animal tranquilizer. They knew, upon opening their eyes, they'd have to deal with the cops. But right now, those large syringes and long needles in the hands of the masked marauders looked decidedly ominous.

Chapter Forty-Eight

I'LL TELL YOU ABOUT THEM

Harris was expecting a phone call from someone with a computerized voice around midnight. However, he got a phone call at 12:16 a.m., and the voice wasn't computerized; it was his captain's. For the past few years, he'd received many memos and attended many lectures about the verisimilitude of deepfake videos and audio. Most of those memos and lectures were quite technical and boring. But he learned one thing; it was impossible to recognize a deepfake without sophisticated equipment and software. At home, he had access to none of those. Therefore, he didn't even have an inkling that he'd just been talking to Rex Dalton and not his captain.

Apparently, an anonymous caller had reported a big mess at the Pink Poodle and Cloud Nine; lots of blood, bodies, a fire alarm, a power cut, and lots of panic. Probably the beginning of a gang war.

Harris was in his car in less than two minutes. The blaring clip-on siren on the roof was flashing red and blue to ensure anyone on the streets made way for him.

More than just a little irritated, he was swearing under his breath. That call from the captain had all but spoiled what he thought would be the perfect end to a perfect night. It was one of the best nights he and his love of more than forty years had in a long time. The movie was excellent, the seafood divine, and the lovemaking heavenly. *If retirement is going to be like this, bring it on, I'm ready, willing, and able.*

All he needed to tick off the last box to make it a perfect night was to put handcuffs on a bunch of child molesters, child sex slave bosses, child rapists, and drug pushers. Those who'd survived the wrath of the US Marshal and his grinning black dog.

"Thanks for ruining what would've been a perfect end to a perfect night," he mumbled. "Instead of taking real nasty criminals off the streets, your humble servant will now investigate pimps fighting over prostitutes.

"How many times have I told you, idiots, we should raid those places and shut them down. But no, you keep on blocking my proposals. Too many adverse reactions. Too many red faces. The pimps are doing us a favor; they're keeping the girls off the streets and safe. No one gets harmed. Let them be; at least we know who they are and where they are. You've got better things to do, like catching real criminals such as thieves, robbers, murderers, rapists, and more."

When Harris was about two minutes away, his radio squawked. It was the dispatcher ordering every patrol car within a five-mile radius to the scene. He was expecting to find the crime scene packed with police vehicles and officers. But it seemed he was going to be the first one there. He was too frustrated and preoccupied to find it odd.

When Harris pulled up in front of the Pink Poodle, he

was indeed the first cop there. It was exactly as the captain had described—darkness, noise, panic, and chaos.

He switched off the engine, got out, and pushed the button on the fob. The doors of the car locked with a beep, the fire alarm stopped, and then the lights in the Pink Poodle flickered to life. Harris stopped and looked at the keys in his hand as though he was trying to find some kind of connection between the car keys, the alarm, and the lights.

And then it struck him; there was indeed a connection, Rex Dalton. That meant the call earlier didn't come from his captain, and probably the dispatcher's radio calls to the patrol cars originated from the same source. As far as he was aware, this was the first time he'd been deepfaked.

The synchronicity between his car's remote and the alarm and lights of the Pink Poodle must've been happenstance.

"How the hell—?" He didn't have time to ponder. He could only hope that the Marshal and his dog were alive, the bad guys dead, wounded, or missing, and the prostitutes alive and safe.

He couldn't help but think he was probably going to have that happy retirement after all.

A few minutes later, Harris entered the Pink Poodle and was pointed at the way through the tunnel to Cloud Nine. On the way, he walked past two men lying on the floor near each other. One was unconscious and gagged with duct tape. His arms and legs were zip-tied. The other was in a white suit, white shirt, and red tie. His white suit was a mess, and he was dead. Two small bullet holes in his forehead explained his condition. Harris left them there with a nauseated feeling, not so much because of what he had just seen but what he expected to find ahead. He continued to the lounge area on the first basement floor of Cloud Nine.

Within minutes after his arrival in the lounge, he was wondering if there was a way to vanish, not as in walking or running away, but as in disappearing in a puff of smoke, like a magician. But he had no magic wand. Just as well, his audience, twelve disheveled, traumatized, and morose teenage girls with lifeless eyes, and fifteen adult women covered in blood having their arms around the twelve children, were clearly not in an emotional state to go through the trauma of a disappearing police officer on top of everything else they'd obviously been through already.

If ever Harris had experienced a classic case of mass catatonia, this was it. The women showed no signs of aggression, fear, or emotion. They were unperturbed by the three groups of blood-soaked bodies lined up on the floor against the opposite wall from where they were sitting in a tight cluster on the floor. And none of them said a word. Their silent stares made his skin crawl. This was a scene from a horror movie.

Slowly, Harris turned and walked to the expired. He turned back when he heard a shuffle behind him. It was a blonde girl who couldn't be much older than twenty. Her hair was matted with blood; in fact, she was covered in it from head to toe. She held a stiletto in her right hand. Harris looked at the knife, then at her. She threw it aside and took a step forward closer to him.

"I'm Eva Hansen; I'll tell you about them… who they are… were."

Harris nodded.

The first group consisted of two men who could've been somewhere in their thirties, but with all the tattoos covering their faces and bodies, it was difficult to say.

"Johnny and Sammy," said Eva. "I don't know their real names. They are what you people who don't know what's going on in this place call pimps. We, who know, call them rapists, drug pushers, abductors, murderers." She pointed back to the children. "Child molesters, animals."

Harris looked at the two naked bodies again. The features that were most prominent were the bleeding wounds where their external genitalia was supposed to be. The second most notable was that said missing private parts were lodged in the mouths of their owners. The third most discernible feature was that both men's upper torsos each had precisely twenty-seven stab wounds in them. One stab wound for every girl in Cloud Nine. Harris couldn't tell which the deceased lost first, their manhood or their lives.

Their feet were tied together with zip-ties, and so were their hands behind their backs.

Zip-ties in a brothel?

Harris had seen most of the weird tools of the sex trade in his lifetime, including handcuffs, but never zip-ties. He saved that thought and returned to his dilemma—nineteen dead, zip-tied men.

At this stage, Harris didn't know there was a body missing from the first group because Eva didn't say anything about TJ; his body wasn't there. Her offer to the detective was to tell him who the dead men on the floor were.

She moved on to the next group. Eleven men ranging in age from thirty-something to sixty-something. "I don't know their names. But I know they own girls like us. For all we know, one of them could actually *be* our owner. They tattoo us. You know, like a car registration to establish ownership. They buy and sell us as it pleases them. They put us in places like this to make money for them by screwing up to ten clients a day and peddling drugs for them. Oh, they usually buy and sell us at auctions that take place one floor below your feet in what is ordinarily the studio where the owners of this place produce pornographic movies, including kiddie porn." She pointed at the children again. "But, fortunately, for six of those girls, we could stop tonight's auction when we overwhelmed these men."

Something bothered Harris about that picture. *Mutiny in a brothel?* Admittedly, this was not a brothel; this was hell. Still, fifteen adult girls and twelve teenage children, unarmed, overwhelming nineteen adult men, gangsters with guns and knives? That was a bit too much for a dollar.

They must've had help.

One Mr. Rex Dalton and his big black dog immediately came to mind. This was the kind of mayhem he thought Mr. Dalton and his dog were capable of.

The eleven men were fully clothed. The only strange features about them were the small holes in the middle of their foreheads and the rather large missing parts of their brains and skulls at the back where the bullets exited. The now familiar twenty-seven stab wounds in the chest were impossible to miss. Whether they were first shot and then stabbed, Harris didn't know, and it didn't matter; either would've killed them.

The guns that he presumed caused the damage to their heads were resting on their chests now. Except for the fat man in the middle, he had no gun on his chest, but he had the routine hole in the forehead and a messy brain, just like his buddies.

"Who's this?" said Harris.

"The auctioneer," said Eva.

Their feet were also tied together with zip-ties, and so were their hands, behind their backs, just like the first group. Their mouths were covered with duct tape.

The third group consisted of six naked dead men. Harris recognized the faces of the sheriff, judge, and politician. The mayor looked familiar, but he couldn't put a name to the face. The pastor he had never seen before, but then he hadn't been in church in donkey's years. Neither did he recognize the principal. Regardless, he would soon know who all of them were.

"Pedophiles caught raping six of the kids back there," continued Eva.

Their bodies had been ravaged, genitals and all. There could be no doubt the killers had taken out their frustrations on these men. Years of it. The only parts they didn't mutilate were their faces.

Why not?

Then it struck him; they wanted the cameras to see those faces.

Just like the previous groups, their feet were also tied together with zip-ties, and so were their hands behind their backs. Their mouths were covered with duct tape except for the judge's; his mouth was not covered with anything. His face was a strange coloration of purple, though, as if he had suffocated.

Eva told him there were eight clients locked in rooms upstairs. They were alive but asleep.

Another eight they had to subdue, thought Harris.

Now Harris's urge to vanish was stronger than ever. He didn't want to abandon the girls, but he couldn't think of any good reason he had to arrest them, although he knew his captain and everyone above him, up to the governor, would crucify him if he didn't.

Maybe he could just tell the girls to go. Disappear. Vanish. Don't come back. But he knew they wouldn't last twenty-four hours without drugs and pimps or doctors and psychiatrists.

He took his cellphone out and called his captain. They needed doctors and nurses who specialized in the treatment of drug addicts. And psychiatrists who can treat children and adults with severe PTSD.

Chapter Forty-Nine

WHO DID IT?

Harris had three questions.

"Who did it?"

The fifteen adult girls all took a step forward as if they were on a parade ground and, as one, shouted, "I did!"

Harris believed them.

"Where were the guards?"

The girls started laughing. "Guards?" said one of them called Suzie. "You must be joking. What you call guards were as bad, if not worse, than the dead men over there. They were not here for our protection; they were here to prevent us from escaping."

"Okay, but where were they when this happened?"

"They got scared when they discovered we'd taken charge of the building under their noses. They ran away."

Harris sensed a half-truth. He decided to leave it at that for now. The fact was the guards were not there.

"Who helped you?"

The reaction gave him some idea of the confusion that reigned during the time of the Tower of Babel described in

Genesis 11 in the Bible. Except in this case, language was not an issue. It was that everyone was talking, and everyone had a different story, yet everyone was telling the truth.

Seven of the adult girls were in the Pink Poodle when the fire alarm went off, followed by the water sprinklers coming on, not long before the lights went out. Jake and Rick had tried to escort them out to the Cloud Nine lounge, but in the chaos, the two men had disappeared. Fortunately, an old couple had powerful pen flashlights with them, which they used to help them all get to the safety of the lounge room in Cloud Nine. Suzie was with them.

The six children who were supposed to go on auction saw a big, masked man put their guard to sleep with a tranquilizer dart, tie him up, and throw him into the elevator like a sack of garbage. The masked man told them to wait and not to worry; someone would come for them soon. He didn't lie. Not long after, a very friendly old couple not wearing masks turned up, unlocked their cages, hugged them, and brought them up here. The lady comforted them, and the old man made them delicious sandwiches and hot chocolate. They hadn't seen any dogs. They didn't see any other masked people.

The six children from the fourth floor below said a masked man with a big black dog entered their rooms first and kept their abusers under gunpoint. Following them were Abbie, aka Eva, and a masked woman who helped them get dressed, took them away from their abusers, and brought them up to this room. When they arrived there, there were a friendly old man and woman, not masked, with the other children. The old couple gave them sandwiches and hot chocolate and were very kind to them.

Four of the adult girls said they were in their rooms with clients and hadn't seen a dog either but were collected from their rooms and brought down here by Suzie and a big, masked man with a gun. Two of the remaining four adults said they were also in their rooms with clients when a masked man with a tranquilizer gun, Lucy, and a masked woman turned up and brought them down there. The eighth girl said one moment she was in her room talking to a big blond man and a beautiful dark-haired woman, no sex, and the next thing she knew was when she woke up here. She saw a man and a woman with a big dog over in the Pink Poodle earlier in the evening but didn't pay them much attention.

So, there was a big dog, thought Harris. He was waiting for someone to tell him about the smile on the dog's face. No one did.

There was also an old couple.

All of them were sure when they arrived in the lounge, the nineteen men were already there. All but one of them were alive. Their feet were zip-tied together, and their hands zip-tied behind their backs. And all but one of them had duct tape wrapped around their mouths. The man without a gag was already dead when they got there.

Harris recognized the judge; he'd testified before him frequently in the past.

Harris finally figured out they were all truthful. It was obvious Dalton had his team split up into smaller teams to rescue the various groups of girls on different floors. By his calculations, there were seven men and women, eight including the dog.

None of the girls volunteered any information about how the nineteen men on the floor on the other side of the room became dead.

But it was unnecessary to inquire about it—it was a case of *res ipsa loquitur.* Literally, the thing speaks for itself.

The only conclusion Harris could draw was that they did indeed receive help. Another was that when the girls' helpers left, which was by his calculations about half an hour before he'd arrived, eighteen of the nineteen men who were now dead were still alive; their hands and feet were zip-tied, and they were gagged, but they were alive.

By now, the place was crawling with police, patrol cars, forensics experts, paramedics, ambulances, two psychiatrists, and a large crowd outside who the police had a hard time keeping in check.

Harris was still walking around in a daze. He was shaking his head. He knew Mr. Dalton and his dog were dangerous, but this...

He stopped. *So, isn't this what you wanted? Twelve, maybe twenty-seven, missing children were found. Twenty child molesters dead. How many years did you spend before you locked up that many? Or saved that many? This guy and his dog did it in less than a week.*

Now he was wondering how to go about extending his service to his country, in partnership with Mr. Dalton and his smiling dog, of course, just for a year. At this rate, they could make LA the safest place in America within a year.

Just then, his captain arrived, and one of the first questions was if Lieutenant Harris had read them their rights and placed them under arrest.

"Who?"

"The girls, Harris, all of them."

"For what?"

The captain had a frown on his face. "Didn't you just tell me they admitted to killing those men?"

"No, I said they executed them. There's a difference. Those men were already sentenced to death. The girls merely executed their sentences. They killed eighteen out of nineteen. One of them was already dead when they got here," said Harris. "But come with me. I want to introduce you to the dead men. When I'm done, you can place the girls under arrest if you think that's the right thing to do."

The captain was a patient man. Harris was a good cop. He went with Harris. When they were done, the captain ordered six more officers to the ladies' protection detail.

Nobody got arrested.

Chapter Fifty

ONE OR TWO EVERY SIX MONTHS

They were back on the *TOMATS* a little before 1.00 a.m. When John Brandt's Magnificent Eight walked into the Ops Room; they were in high spirits. They had TJ, the criminals, dead and alive, were in police custody by now, and the twenty-seven girls had been rescued. But then things took a turn none of them expected. They found a pale-faced Greg and Rehka in the Ops Room. They looked as if they were about to be sick at any moment.

"What's up?" said John.

"Have a look at this," said Greg somberly.

He rewound the tape and showed them what happened in the lounge at Cloud Nine after they left. It was macabre. A scene from a zombie apocalypse movie.

It started when Eva went out of the lounge and came back a few minutes later with an armful of plastic bags filled with guns and knives.

One by one, the fifteen adult girls walked down the row of comatose, zip-tied, gagged men and stabbed them in the chest. Some stabbed twice, others stabbed only once. But each man received exactly twenty-seven stabs to the chest, except for the last six men who got cut to pieces. The ten traffickers and Fatman got shot in the head with their own guns before being stabbed. Johnny and Sammy lost their manhood first, then their lives.

All of them except for Christelle, Greg, and Rehka had killed in the line of duty. But never like this. Yet, they were sympathetic to the girls. Were it not for the murder charges that would follow if they were arrested, all of them, including those who had never killed before, would've killed the bastards themselves but with a bullet to the head. But then, none of them, except Rehka, understood what those girls had been through.

"They're going to be arrested," said Josh.

Everyone except Rex agreed.

"I don't think so. Let's keep watching the tape."

They did and listened carefully to Harris explaining to the captain who the dead men were.

"My God!" said the captain. "These lowlifes were not murdered; they were merely executed, as you said. Those girls need protection, not prosecution. I want six more officers protecting them day and night wherever they are."

Rex didn't miss the little, nearly imperceptible smile on Harris's face. He looked at his watch; TJ should be coming around about now.

John called Dan Curtis and told him to come over for a cuppa joe that would wake him up and keep him awake for the next few days. Dan arrived an hour later.

In the meantime, Rex and Digger were in the gym next to

the engine room. It was a well-equipped little gym, sound-proof, with cameras, microphones, and all.

TJ's moaning and groaning were growing louder and louder. He was dangling spread eagle off a crossbar with his feet about six inches from the floor.

The carpet was covered with a blue plastic sheet. If TJ had noticed it, he would've known what it meant. The owner of the gym didn't want a mess on the carpet. And if he had more time to think about it, he would've figured out that although gyms were places where people usually went to improve their health, he was probably not going to get any health benefits from this session. He was too preoccupied with the pain in his shoulders and the growing difficulty in breathing from hanging by his arms in the crucifix position to pay attention to anything else.

The pain had finally brought him completely out of his ketamine-induced coma.

A tall man with an athletic build, dark hair, and penetrating dark eyes stood in front of him, and a big black dog was next to him. He recalled seeing the dog and those dark eyes behind a black ski mask the last time he was conscious. Both of them looked exasperated. The dog was snarling and growling. The man had a gun in his hand and what TJ thought to be the look of the Grim Reaper on his face.

"Okay, I'm Rex Dalton, and this is my best friend, Digger. I ask the questions you answer them. You lie, the dog *will* know, and he *will* attack you for it, and I *will* shoot you for it.

"First question, do you understand the science of crucifixion?"

TJ moaned and shook his head.

"I thought so. Too busy molesting and killing children.

Nevertheless, here's the story. Contrary to popular belief, it was not the Romans who invented crucifixion; it was the Persians, the forebears of today's Iranians. Three to four hundred years before Christ. To this day, it is still regarded as one of the most excruciating deaths ever devised by humans. Hence, the English language uses the term 'excruciating' to describe intense pain. In the days of yore, this brutal punishment was typically reserved for rebellious slaves, revolutionaries, and the most heinous of criminals. Over the ages, it has been abandoned as a punishment for all crimes except for heinous criminals, which means you and other scumbags of your ilk—child abusers and child killers. I won't bore you with all the scientific details of what happens to you during the crucifixion, except that you'll slowly suffocate to death over six hours to four days."

TJ was crying like a baby. "I won't lie, just let me down, and I'll tell you all you want to know."

Rex ignored him. "Where's my daughter, Courtney Lloyd?"

"Court… Oh, Rosie?"

Rex didn't respond. TJ knew who he was talking about.

"I was told to deliver her to Manza's estate outside Malibu. I can't remember the specific date; it was a few months ago."

"Is she alive?"

"Oh yes, she is. Her job is to entertain the cream of society when attending private parties, functions, fundraising events, weekends on luxury yachts, etcetera. She rubs shoulders only with the wealthy and powerful. She's a lucky girl; she gets treated like a princess. Please let me down."

Rex felt the anger rising. "Yeah, to be raped by rich and powerful pedophiles is a privilege—how lucky can a princess be?" His trigger finger was itching mightily.

Digger whined softly.

Not yet. Keep cool. We need more information.

TJ was wise enough to keep his mouth shut.

"Where is she right now?"

"I don't know, but if she's not with one of Manza's friends or acquaintances, she'd be at the estate."

"Where exactly is this place?"

Within minutes after TJ told them it was known as Dorset's Vineyard, outside Malibu, Greg and Rehka had it pinpointed and were collecting data from Google Maps, CIA satellites, and other sources.

"Are there other girls?"

"Yes, five, including Rosie."

"Who is Manza?"

"I've never—"

Digger stood behind TJ. It was as if he were just waiting for this moment. And who could blame him? This was, without doubt, the most boring mission he'd ever been on. This guy reeked of evil. Yet, apart from a few growls, yaps, snarls, and so on, he felt like a spare tire locked in the trunk. He jumped forward and ripped into TJ's left calf muscle.

Rex let Digger go for a while before telling him to stop. When Digger stepped back, ever so reluctantly, he was just getting into it. Rex kept his promise and shot TJ in the right knee.

The scumbag was screaming and bleeding profusely, and then he passed out.

Rex broke an ampule of smelling salts, aka ammonia inhalant, under his nose. It brought him back to full alertness within ten seconds.

TJ immediately started moaning and groaning and swearing and crying but soon regained enough of his senses to realize how stupid he was to upset an aggressive canine lie detector and the Grim Reaper with a loaded gun and an itchy trigger finger.

"Robert Dorset!"

Rex drew a long, slow, quiet breath. "Marion Cooper's dad?"

"Yes!"

One of LA's foremost investment bankers. My ass. Foremost blackmailer. Extortionist. Child sex slave owner. Human trafficker. Scumbag in chief.

Rex thought he'd made a breakthrough in the search for his daughter; he did, but he had no idea what else he was about to unearth.

"Josh, please do me a favor," said Rex over his molar mic. "Sedate that bitch and tie her up. I don't want her to hurt herself."

"Consider it done."

———

"You killed Elizabeth Clayton, Beth, she was only sixteen—"

"I don't know who you're talking—"

Digger's teeth sunk into TJ's groin.

He roared in pain as Digger ripped his pants apart and crushed his privates, turning the macho pimp into a soprano.

TJ was getting weaker from pain, blood loss, and lack of oxygen. His screaming sounded like groans. In a whispered tone, he started begging and pleading for his life.

Rex ignored him and let Digger carry on for a while longer. Then he took his knife out and cut the duct tape holding his arms to the crossbar.

He hit the floor with a thud like a bag of trash.

Rex had to stop Digger from ripping his throat out.

TJ passed out again and was brought back by the smelling salts, but it took much longer this time.

He told Rex in much detail what he did to Beth.

"How many have you killed like that?"

TJ shrugged. "Ten. Twelve, maybe more. I don't keep score. One or two every six months or—"

He stopped mid-sentence when the first .22 round hit him between the eyes. He probably didn't feel the second round penetrating his forehead.

Chapter Fifty-One

I'VE GOT EVIDENCE

It was almost 5:00 a.m. Around the table in the Ops Room on the *TOMATS* were John, Christelle, and Dan Curtis. On a side table were sandwiches and an espresso machine that produced near-lethal strength coffee, according to Dan's taste buds. Apparently, his hosts had taken the antidote because they kept on drinking the stuff as if it were water.

Rex, Catia, Digger, and the Farleys, guided by Greg and Rehka remotely, were on a reconnaissance trip to check out Robert Dorset's vineyard. According to the media, it was the venue from where a hopeful for the top job at the White House, Sidney Fuller, was going to announce her candidacy tonight and raise funds for her campaign. And according to TJ, Courtney Lloyd and four other children were held captive at this venue.

John, on condition of anonymity, told Dan what happened at the Pink Poodle and Cloud Nine. He mentioned neither names nor did he mention a dog. He showed neither pictures nor mentioned numbers; he gave

Dan as much detail as he required to make a call to Captain Hillman, Lieutenant Harris's boss.

Dan was shaking his head slowly when John finished. "This was a newsworthy story by the time the phantom force you talked about left Cloud Nine. The news would've made it all the way to the East Coast."

"Precisely. And the media focus would be on the mysterious welldoers who brought the bad guys to justice and saved twenty-seven girls."

Dan nodded slowly. He hadn't thought that far ahead yet.

John continued. "You would've scored a few brownie points with your editor and maybe received one of the end-of-year in-house rewards. No pay increases, no promotion, just another certificate and a pat on the back for doing your job."

"What are you getting at, John?"

John ignored him and continued. "But now the story can reach the entire planet. Dan Curtis will be the one to beat if you want the Pulitzer. The only problem is the focus will now shift from the phantom force, as you call them, to the twenty-seven girls who led a successful mutiny against their bosses. And the world's sex traffickers will be seriously worried."

"They'll want to kill all of them," whispered Dan.

"Exactly," said John. "They'll put contracts out on them, Dan. They'll want to send a message to the world's sex slaves. Don't even think about it."

"Okay, why did you tell me all of this if you don't want me to publish the story?"

"So that you can phone Captain Hillman, he's—"

"On my speed dial." Dan held up his phone.

Captain Hillman didn't have time to go home to have breakfast with his wife before going to the office. On the way to work, he made a slight detour through a McDonald's drive-through and got breakfast, including the coffee. He expected it to be a long day. But he'd forgotten how many layers of bureaucracy were between him and the governor of California. Everyone would have instructions for him.

He didn't even know of the blacklist.

Hillman was still hungry when he lobbed the last food wrapper in the wastebasket next to his desk. He took a sip of the lukewarm coffee right as his mobile phone rang. "What's up, Dan?"

"Captain Hillman, sorry to trouble you so early, but I heard a rumor about a tragedy at two downtown nightclubs, the Pink Poodle and Cloud Nine. Tell me about it."

Dammit!... Or... wait a second...

"Yeah, it's a sad, sad story. Come over, let's have a coffee and a chat. You're buying."

To Dan, it was obvious the captain was up to something. Hillman was a nice guy. But he'd been a cop for long enough to be circumspect when dealing with the media. Extending a coffee invitation to a journalist was anomalous.

Over coffee and pancakes at IHOP, the captain talked, and Dan listened. It was as if he and John Brandt had caucused. Except, the captain had a different solution for the problem. He wanted Dan to spin the story so that the girls were innocent and the dead child molesters were the victims of gang rivalry. In his opinion, that would cause the least amount of trouble for him, the Chief of Police, and everyone up the ladder to the Governor.

"Not a bad idea, Captain, except that the gangs will

know the truth. And we can bet all we have, they're going to put contracts out on those girls. They can't afford to let the geese that lay golden eggs for them rebel against them, can they?"

Hillman's eyes shot wide when the full impact of what Dan was saying struck him.

Dan saw it and added another tidbit just to reinforce the risks. "My source also mentioned something about computer hard drives and storage devices with video recordings that might cause a firestorm of epic proportions."

Hillman hadn't seen any of the videos, but he had seen the stacks of computers confiscated. He'd seen the studio, and Harris had told him what it was used for, and the girls told him what they'd find on those hard drives.

"I've put six officers on a protective detail for them," said Hillman. "But now I think sixty might not be enough."

"How about protective custody or witness protection?"

Hillman nodded and smiled. Dan had given him an idea. "Yep. But that's FBI and US Marshal territory."

Dan almost smiled. That's precisely what he and John wanted; to let a joint CIA-FBI task force handle this. "Is that going to be a problem?"

"No, I don't think so. I'll call them right now."

Captain Hillman didn't ask who his source was. Maybe he knew it would be a waste of time; Dan would've been ready with one or more of the standard answers, which would all come down to one thing—I am not at liberty to say.

Chapter Fifty-Two

NOLLE PROSEQUI

It was shortly after 8:30 a.m. when Rex, Catia, and Digger in one of the RAV4s drove past the guarded main entrance to Dorset's Vineyard. Josh and Marissa were in the other RAV4 about two miles away.

The fifteen-million-dollar Dorset's Vineyard was an awe-inspiring hundred-acre estate situated atop a hillside, offering a panoramic view of the vineyards in the valley below. The remarkable seven-bedroom, seven-bathroom home showed off Victorian-style furniture and decorations. There were accommodations for overnight guests and staff. There was also a guest house and five two-bedroom modular homes. For the equestrians, there was a luxury ten-stall barn with horses. An ample supply of well water, a vast solar farm, and a large array of Tesla batteries kept the estate off the grid.

It was hard to believe that such an idyllic place, so serene, could be home to as much evil as TJ told them.

Greg and Rehka found a few traps and obstacles on their way into the computer and security systems of Dorset's

Vineyard. It slowed them down by a full fifteen minutes. But once they were through the firewall, Rex and the team became privy to what was going on inside. They soon knew the location, angle, and arc of vision of every security camera inside and outside. They knew where the electrical control panels were. They had plans for every building on the farm. They knew where the motion detectors for the security lights were and the laser tripwires and the alarms. And the guardhouse and the guards.

They were not surprised to find that every nook and cranny, including the bathrooms and toilets of Dorset's Vineyard, was under electronic surveillance. The exception was Dorset's bedroom. But they learned their lesson at Cloud Nine. The most horrific horrors could be hidden underground and recorded on a separate system.

Rehka compiled a folder about Dorset and shared it with the team. He was like an iceberg. Most of it was below the waterline—invisible.

He was a mediocre student at school; he neither shined in class nor in sports. He was good-looking but didn't have a girlfriend. He had a circle of friends, but he was not nearly as popular as in his adult life.

He enrolled for a bachelor's degree in quantitative economics and econometrics. It's a field of study focusing on the analytical and applied aspects of economics, including forecasting, program and business evaluation, benefit and cost analysis, and economic impact analysis.

It was exactly what it seemed to be—a bridge too far for a proven academic underachiever. Over the course of the next eighteen months, his enthusiasm for academia waned. By the end of the first semester of his second year, he was suffering from a severe lack of ambition and interest and gave up his studies.

So far, so good; that was not a unique story. But then came the anomalies.

One of his girlfriends' dads, an extremely rich man who'd made several fortunes in the pharmaceutical industry, was on the school board of a posh private school and procured him a position at the school teaching economics. Dorset always referred to him as Rich Dad, after one of the main characters in Robert Kiyosaki's bestselling book, Rich Dad Poor Dad.

He married when he got the teaching job. They adopted Marion in the first year and remained married for six more years.

Of his decision to get married, he often said, "That was when I was young and sexy and stupid. Now I'm not stupid anymore."

As can be expected, he was a hopeless teacher. Many complaints were leveled against him for being clueless in the classroom, and there were persistent rumors that some girls perceived him to be making sexual advances toward them.

He resigned before he got fired.

Rich Dad came to the rescue again and introduced Dorset to his investment advisor, who offered him a job.

Dorset was an inept teacher, but despite his lack of knowledge and experience as an investment advisor, he did much better for himself. Within two years, he was a partner and eighteen months after that, he started his own investment business. Rich Dad was his first client, and his former business partners were secretly wondering if it was possible to commit the perfect murder.

Twenty years later, Rich Dad was still his only client, officially. Robert Dorset was worth a little over seven hundred and fifty million. Three-quarters of the way to billionaire. One of the explanations was that he must have had numerous well-to-do and happy clients who wanted to remain anonymous.

There were a lot more questions than answers when it came to how Dorset made his money, another part of the iceberg that was below the waterline.

His rather large circle of powerful friends, which included two former presidents of the United States, various well-known foreign dignitaries, including aristocrats, governors, senators, congressmen and women, high-ranking law enforcement officers, mayors, generals, and directors, caused much speculation—yet another part of the iceberg under the waterline.

Rich Dad was in the news for a short while, about five years ago, when he was investigated by the police for accusations of statutory rape. The investigation ended when the plaintiff and her parents suddenly decided to withdraw the charges. For a day or two, rumors swirled that it was an undisclosed sum paid to the plaintiff without an admission of guilt, which secured a *nolle prosequi*. According to the Oxford Dictionary, *nolle prosequi* is a formal notice of abandonment by a plaintiff or prosecutor of all or part of a legal suit or action.

Chapter Fifty-Three

REMEMBER HER?

Josh and Marissa were parked under a tree next to the road on top of a hill about three miles away from Dorset's Vineyard. They had two painting easels set up next to each other, white coats, straw hats, canvas, paint brushes, pallets, iPads to control the drones, and all. It was a beautiful day, not a cloud in the sky, ideal for artists looking for a perfect day to visit the perfect view. And, of course, it was also the perfect day to inspect Dorset's Vineyard through the cameras mounted on the two drones loitering over the homestead streaming back high-quality images to them.

They had one spare drone as a backup and eight batteries; two keeping the active drones in the air, two fully charged, ready to be swapped out, and four being charged.

They'd already decided that no one would see their paintings. But if anyone could look at Marissa's painting, it would be obvious she had an artistic streak in her. Josh, not so much. It was evident that he thought the paintbrush was to chew on and the cotton balls to be dipped in paint and thrown at the canvas. He explained that was how famous

284

abstract impressionists, such as himself, created their masterpieces.

Fortunately, the Farleys were much better drone pilots than artists. Between them and the IT gurus on the *TOMATS*, they learned everything about the place in a few hours; everything that was on the plans and everyone that lived and worked there except Courtney and four other child sex slaves.

Dorset was there. So was his eighteen-year-old girl-friend. There were four cleaning and kitchen staff, female and very young. "Undoubtedly below the age of consent," said John. They lived in the prefabricated houses. There was also a manager, a kind of chief of staff, a chef, a middle-aged lady, and three farmhands, young men in their twenties.

All but Dorset, his blonde girlfriend, and the middle-aged manager were Hispanic. Rex and the others couldn't help but wonder if they could be undocumented nonciti-zens, previously known as illegal aliens or illegal immi-grants. It would keep the overheads down and ensure no one would talk about what was going on there lest the police or ICE came knocking on their doors.

According to the logs of the electronic time tracking system, the private security company provided Dorset with six guards who worked eight-hour shifts in pairs.

The caterer and staff were expected around 10:00 a.m. The VIPs, with their entourages of security details and bootlickers, would arrive at around sunset.

It was about 11:00 a.m. when Rex parked their SUV next to the road under a tree with a few wooden benches about a mile away from Dorset's Vineyard. He, Catia, and Digger got out. Catia took her backpack out from the back and poured them each a mug of coffee from the stainless-steel thermos. Digger got a handful of turkey jerky.

Rex took a few sips of his coffee, got up, and retrieved Courtney's t-shirt, stored in a plastic zipper bag, from his backpack.

Digger was cozying up to Catia, trying to make her feel rotten for not parting with more of the turkey snacks. But Rex ruined his plans.

"Hey, buddy, would you mind coming over here for a moment? I need your help."

Digger ignored him and looked at Catia and then at her backpack, where she'd returned the bag of treats. But she waved her finger and said, "No, you've been called." She pointed at Rex. "First, find out what he wants, and then we can continue the battle of wills."

The smile disappeared from Digger's face as he admitted defeat, but he got the last word in with a soft growl. Which she thought meant something like, "O-k-a-y."

But Rex started laughing.

"What?"

"You don't want to hear what he told you to do with that jerky."

Catia feigned shock when she looked at Digger. "Digger!"

But he paid her no mind. He was staring at Rex.

Catia laughed. "The sooner you have that fatherly talk with our boy, the better. One of these days, he's going to embarrass us."

If Digger were disappointed that Rex had no snacks for him, he didn't show it. He was all business when he sat down in front of him, panting, tail wagging, and all, as if to say, "This is what I've been waiting for."

Rex held the t-shirt out for him to smell. "You remember her?"

Digger whined softly.

"Hey, I didn't say you're stupid. I just wanted to know if you remembered."

Digger just stared at him. No smile. No panting. Tail unmoving. He was irritated. Maybe Catia should've given him the jerky.

"My, my, we *are* testy today, aren't we?"

That's when Rex realized Digger had probably stored her scent in his nostrils or brain or both, since he'd let him smell it for the first time about ten days ago. Now he also understood Digger's gripe. It was the same as someone asking him if he knew which end of the gun to point at the bad guys.

"Okay, I'm sorry, I forgot about what a super smeller you are. So, here's the thing you can help with. According to TJ, Courtney is here, and I want to know if it's true."

The smile was back on Digger's face when he yapped twice.

"Okay, okay, hold your horses. Let's finish our coffee, and I am sure if you twist Mom's arm enough, you might just get more turkey. And no, coffee is still bad for dogs, same as chocolates and beer."

Digger's groan could've meant only one thing, "Okay, in that case, go give yourself a coffee enema." He turned and went back to Catia for more jerky, despite telling her to stuff it just a few minutes ago. It was a fundamental right to change his mind whenever he wanted.

"You're definitely not in a good mood today."

Digger ignored him.

Rex shrugged. "But if you don't want to talk about it, I can't help you."

Catia was just shaking her head in bewonderment as she listened to Rex and Digger. She still didn't know if Rex was talking to himself or if he and Digger were having these impossible conversations. The outcomes of those conversations, whether they were with Digger or himself, and as crazy as they might've sounded, saved the world from war many times.

Chapter Fifty-Four

YOU SURE?

They were finishing their coffees and turkey jerky while they fitted Digger's tactical harness and clipped on only the little camera between his ears and the microphone onto the harness on his chest.

A thought crossed Rex's mind, and he looked at Digger. "You've already locked onto her scent, haven't you?"

Digger looked at him with a smile on his face and whined softly.

"Aha, I thought so," said Rex.

"Ah, c'mon, Rex," said Catia. "We're more than a mile away from the place. It's impossible."

"One mile is nothing for our boy, my dear. In ideal conditions, he can pick up a scent from as far as twelve miles."

Catia was shaking her head as she looked at Rex first to see if he was serious. He was. Then she looked at Digger and concluded he was serious too. "So, you say she's there, and you're going to show us exactly where?"

Digger licked his lips and looked at her backpack. "Ah, I

see; you've mastered the art of extortion. No jerky, no answer, right?"

Digger didn't answer. He just sat down and licked his lips again.

He got two more pieces of jerky and wolfed them down in as many gulps.

"He says the answer is yes," said Rex.

Catia was shaking her head. "O-k-a-y, but only because I trust you won't lie to me."

They shouldered their backpacks, assembled their multi-functional unbreakable aluminum alloy hiking sticks, which were hiding fifteen different tools ranging from a knife to a powerful monocular, and hit the road. They wanted to visit a few of the boutique wineries in the idyllic area surrounding Dorset's Vineyard.

It was after 2:00 p.m., and still no word from Digger. But Rex had long since learned to trust Digger's senses like a pilot trusted an airplane's instruments.

Digger told them Courtney was there, and Digger would never lie to him. His frustration was that his daughter was locked up in one of the buildings right in front of his eyes, probably below ground, alone, drugged, abused, afraid...

But until Digger could point out which building, he couldn't go in, definitely not during daylight; he and Digger would be dead in short order.

They were on the last leg of their hike. The walkway was about three yards away from the electrified eight-foot diamond mesh fence with rolls of razor wire topping it off. The only difference between this and a Nazi concentration camp was the lack of guard towers with guards and machine guns. But there were motion-detector security flood lights and CCTV cameras, looking inward and outward, on top of every second fencepost.

Greg and Rehka assured them there were only security cameras on private property, but they made sure those experienced glitches when the Daltons passed by, including Dorset's Vineyard.

Just then, Digger stopped, turned ninety degrees to his left, sat down, yapped once, softly, and stared straight at the guesthouse. It was about a hundred and twenty yards from their position, and there was an almost imperceptibly slight breeze coming from the house toward them. According to the council's plans, it was a single-story two-bedroom dwelling with the usual amenities. It had a red, tiled roof and was built in a Spanish hacienda style. The guest house was a good hundred yards away from the nearest building in any direction.

"You sure?"

The look Rex got from Digger said it all. The canine version of the middle finger. Digger could be antsy when he was second-guessed.

"Yeah, I know to you it sounds like a stupid question. But if she's not there and we get caught, mommy and I are going to jail, if we're not dead, and you to the orphanage, also known as the dog pound."

Digger didn't even bother to look at him. He just snarled softly.

Rex took Digger's water bowl out of the backpack, poured some water, and put it in front of him. Rex drank the rest of the water in the bottle. Catia took an electrolyte drink out of her bag. All the while, they were talking to the rest of the team via their molar mics.

In the meantime, Josh and Marissa activated the thermal imaging cameras on the drones and hovered them about three hundred yards above the guesthouse. "Above ground, there's no one in that building," said Marissa. "We can't tell if there are rooms below ground."

"What we need is ground penetrating radar, but our drones are too small for that," said Rehka.

"Well, Digger told us she's there," said Josh. "So, I suggest we go in the old-fashioned way, breaking and entering."

"Yep, but don't forget, tonight the place will be crawling with more than thirty VIPs and their security details," said Rex. "Maybe plainclothes police, too. So, we'll have to think of a quiet entry."

"And, if the media and the polls are to be believed, the first female President of the United States and her husband will be there, too," said John.

"Well, looking at where a patriarchal White House has landed us since independence," said Josh. "I'm not surprised people are ready to give a matriarchal White House a go. But I wish I could let them know not to vote for this matriarch until they've had a look at some of her friends. Perverts. Child molesters. Scum. Even if she's not one of them, are they okay with her accepting their money and favors?"

"Unless, of course, she has no idea how evil some of her benefactors are," said Catia.

"Plausible deniability," said Josh, "the politician's credo."

"But we all know those campaign contributors expect quid pro quo," said Greg. "So, what has she promised them?"

"That's the million-dollar question," said John. "Perhaps we'll get answers eventually. In the meantime, let's plan for tonight."

"The challenges are bigger than last night," said Josh. We have to overcome the guards, the guests, and their security details, plus Dorset and his staff. And tonight, they'll not be spread across different buildings and levels like last night."

Rex nodded. "We'll have only one chance to surprise them."

"Why don't we surprise them by just grabbing the children and running?" said John.

"And let them get away with it?" said Josh. "I've been looking forward to putting at least a couple of rounds into Dorset's ass."

"Then we'll have to neutralize them somehow," said Marissa. "Any ideas?"

"We can take care of the fence for you," said Greg. "We'll disable the cameras and switch off the electricity to the fence; all you'll have to do is cut through the wire and walk through. We know where the laser tripwires are."

"What's the best time to go in?" said Catia.

"I think early morning, after the party," said Rex. "After everyone has gone home."

"Okay," said Christelle, "back to Marissa's question. How do we neutralize them? We know knockout gas is best left to the moviemakers."

"Sedatives in the food?" said Marissa.

"But for that, we need to get into the kitchen," said Josh.

Rex was scratching Digger's back slowly—deep in thought.

Why not make Lieutenant Harris's dream come true?

You mean let him and his men come and surprise them?

Exactly.

Now there's a plan I like!

Rex said, "Digger reckons we should involve Lieutenant Harris. But this time, we'll lock the girls up. Except for Courtney, she comes with us."

"There's a plan I like!" said John.

Rex smiled a little.

John and Digger had a rough start at the beginning of their relationship. John referred to him as the "damn dog" and kept telling Rex how stupid it was for a CRC agent to go around with a "damn dog." Digger was not happy with John Brandt's rudeness, and he wasn't afraid to let John have a piece of his mind. Fortunately for him, John didn't speak canine. But since then, they'd worked out their differences. Nowadays, John thinks of Digger as his best agent and protector of his children.

"All on board with Digger's plan?" Rex wanted to know.

There was no dissent.

They already had access to the computers since about six in the morning. They knew what was going on inside. The problem was the same as at Cloud Nine; they didn't know what they couldn't see, and the only way to fill the gaps was to get inside or capture and question someone from inside.

The caterers came in three trucks carrying the food and wine, and everything else needed for the event. The trucks bore the signage and logos of the prestigious Los Angeles Gastronomy Services.

The advance team of security guards of Sidney Fuller arrived at about midday to inspect the place and sweep it for surveillance gadgets.

They arrived in two black 4x4 SUVs with heavily tinted windows. Their vehicles were registered to one of LA's top-rated private security agencies, Executive Services. Once Sidney Fuller had been officially nominated by her party, she'd be entitled to Secret Service protection. But that was still more than a year into the future. The primaries had not even kicked off.

Rex was wondering if he could get the cooperation of these guards or those at the gate. "Greg, Rehka, what do you have on the guards?"

"There are six on duty this month. Apparently, they rotate every month," said Rehka.

"They're not what I'd call highly trained. They received two weeks of training. They know how to fire a weapon and carry licensed side arms, but only when on duty. Two of them have military training in logistics and supply. No battlefield experience. Three of them have one or more convictions for petty offenses."

Rehka continued and told them that changing of the guards happened three times a day, 7:00 a.m., 3:00 p.m., and 11:00 p.m.

"Okay," said Rex. "What do you know about the guards going on duty at eleven?"

Chapter Fifty-Five

VISITING THE GUARDS

It was almost 3:00 p.m., sunset was at 7:04 p.m.

The target was the two guards who'd go on duty at 11:00 p.m. The IT team had their cellphone numbers and were tracking their GPS locations. Their home addresses and a few personal details were in their company's HR system, to which Rehka had unobstructed access.

They were Hispanic. Twenty-two and thirty, respectively. Their English was at the lower intermediate level. They were single. The rudimentary HR system made no mention of their residency status, i.e., if they were citizens, permanent residents, or on work or study permits. They shared a unit in a dilapidated apartment block that was less than half an hour's drive away from Dorset's Vineyard.

There was a soccer game on, and their team was playing. They'd ordered Mexican takeout and beer. The TV was on high volume. They were eating and drinking and loudly cheering for their team. But then, without warning, things went haywire.

First, a man and a woman, both in FBI tactical jackets and black ski masks, walked in and stood in front of the TV, facing them.

Second, the TV went dead.

Third, a snarling big black dog with fangs like a lion sat down between the FBI agents and also faced them.

When they made to jump to their feet, the silenced guns, which materialized and pointed at them, and a low growl from the dog made them freeze in their chairs.

The FBI man ordered them, in fluent Spanish, to lie down on the floor, face down, hands behind their heads, and not make a sound or a sudden move; unless, of course, they wanted to have their throats ripped out by the dog or, if they preferred, rather be shot in the head.

Next, the man zip-tied their hands behind their backs. Their legs got duct-taped together from their knees to their ankles. They didn't carry IDs or guns.

They were pulled back to their feet and shoved back into their easy chairs.

"Now listen carefully; your lives depend on it. Answer quickly and honestly. Don't even think about lying. The dog will rip you to pieces if you do. Understood?"

"Yes!" they yelled in chorus.

"Please don't shoot us. We've done nothing wrong. We will cooperate." The older man had established himself as their spokesman.

"Good. You will live much longer with an attitude like that. You are illegally in the country, right?"

"Yes."

"Your boss knows about this, right?"

"Yes."

"And you're getting paid much less than the others who are here legally, right?"

"Yes."

"Okay, we won't worry about any of that for now. Let's see if you're honest hombres. Tell me everything you know about the Dorset hacienda and the people who live and work there."

They were about to be disappointed. Instead of the guards telling them what was going on and where Rex's daughter was kept, they told them they weren't allowed to know anything about this place and the people.

"We're only responsible for the gate and watching the security camera feeds. We've been working for our company for more than three years and have been on guard duty there only three times, one month at a time. So, we haven't had much opportunity to learn about the place and the people.

"We report anything irregular to the property manager and our boss. Other than the manager, we've met no one living there in person. We know some of them from a distance. They're forbidden to talk to us, and we to them."

Digger seemed to be happy with the men's answers so far. Rex was also watching them closely, and so was the rest of the team through the camera on Digger's harness. It was good that the guards were honest, but their lack of knowledge didn't help the team at all until Rex asked, "Are all the Hispanic people at the hacienda illegal immigrants?"

"Yes. Same as us."

Click. Rex knew how he could approach Lieutenant Harris to persuade him to come over tomorrow morning, early.

"How do you know?"

"That's what the manager told us. The hacienda is like a

safe house for them. Until Mr. Dorset can arrange for their papers."

"So why lock them up and guard them? Are they not supposed to be free in their new country? I thought that's why they came here."

"I don't know the answer to this."

"How many visitors do you get, and how do you record their visits?"

"Ten to fifteen per week. We keep a video log of everyone. Registration numbers, videos from all angles as they pass through, plus their voices are recorded by our body cams."

"What do you do with the videos and voice recordings?"

"We have to give them to the manager every day."

"Have you ever been to the main house?"

"No."

"Have you ever recognized any of the visitors?

"No." As he said that, he looked down and to the right. A telltale he was lying.

Digger growled.

Rex decided to let it go and raised his finger to call Digger off. Rex preferred to maintain a good relationship with the guards to eventually get their cooperation. The video and audio files will have the information.

Rex told them that a SWAT team was going to raid the place, and if they helped the advanced team get in, it might count in their favor when it came to matters of immigration.

But that was just one part of it. Rex told them what evil they'd been protecting all this time and that the police would be seriously pissed when they found out what was going on inside the confines of the barbed wire fences, and they, the guards, might find themselves in custody and then the police might uncover the immigration issues and so forth.

They agreed one hundred percent with Rex; it would be an excellent idea to walk off the job as soon as the FBI's advanced team was inside. They'd find another employer, far away from here. And Rex could count on their full and fearful cooperation.

Greg had already invaded both their cellphones with the help of Pegasus.

This time no one had an issue with setting child molesters free. These guys came to the land of opportunity for a better life. They'd kept their noses relatively clean, found themselves honest jobs, said their prayers, and paid their taxes. If only the guards that went free last night had résumés that read like those of the two illegals.

Without their help, Rex and the team would have had to cut power and fences to get in. Now they could drive up to the front door of the main dwelling if they wanted to.

Chapter Fifty-Six

THE VISITOR

While the Daltons paid the guards a visit, the Farleys kept a watch over Dorset's Vineyard. Throughout the day, vehicles came and went. The high-resolution cameras on the drones enabled them to get a good look at the occupants of those vehicles. There was nobody of interest. It was a little after 4:00 p.m. when a limousine driven by a chauffeur with a gray-haired female passenger in the back pulled up to the front gate. Everything from the vehicle, the chauffeur, the lady's demeanor, and the guard's body language broadcasted preeminence. The limo and passenger were practically waved through the gate.

While Greg and Rehka queried various facial recognition databases, John's mind was working overtime. He'd seen that face before. Not recently. But the face was out of context in this environment, and that's what his brain needed, context.

He was playing around with the zoom function of the image software on his laptop while his mind was paging through the chapters of his life. Most of the footage from the drones and the guards' videos that Greg had access to was of poor quality, but there were a few images of sufficient quality to trigger memories from a time when he and Christelle were thirty-odd years younger—the time when Dorset's visitor was a brilliant young KGB spy.

"Christelle, I need your help. I think I know this woman. Greg, can you broadcast my screen to the TV?"

Greg did so.

"Look carefully and think back thirty-plus years."

John zoomed in and out on a few images and studied his wife's beautiful face for a sign of recognition. And there it was, her eyes widened for a fraction of a second, recognition.

"Of course, you'd remember her; that's Irina," said Christelle.

John nodded. "Thanks. I thought I'd lost my mind. Okay, everyone else, the lady in the back of that Limousine was Irina Kutuzova, an old acquaintance of Christelle's and mine."

"A Russian spy?" said Catia.

"Yes."

"And the two of you had business with her?"

"Yes."

"And as soon as this is over, you and Christelle are going to tell us the whole story?"

"Yeah, but only if you make us a nice Italian dinner," said Christelle.

"Deal."

"So, what's your friend doing here?" said Marissa.

"No idea," said Christelle. "But it seems she's expected."

It was for situations like this that Greg promised himself to enhance Pegasus to fly for much longer distances, and then it struck him that for his current situation, the solution was staring him in the face. He already had control of their internet router, he only had to deploy Pegasus there, and it would propagate itself to every connected device.

By the time Dorset and Irina Kutuzova shook hands, Pegasus was installed on the router. By the time they reached the study and had a glass of wine in hand, and were ready to talk business, Dorset's phone was broadcasting to Greg's 'listening post.'

"What happened at Cloud Nine?" Kutuzova started.

"I'm still investigating, but it's not progressing well; everyone who could tell us is dead or missing. Marion is self-isolating because she's got COVID. She doesn't even know what happened. TJ has gone silent. No response from him at all."

"Does this not worry you?"

"Of course, it's worrying, but how does that change anything. It's not going to make the dead alive, is it?"

"Why haven't you contacted me?"

"And how would you have prevented any of this?"

"Don't try and be smart with me, Robert. We brought you to this country. We set you up in the lap of luxury, we made you obscenely rich, and all you had to do was stay below the law enforcement radar, collect, and pass on information. I've got a message from the President for you, verbatim. 'This is a disaster. You're responsible, and you're replaceable.'"

The color drained from Dorset's face. "What do you want me to do?" His bravado was gone.

Kutuzova held up one finger. "Find those bitches, all of them, and kill them." She raised a second finger. "Find out who helped them and kill them." She raised a third finger. "There is a drug pusher who survived and is in police custody. Take care of him before he starts making plea deals."

Dorset nodded.

"Oh, and Robert, one more personal message from the President. 'No more screw-ups or you'll find out the rumors are true; the Siberian gulags have never been shut down.'"

Dorset swallowed hard.

"Now, get someone to fetch my luggage from my car and show me to my room."

Chapter Fifty-Seven

DADDY'S FAVORITE

It was approaching 6:00 p.m. Rex, Catia, and Digger had rushed back to the *TOMATS* to talk to Cooper. She hadn't cleaned the room as instructed. The place smelled foul.

Cooper woke with a burning sensation in her nose and eyes from the smelling salts. She saw Rex, Catia, and Digger, and the look on their faces scared her. She'd tried strangling herself with the electric cables but found she couldn't do it. A yellow belly.

Rex pulled her to her feet by her hair and shoved her into a chair.

Cooper was screaming in pain. "What the hell are you doing that for?"

"Manza. Start talking."

Cooper knew it was all over. All that remained was her execution. She hoped it would be a bullet to the back of the head. Not to the face; she hated the idea of turning up on the other side disfigured.

I should've tried harder. Maybe I should've swallowed the cleaning chemicals.

"I won't tell you anything."

"Suits me," said Rex. He grabbed her hair and twisted her head so that she was facing Catia's laptop screen.

Catia started the video of the massacre at Cloud Nine and showed her pictures of the bloodied body of TJ with the small bullet hole in his forehead, unmistakable.

Finally, Catia showed her pictures of the three girls on the yacht. "Oh, all three girls have expressed a desire to see you. There are also the twenty-seven over at Cloud Nine. Some of them remember you very well, others have never met you. Notwithstanding, they all want to meet you."

Cooper couldn't get any paler. She wasn't going to the bottom of the ocean with a hole in her head. She was going to turn up there in hundreds of small pieces. Her eyes were wide as she feebly tried to wiggle out of her restraints.

Rex and Catia stared at her, emotionless, as she went on a profanity-laced rant. The damn dog was grinning at her. And then, a few minutes later, as if someone had flipped a switch, she started sobbing, and when she still got no sympathy, she sniffed a few times, took a deep breath, and spilled the beans. All of it, like a true traitor.

"TJ probably told you Robert Dorset is my dad. He's not."

Neither Rex nor Catia wanted to believe what they were hearing. They were watching Cooper for the telltale micro-expressions of someone who was lying. There were none. They watched Digger for any signs. There were none.

Cooper told them she and Robert Dorset were not related at all. Not even distantly, unless they were regarded to be related because they were both brought to America as children.

Dorset had been adopted by an American couple of Russian origin from a Polish orphanage when he was eight.

His new parents had been living in Poland for fifteen years before immigrating to America. His new family changed his name from Jarosław Bielszowicki to Robert Dorset, his adoptive parents' American surname.

They were Soviet agents but were not required to do any spying. They only had to ensure Robert and his adopted siblings, a brother from Bulgaria, and a sister from Ukraine, received an American upbringing, accent, mannerisms, and all. Oh, and they had the help of a 'family friend' who not only helped them financially but also helped them instill in the children a love for Russia and hatred for America.

Robert got married to an American woman, Dorothy Cooper, whose parents moved to America in September 1992 from Estonia, a year after the end of communism.

Mariyan Tsitsishvili was adopted by the Dorsets from a Georgian orphanage a few days after her seventh birthday. They renamed her Marion. It was only after her parents divorced that she started using her mother's surname—on her dad's insistence.

Rex recalled several high-profile cases of Russian spies operating within the United States uncovered during the Obama administration. Those cases reiterated the views of not only Rex and his team but quite a few security experts as well; the West was the only party in the Cold War that believed it ended in December 1991 when the Soviet Union ended.

It was obvious Russia had not stopped hating America; they were still running widespread espionage activities in America.

Sleeper agents are trained to blend in with their surroundings and avoid suspicion. They're used to gather information ranging from political and military intelligence to economic and technological secrets. They may also conduct covert operations, such as sabotage, espionage, and influence campaigns.

"And don't forget daddy's favorite," said Rex.

"What?"

"Blackmail."

"Of course," said Cooper. "And for that, you need kompromat."

The word kompromat is derived from the words compromising and material and refers to the gathering and using of compromising or incriminating information against a target for blackmail, manipulation, or extortion.

This was no longer only about Rex and his team versus the pimps and pedophiles holding his daughter; this was about archenemies with more than eleven thousand nuclear weapons between them to settle their disputes.

Chapter Fifty-Eight

STAY ON THE LINE

Martin Richardson was the deputy director in charge of CIA operations. During his tenure at the CIA, Richardson saw the Soviet Union dissolved, the rise of Islamic radicalism, the emerging threat from the People's Republic of China (PRC), and Russia's annexation of Crimea and invasion of Ukraine.

It was 10:00 P.M Sunday in Virginia. Richardson and his wife had gone to bed an hour before. They'd just switched off the lights when his secured mobile phone started ringing. "May you get a cramp in your ass," he muttered before looking at the phone's screen. "Dammit, John Brandt, what the hell have you done now?"

"It's entirely possible that we've irritated your bosom friend, Stas, more than just a little," said John.

In Russia, surnames, especially in formal ways, are written first, then the first name, then a patronymic name based on the father's name. The patronymic name is important as it's polite to call somebody by their first and patronymic names. So, Krivkov Stanislav (Stas) Ivanovich's surname was Krivkov, his first name Stanislav and Stas his nickname, and Ivanovich his father's name. The polite way to address him would be Stanislav or Stas Ivanovich—if you were on a first-name basis with the President of Russia.

The line went deathly quiet on Richardson's end.

Krivkov was an authoritarian, offensive, and expansionist leader. He didn't tolerate political dissent. He suppressed press freedom and didn't hesitate to crack down on his opposition. He was overly aggressive in his foreign policy, as demonstrated by his involvement in the conflict in Syria because Russia's only Mediterranean naval base for its Black Sea Fleet was in the Syrian port of Tartus. His annexation of Crimea in 2014 and the invasion of Ukraine in 2022 were the first steps to realizing his dream of expanding Russia's territory and restoring it to its former glory. In short, like Hitler and others of his ilk, Krivkov was dangerously ambitious.

"You've heard about the war in Ukraine?" said Richardson, his voice dripping with sarcasm. "It was in all the newspapers for a while. You might not know this, but it is this administration's policy to do nothing that would escalate the conflict between us and Russia. And that includes not offending the Russian President."

"Yeah, I've heard about that, but your buddy, Stas, is still fighting the Cold War," said John.

"John, the Cold War ended in 1991. We won."

John sighed. "I know that's what *you* believe, or rather what the politicians are *telling* you to believe. But I've told you before wars don't end because one side declares victory. To end a war, one side must be obliterated or surrendered. Nobody was obliterated, and nobody surrendered, Martin. The sons of bitches are still fighting the Cold War."

"C'mon, spit it out, John. The suspense is killing me."

"We've unearthed a Russian spy network, the likes of which you couldn't imagine. Forget about horror movies; not even in your worst nightmares can you dream up something like this."

The silence from Richardson's end lasted for almost half a minute. He had known John Brandt since joining the CIA. John was as solid as the Rock of Gibraltar. "Do you have, I mean, what evidence—"

"Oh yes, I've got evidence. Witnesses, dead and alive. High-quality videos with faces, names, and dates. Confessions, handwritten and videotaped. Two prisoners, one a psychopath, the other a drug pusher. Fifteen adult girls, addicted to drugs, sex slaves, but, thank God, alive. Another fifteen girls, minors, child sex slaves, addicted to drugs and, thank God, also alive. And last but not least, twenty-one very dead sexually perverted male miscreants—"

Richardson chuckled. "For a moment there, I thought you said twenty-one dead."

"That's precisely what I said, but I miscalculated; there are actually twenty-two; one of the scumbags threw himself off a building."

"Twenty-two dead?" said Richardson slowly and softly and repeated it. "Twenty-two dead. Who killed them? Except the one who threw himself off a tall building. I take it he didn't stab or shoot himself in the back before he jumped?"

"Martin, the best is you shut up now and don't interrupt me until I'm done. Okay?"

"Whatever, I am screwed, whether I hear all or none of it. I'm listening."

"Good. We also came across something akin to a thermobaric bomb. You know, those bombs with names such as

MOAB, mother of all bombs, the most powerful non-nuclear bomb in the US arsenal."

Richardson was breathing heavily.

"Except, this bomb is a list. It contains the names and details of five-hundred and fifty-six individuals. The who-is-who of sexual deviants in the hallways of power; politicians, military leaders, law enforcement and intelligence officers, justices, business leaders, bureaucrats, clergy, educators, and so forth."

Richardson sighed noisily.

"There's not a pie in which they don't have a finger, Martin. And this is only in California. For all we know, they could have setups like this across the country. Can you imagine one of them in D.C.?"

Martin couldn't help himself. He had to know. "So, where does Krivkov fit into the picture?"

"His spies own that list, and they're milking the people on that list for information, money, favors, votes; use your imagination."

Richardson's silence was deafening.

"What else do you need?"

"I need you to stay on the line while I get Howard on this call." Howard Lawrence was the Director of the CIA, Richardson's boss.

Chapter Fifty-Nine

IN CONCLAVE

Five minutes later, Lawrence joined the call. Half an hour after that, the three of them were in conclave with the President of the United States and the Director of the FBI, Harrison Douglas, via secured video conference.

John briefed the newcomers when the president and Douglas joined. There was a protracted silence when he ended. The president spoke into the silence. "I don't know about you, but I say this is an act of war."

Everyone agreed.

"What scares me most is that neither the police nor the FBI or any other law enforcement agency knew about this? Not even a suspicion?"

It was an uncomfortable question. The three questions civil servants feared most were: What did you know? When did you know? Why didn't you know? The latter was what the President was asking.

"Mr. President," said John, "my people had the same question and concluded that some law enforcement officers know all about it but were blackmailed or extorted to not reveal what they know. When one looks at the blacklist, I referred to earlier, it's quite conceivable that law enforcement was blocked by their masters, such as the mayors and politicians in their jurisdictions, all of them beholden to Russian spies who have dirt on them."

The look on the president's face said it all.

John continued and gave the president more information about the sophisticated surveillance equipment and the blacklist.

"Someone on the inside helped the child molesters?"

"Yes, sir, child molesters themselves, and we expect to find some, if not all, of them on the Russians' blacklist."

The president had a pained expression. "Let me see if I understand what's going on in this garbage dump. On that list, we'll not only find high-society child molesters but also child molesting traitors and spies, right?"

"Precisely, Mr. President," said Lawrence.

The new round of silence that erupted gave everyone time to consider the gravity of what they'd heard. None of them had any illusions. This was trouble—a tsunami of it.

"We need to know how many more of these establishments there are across the country," said the President. "That intel can't be collected fast enough, and even then, it might be too late. We need to find and rescue those children, and we need to inform Five Eyes." It was an alliance between the intelligence agencies of Australia, Canada, New Zealand, the UK, and the US, to share information of political or military value.

"So here are my priorities. The critical issues uppermost in my mind are the victims, the Russians, the traitors, and the pedophiles.

"The children get taken care of immediately," said the president.

Everyone agreed. There were twenty-seven girls from Cloud Nine, three on the *TOMATS*, and nine at Dorset's Vineyard. Thirty-nine in total. Fifteen were above the age of consent, and twenty-four were children between twelve and sixteen.

The president continued. "Second, I want every child sex slave found, and I want them taken care of physically and mentally. I want them protected as thoroughly as, or better than I am.

"One brothel in downtown Los Angeles gets raided and, in the process, twenty-seven sex slaves are discovered in one place. So far, thirty-nine, twenty-four of them are kids. How many more are enslaved across the country? Thousands? Tens of thousands? I'm ashamed, and I'm going to fix this.

"Furthermore, from that one blacklist, they've collected five-hundred and fifty-six names. How many more blacklists and traitors and pedophiles are out there? We don't know, and we better find out quickly. Bring in the National Guard if necessary."

It was the National Guard's job to respond to domestic emergencies, overseas combat missions, counter-drug efforts, reconstruction missions, and more. If this was not a domestic emergency, then what was?

"Three, damn you, Krivkov! All is not fair in love and war. You've removed all doubt about how demented you are. How could anyone in his right mind justify the abuse of children? I'm sickened to see to what new lows you've sunk. Of course, the relationship between us had taken a nosedive the last few years. We let you have Crimea just to keep the peace. We didn't fight you in Syria; we fought ISIS and left you alone just to keep the peace. We couldn't stand by and let you take Ukraine, the breadbasket of Europe, or let you starve our European allies of gas and oil. But we didn't put boots on the ground, just to keep the peace."

The president stopped talking and looked up. "Sorry, I got a bit carried away there. What they're doing here is like a Cold War spy operation, but the most atrocious I've ever heard of."

John and Martin were nodding. John was a spy in the Cold War. Martin was a mission support specialist then. The rest of the attendees had read the books and seen the movies, and heard the stories.

"The thing is, Mr. President," said John, "this operation originated during the dying days of the Cold War when Krivkov was a young KGB officer on the up and up. He was the one who dreamed it up and sold it to his superiors.

"We, the CIA and the French DGSE knew about it. It was duly reported and documented, but then, 'peace' broke out," he made air quotes, "when the West unilaterally declared the end of the Cold War and claimed victory, that report got archived or destroyed.

"Sir, with all due respect, it's nothing but obvious the Russians have never aborted the operation because, for them, the Cold War has never ended. Russia was humiliated, not defeated. We all know Krivkov wants the old Russia, feared by everyone, back."

"That has become crystal clear to me over the past hour. I'm seriously tempted to call that SOB and give him a piece of my mind."

Martin drew a sharp breath.

"Don't worry, Martin, I won't." The president was smiling.

John said, "Mr. President, if I may, there's one more critical matter I'd like to put on the table; Sidney Fuller."

"Why her?"

"If the polls are to be believed, which I never do, but I must admit I've been wrong many more times than they were, Sidney Fuller will be your successor."

"As for trusting the polls, 2016 springs to mind. Are you suggesting Sidney Fuller is involved or has been compromised?"

"No, sir, but I'd say it's critical to have a conversation with her about the bad company she's keeping. They've been waiting nearly forty years for an opportunity to get a Russian-controlled puppet in the White House. So, the big question is probably, does she know what her friends are up to or not?"

The president had a dilemma. Party politics and patriotism had become two different worlds. Sidney Fuller was of his party but was not his choice for President. He hadn't announced his support for anyone yet; it was way too early.

He knew Sidney Fuller would've loved nothing more than getting the president's tick of approval in public right now. But she'd have to wait until she got the nomination, which would be highly unlikely if just a fraction of what was said in this meeting tonight leaked to the press. Even if it was just a rumor, it would ruin her candidacy in a matter of days. He would never do that to her. But if she were in cahoots with the Russians and their child molester spies, he wouldn't leak anything to the press; he would tell them in person at the press conference immediately after he had her arrested.

Talk to her or let her be if she's not a spy. Election interference is a serious matter. But then, it is also expected of me to help candidates of my party get elected. I need more time to think this through.

"Good point, John; I need to think what the best approach will be."

Chapter Sixty

RULES OF ENGAGEMENT

"John, I want to know how you came by this information," the president said.

John was taken aback. The president knew it was standard operating procedure that he would only ask for the source of information when he needed to know. So, John asked him, "On what basis do you *need* to know that information?"

The three government officials in the room drew a collective sharp breath.

But the president took it in his stride and smiled. "I need the information so that I know who to pardon and why. Or are you trying to tell me the drugged girls with no weapons or training overpowered twenty-one men, hardened criminals with weapons, and scared a bunch of trained and armed guards into running away? Come to think of it, I need the girls' names as well, for the same reason."

"Apologies, Mr. President, I had to ask, and I'm happy that you have a *need* to know."

Lawrence and Douglas were breathless. Richardson was

smiling; John's mind was back in the CIA, forty-odd years ago. That's how they did it back then and how it was supposed to be today.

"And no, sir, the girls didn't overpower those men; my people did. The girls merely executed them after my people left."

The president nodded. "And that's why I need their names, so I can pardon them. Maybe I should decorate them while I'm at it. Please continue."

John didn't have much use for politicians, but he'd met this president personally on a few occasions. One such occasion was a private dinner with him and the First Lady in the West Wing when he and Christelle, the Daltons, the Farleys, and Digger were invited after the last operation in China. He trusted this man because he was honest and took his job as this country's commander-in-chief seriously, and he would not go back on his word.

He started with Beth Clayton and continued until he reached the present and backed his narrative up with photos and videos. He left out the part about how Rex hoodwinked Harris into giving him the original information. He first wanted to be sure the president was going to include that transgression and Rigoberto's assisted nosedive from the rooftop in Rex's pardon as well.

Despite having been given this information by John during the briefings, it differed greatly to be shown what he had talked about earlier—much more shocking and infuriating. It was a visual tale of human misery that left the audience speechless with rage as he flipped through the sickening images and video clips.

When John finished, the president spoke first. He was white in the face. He spoke softly and measuredly. "How is this even possible? In any country? I feel as if I have failed the American people. This has been going on, on my watch, under my nose, and my predecessors.

"How sick must one be to do these things to children? Rape, sodomize, and kill children in the name of espionage?

"I'll tell you this; I've got eighteen months left in this office. From this moment, the eradication of these vermin is one of my highest priorities. Rex Dalton's daughter and four others are at that vineyard. There could also be four Hispanic children in the same situation. I want them rescued immediately. I don't care about Sidney Fuller's party; crash it. But those children are out of there before the sun comes up. Give those children the same protection as the others. Make sure not a single strand of hair on their heads is damaged."

"What are our rules of engagement, sir?" said Douglas.

"Arrest as many of them as you can and use as much force as is necessary to overcome any resistance. Foremost, protect those girls; shoot to kill but keep the kids alive.

"Arrest Dorset and his lieutenants and question them.

"Arrest and confiscate anyone and anything that can be used as evidence, including the computers, videos, and pictures on that farm."

"Thank you, Mr. President."

"Keep me posted. I want you to work with Howard and every law enforcement and intelligence agency you deem necessary to assemble a joint Taskforce and go after them everywhere. Dollars to donuts, there's at least one of their brothels in the Washington swamp. Get all children to safety. Find the pedophiles and the traitors and arrest them. No bail. Put them in protective custody to protect them from the Russians, and while you hold them, interrogate them."

Everyone was in agreement with the president.

"Finally, spare nothing and nobody. I will put my orders in writing, and if anyone gives you any trouble, phone me directly; don't go through the switchboard."

"Mr. President, I suggest we also lawyer up as quickly as possible," said Douglas.

The president nodded. "Agreed. I'll take care of it."

"Mr. President, I have one request," said John. "It's about Rex Dalton and his team and a certain LAPD vice squad detective."

"Shoot."

John told them how Rex went about using his US Marshal credentials to get the initial tranche of information from Lieutenant Harris, which set Rex and the team up to launch their own investigation and operation to find his daughter.

When John was finished, the president was smiling and shaking his head. "One day, John, you and I need to sit down and have a beer while you tell me everything about Rex Dalton."

John started to say something, but the president held up his hand. "Yeah, yeah, I know I must have a need to know. I have one. I can't give him retrospective pardons if I don't know what they're for. Good enough for you?"

"It is, sir."

"He must be one of the most resourceful people I've ever had the privilege of knowing. America owes that young man and his team and that dog a great debt of gratitude. We would be fighting the Chinese now were it not for him. What's your request?"

John told the president.

"Give me the telephone number and consider it done," said the president.

Chapter Sixty-One

A CALL FROM THE PRESIDENT

It was shortly before 2:00 a.m. in LA when Captain Hillman's phone rang. He was asleep next to his wife of thirty years. The Cloud Nine incident had not reached the ears of the press when he went to sleep, but now it probably had. Why else would anyone want to phone?

He brought the phone to his ear, ready to tell the caller why clocks and watches were invented before he was going to get rude. But the lady's voice on the other end didn't give him an opportunity to implement his strategy. She told him she was a phone operator at the White House and Director Harrison Douglas of the FBI wanted to talk to him. Urgently. He was expected to stay on the line. He did. Getting a call from the White House was a first for him, and so was a call from the Director of the FBI.

Now the Captain was fully awake, on his feet, next to his bed. His mind was in overdrive. He was expecting a call from the FBI informing him they were taking over. In fact, he was very much looking forward to that call from the FBI office in LA, even at 2:00 a.m. on a Monday.

The factions who had orders for him about how he should be handling the Cloud Nine mess were many. One faction didn't want to hear about it. He was happy to oblige. One faction wanted the case buried so deep that no one would remember it. He couldn't please them. One faction wanted the names of everyone. They needed them to stay in the run for the Pulitzer Prize. He told them he was not at liberty to share that information with them. One faction, overpopulated by politicians, thought the names of the clients were the most important to them; some of their opposition's names could be on that list. He couldn't make them happy, either. Another faction insisted the facts needed to be pruned and presented with a bit of a spin. And so forth.

The problem was all of them outranked Hillman, therefore, felt entitled to issue orders to him. This case wasn't a day old and had already aged him by at least a year.

Nevertheless, this was not the call he expected.

The Director of the FBI is at the White House? Another set of orders? Or worse, the FBI wouldn't touch this case with a ten-foot pole and wanted him to continue with it.

He answered carefully and politely. The man on the other end said what his name and title were, and that agreed with what the telephone lady said. Hillman said nothing. The Director had called him. Speak only when spoken to.

The FBI director told him that he was in the Oval Office with the president, who wanted to talk to him. The telephone lady said nothing about talking to the president. *Is this a joke?* He didn't ask. *So? What now? Tell the Director of the FBI you won't talk to the president because nobody forewarned you?*

Hillman was still wondering what to do when the president came on and told him who he was, his title, and so forth, and said, "Captain Hillman, I want you to listen very carefully to what Director Douglas and I tell you, okay?"

"I will, Mr. President." Hillman had regained some of his composure.

"I'm putting us on speaker now. First, I've been fully briefed on the events at the downtown brothel last night. It has become a matter of national security. I want you to hand the case over to the FBI forthwith."

Thank God!

"Yes, Mr. President." He refrained from telling the president what a pleasure it would be to follow that order.

And then the matter took a surprising turn. The president wanted Lieutenant Benson Harris embedded in an FBI SWAT team about to go on a raid. He wanted Hillman to inform Harris that he was to be dressed and armed in no more than thirty minutes.

What has Harris been hiding from me?

"Questions?"

"No, Mr. President." He felt the urge to let out a long sigh of relief but controlled himself.

Douglas said, "The FBI agent in charge should be knocking on your front door any minute now. His name is James Winger."

They exchanged goodbyes and ended the call.

No one timed it, but if they did, it would've shown it was precisely sixty-seven seconds before the knock on the front door came.

Just enough time for Captain Hillman to put on pants and a shirt, walk to the front door, and switch the porch lights on.

He invited FBI special agent Winger in and led him to the kitchen table, and started coffee for both.

Hillman knew he wasn't going back to sleep. A proper

case handover was not an argument between the police officer and the FBI dude, as portrayed in the movies. It was a long and tedious process. Notwithstanding, Hillman had no doubts that this one would break the records and be over in an hour.

"Is Harris ready?"

"No, I still have to tell him. Between chatting to your director, the president, and your arrival, I haven't had time to call him yet." He took his phone out while talking; it was already ringing on Harris's side.

As expected, Harris had a mouthful to say about the ungodly hour of the call.

"Yeah, I know all of that," said Hillman. "You can file a formal complaint later. In the meantime, the Director of the FBI and the President of the United States phoned me and ordered me to tell you to raise your ass from your bed, dress up, and wait at your front gate for an FBI SWAT team to pick you up. They're going to raid another brothel. I don't know why, but maybe they reckon, after last night, you're the resident expert on brothels. Who knows? Whatever their reasons, the president wants you to go there with them. I don't know anything else."

Harris was too stumped to query the President of the United States or speak in full sentences. "Uh-huh."

"Do you know anything about this? Anything I should know?"

Harris grunted something, which his captain took for a no.

"Okay, get ready; your ride will be there soon. Get in touch when it's over. Don't do anything stupid like getting yourself shot or killed. Be careful and be safe."

Chapter Sixty-Two

THE ADVANCE TEAM

The clock on the wall said it was 3:10 a.m. in LA. The changing of the guards was four hours ago. The party was over. The guests had left. Dorset had invited Sidney Fuller and her husband to spend the night in the guesthouse.

Marissa and Josh kept their drones circling above and streamed the video back to the *TOMATS* and the team's mobile phone screens. They were in their cabin on one of the guest farms about a mile away from Dorset's Vineyard.

John, Christelle, and Declan were also in a cabin on a different guest farm neighboring Dorset's Vineyard, following Rex and company's progress on a laptop screen.

Since getting the drones up, Josh and Marissa had quickly established that there were eight humans in four of the prefabricated houses, the quarters of the child sex slaves. The fifth one seemed empty. The thermal imaging cameras said there were two people in the same bed in the master bedroom of the guest house. Presumably, the Fullers.

Less than an hour ago, Lieutenant Harris stood inside his house dressed in police battle fatigues. The body armor was invisible beneath his shirt, and his police-issue nine-millimeter pistol was in his underarm holster. Four extra magazines were distributed among the inside pockets of his suit jacket. His night vision equipment was in a small canvas carry bag.

At 3:35 a.m., a white hybrid Toyota RAV 4 with tinted windows pulled up at his front gate. He quickly hugged and kissed his wife, picked up his bag, and headed for the waiting vehicle with more than just a little apprehension. He felt he'd been treated like a junior beat cop. But then it seems his captain was treated the same way by the President of the United States and the Director of the FBI.

He headed for the rear passenger seat behind the driver, but the window rolled down when he was a few yards away, and a woman with an Italian-sounding accent said, "You're our guest of honor. Front passenger seat, please."

"Good to see you again, Lieutenant Harris. Welcome, and thank you for joining our mission," said the man behind the wheel.

"If I knew you were coming for me, Mr. Dalton, I wouldn't have worried so much."

"Please call me Rex. Behind me is my wife, Catia, and behind you is my friend Digger, who you've already met."

Harris turned and shook hands with Catia and waved at Digger, who yapped at him and stuck his right paw out.

Catia laughed. "He's offended that he didn't get a handshake."

Harris said, "Apologies, Digger," and shook the dog's paw gently. "How are you?"

Digger was smiling and growled softly.

"What have I done wrong now?"

"He says he's doing great how about you?"

Harris turned back and stared at Rex, wondering if this was what the looney bin looked like from the inside. Or was this the latest version of The Matrix in which they've replaced the telephone booth with an SUV? He shook his head slowly. "You people speak to a dog? And he speaks to you?"

"Of course," said Rex. "He's our best field agent."

Catia interrupted. "Rex and Digger talk. Rex is fluent in Caninenese; I only know a few words."

Harris could feel his wallet in his back pocket. It gave him some comfort. He had cash and credit cards in there in case he wanted to call a taxi or Uber to take him home.

But Rex must've sensed his unease. "Okay, when this is over, Catia and I will demonstrate what Digger can do. Let's talk about the raid. But first, Catia has to fit you with one of our team communication devices."

Harris turned to Catia, and she explained to him how the molar mics worked and asked him to open his mouth wide, like at the dentist.

When Greg activated his device, and the first sounds came through his jaw straight into his brain, Harris yelled and swore and apologized. However, within a few minutes of practice, Harris seemed to get the hang of it.

Rex continued. "Are you aware the president has sanctioned tonight's operation and everything that precedes tonight?"

"Yes, I am."

"Good. So, here's what we have in mind for tonight."

Instead of an hour, it was going to take forty-five minutes to reach Dorset's Vineyard. That was because of the flashing police light clipped to the roof of the vehicle on the driver's side. Rex would give the speed limits no mind.

It was not nearly enough time to brief Harris about all the events since they'd last seen each other. But it was more than enough time to understand his role in the mission, which boiled down to being an observer and, when necessary, arresting those who were so unfortunate to have survived the raid. Regardless, Harris appreciated the gesture.

"So, how many are in this team tonight, Rex?"

"WYSIWYG."

"What?"

"What you see is what you get."

There was a long silence during which Harris first had to decode that before he could wonder if now would be a good time to go back home. "You mean we're the team? Three humans and a dog?"

Rex laughed. "Just pulling your leg, Lieutenant. We're nine humans and a dog."

Digger stuck his nose between the front seats and growled.

"What's wrong?" said Harris.

"He doesn't want to believe that he's not human. He thinks of himself as a human with different features. He just wanted to make sure I remembered that."

Harris was looking out the window. *Two schizophrenic special operators were already nagging him. Now a dog with a human complex, their best agent, no less. It must be these molar mics talking right inside the brain. They're bound to drive anyone crazy. But the dog isn't wearing a molar mic.*

Just then, Digger pushed his head between the seats and whined softly.

Harris's blood ran cold at the question popping up in his mind. *'So what's your problem with me?'*

But Rex said, "Can you hold two minutes, buddy? We're almost there."

Rex was grateful for the guards who'd shown up as promised. They had enough time to run away; they hadn't. He would be happy to put in a good word for them at their deportation hearings or with the president.

Chapter Sixty-Three

DID YOU RECOGNIZE HIM?

The lights inside and outside the guesthouse were off. They wore ski masks, and had their night vision equipment, silenced Glock .22 pistols, and tranquilizer guns. Rex found it odd that despite all the security guards surrounding the future President of the United States earlier, there were now only two. They were outside the house, on the bench in the garden, both asleep after an extraordinarily long, uneventful day.

They never heard anyone approaching and stirred only lightly when the tranquilizer darts hit them.

"They'll have a lot to explain when they wake up," said Josh.

That they'd been on the protection detail of the president before she got elected would've looked good on any security guard's résumé. But then, 'falling asleep on duty' on their dismissal notices would not go down well with any potential employer. The worst of it all would be their inability to tell the FBI in whose custody they'd wake up, gagged and zip-tied, about three hours after their last memory, what happened in between. Their principals would be missing, and they'd have to explain why they reeked as if they'd taken a skinny dip in Dorset's wine barrels. Those were not only career-ending missteps. They would be unemployable in the security industry for life.

Marissa gave Rex and company the clearance to go through the backdoor. Digger insisted that Courtney was in that house; therefore, he was in the lead. They first swept the house and confirmed that the drones were right; there were only two people in the house, Sidney Fuller and Irina Kutuzova, together in the king-size waterbed in the master bedroom, both naked and engaged in the act of adultery.

A ketamine dart from Rex's gun assured that Ms. Fuller would sleep for two hours. The dart from Catia's gun had the same effect on Ms. Kutuzova. A minute later, their hands and feet were zip-tied, and their mouths duct-taped.

Harris said nothing. This gave new meaning to the concept of protective custody. The ladies *were* in sexual offenders' territory. It could be perilous out there. Better safe than sorry. Fruit of the poisonous tree? Absolutely. But that would only be relevant if they got charged with a crime. There were no arrests or charges yet.

Rex was wondering so loud; everyone could hear him over their molar mics. "Where could Mr. Fuller be?"

"We know he hasn't left," said Rehka. "I can't see his GPS location. His phone must be switched off."

While Rex and Catia were busy securing the ladies, Lieutenant Harris observed. Digger was nearby, just in case. But he was impatiently whining every few seconds as if to say, "C'mon you, hurry up. I want to take you to Courtney."

When Rex and Catia were finished, Digger spun around and followed his nose to the sliding door in the kitchen, which they expected to reveal a pantry. It didn't. It revealed the top of the stairs going down to an underground level.

Rex told Greg, "Count slowly to ten, then flip the mains on."

When Rex and Digger arrived on the floor below, he hastened to switch off Digger's and his night vision goggles. When the lights came on two seconds later, he had his gun pointed at the people on the bed.

Catia and Lieutenant Harris arrived shortly after.

Josh and Marissa were outside, keeping overwatch with their drones. John, Christelle, and Declan were keeping an eye on the prefabricated houses, waiting for Rex and company to join them as soon as Courtney was safe. Thanks to the body cams they were all wearing, including Digger, everyone on the team could see what Rex and his companions were seeing.

———

The subterranean area below the guesthouse was an extra-large bedroom, resplendently decorated and furnished, exuding luxury from every corner. The centerpiece was a majestic four-poster bed boasting intricately carved wooden posts supporting a sumptuous canopy of delicate silk. Rich velvet drapes cascaded down each side, creating an intimate and cozy cocoon. The opulent, hand-tufted bedding featured an array of plush, jewel-toned pillows. Glistening chandeliers cast a warm glow, illuminating the ornate, gilded moldings that adorned the high ceilings and the lush, patterned wallpaper that lined the walls. Elegant furnishings, including a gleaming antique armoire and a delicate, hand-painted vanity, completed the lavish scene, ensuring that this bedroom was a true sanctuary of sophistication and comfort.

Dorset's recruitment room.

According to Greg and Rehka, this room and every room upstairs had been fitted with international espionage-level surveillance equipment, even the toilets and bathrooms. Dorset's 'friends' who were privileged enough to be invited to spend a night in this guesthouse came out completely compromised and beholden to him—for life. The computers running the surveillance system were in a hidden closet in the hallway on the ground floor. Greg and Rehka were already making copies of all surveillance footage going back years.

On the bed were two people. Rex recognized both from their photos. He couldn't recall the name of the fifty-five-year-old naked man lying on his back. The naked sixteen-year-old child next to this man was his daughter.

She was shaking, on the verge of hysteria.

Rex could never describe to anyone the feelings that washed over him at that moment when he first laid eyes on Courtney. In his subjective opinion, she was the most beautiful child in the universe. Auburn hair, her mother's deep green eyes, and a perfectly formed little nose. Even though he knew he wasn't going to see one soon, he didn't have to use any imagination to visualize what an angelical face she'd have when she smiled. The urge to rush to her, pick her up in his arms, and tell her that she was safe, was near insuppressible. But he knew he would only scare her more if he did.

Since launching this operation, Rex and his team had learned that nothing could prepare them for the wickedness and corruption they'd encounter along the way. Apart from the vexing resentment, it was impossible to begin to understand how twisted a person must be to rape, abuse, and murder defenseless children.

Rex had promised himself if this mission led him to a situation like this, where he'd find the rapist in the company of his daughter, as he just did, that person was going to die.

Digger was on the villain's side of the bed, snarling and growling, begging Rex to let him execute the sentence.

Rex was tempted. He realized his finger was curled around the trigger of his pistol pointed at the man's forehead. Slowly, he let go of the breath he didn't realize he'd been holding and eased his finger off the trigger but kept the gun trained on the man's face.

No one would've blinked an eye if he'd emptied his gun into the face of the scumbag who had raped or was about to rape his daughter. However, he had two compelling reasons to break the promise to himself. Well, not break it; just delay it. He wouldn't shoot the man in front of his daughter. And this man's identity was bugging him. He had seen that face before. He had a gut feeling it was important to know who he was and hear what he had to say before shooting him.

Catia was the first to realize that Courtney's abject fear was because they must've looked decidedly alien in their night vision goggles and ski masks, not to mention the fear the guns must've instilled in her. She returned her gun to its holster, took the headgear off, walked to the bed, took her own jacket off, and covered Courtney.

Harris stood to the side, quiet. He'd also removed his night vision gear and ski mask. His gun remained in its holster.

Rex watched his daughter as he removed his face wear. He saw Courtney's eyes shoot wide for a fleeting moment and wondered why. But there was no time for questions now. He had to put her at ease first.

"Courtney, we've come to rescue you. Your mother and Reece asked us to find you. Please don't be afraid; you're safe now. We're taking you back to your family."

She nodded slowly, then said, "I... I... know you. You're... you're... my... my dad."

"Yes, I am. But how—"

"Reece looks just like you—" She broke down in tears as relief washed over her.

Rex took two steps, picked her up from the bed, and held her in his arms like a baby.

Digger whined. Obviously, he was happy to see Rex and his daughter together, finally.

The man on the bed made the first sound since Rex and the others entered the Hadean den of evil. His bladder had forsaken him and emptied itself on the silk linen. The loud sigh admitted defeat. Obviously, he'd figured it out; if this man with the dark eyes and the vicious big black dog was indeed this girl's father, he'd soon be a dead man.

Rex held Courtney for a while longer, whispering to her. "It's all over, Courtney. You're safe. You're going home with us."

He nodded to Catia. She nodded back. He whispered to Courtney, "I want you to go with Catia now. Our friends are waiting for you upstairs. I will join you shortly."

She nodded.

Catia put her arm around the child's shoulder and steered her up the stairs where Josh and Marissa were waiting for them. She spoke to Courtney in a soft and comforting voice, like a mother.

Digger's attention was flipping between the villain on the bed and the sobbing Courtney. He remained on his haunches next to the bed two yards away from the man. He groaned and growled and snarled and yapped, begging everyone who'd listen to let him rip this trash to pieces.

But Rex kept waving his finger.

Frustrating.

When Catia and Courtney were gone, Rex turned to the man on the bed. Gray hair rimmed his bald head. Rex knew the face, but the pictures in his photographic memory showed him with a luscious bunch of gray hair. He removed the man's hair in the picture. *Gotcha!*

He had absolutely nothing to say to the weasel on the bed. He spoke to Greg. "I take it everyone can hear me?"

"Yes, they can."

"Do any of you recognize this child rapist on the bed?"

Silence.

"No," said Greg after a few moments, but I'm running a facial recognition query at the moment."

"Don't bother; this is Nathan Fuller, Sidney Fuller's husband. Look up the public pictures of him and imagine him without the wig."

Lieutenant Harris had a slack jaw. He sunk into the reclining chair two steps away. He'd climbed into Rex's vehicle an hour ago, fully expecting to see some bad guys go down tonight but, in his mind, the bad guys had no names and no faces until now. This was not just trouble; this was a disaster. Sidney Fuller's run for the White House would end on the same night she announced her candidacy. *Unless... Nah, stop right there; too ghastly to contemplate. I'll be retired when she gets elected. Yeah, let's hope someone else will stop her before she can sell the country out to Russia.*

"Dear God!" sighed John.

That was how everyone felt.

"What a screwed-up family," said Josh. "Upstairs, Ms. Fuller is practicing infidelity and treason, while downstairs, hubby is raping a sixteen-year-old child. I wonder if they're aware of each other's extramarital activities?"

"Don't be surprised if they claim that all these years, they were unaware of what low lives they were married to," said Christelle.

"Why don't we put them out of our misery and shoot them now?" said Josh.

Rex was also wondering if the president's pardon would include him shooting the vermin. There were two ways to find out if he'd get a pardon; phone the president and ask, then shoot, or shoot the bastards and ask the president after. He liked the second option better.

Harris started rethinking his retirement plans. Who was going to protect his children and grandchildren if he didn't? There would be one condition, though, he'd insist on working with the US Marshal's team, including the smiling dog who thought he was human.

Chapter Sixty-Four

LET ME KNOW WHEN IT'S DONE

Once Courtney was away from her assailant, although still frail and emotional, she wasn't so scared anymore and started regaining her composure. And started trusting Catia and the Farleys.

Very carefully and tenderly, Catia began to question Courtney about the other children.

What she told them confirmed their information was correct; there were eight more children kept in the prefabricated houses. Four of them were Hispanic. Courtney had befriended them and knew their stories. Spanish was one of her school subjects, and she was near fluent in it.

The Hispanic girls had been smuggled across the southern border and delivered to Dorset's Vineyard, and instead of being given the opportunity to receive an American education, they were forced to work as kitchen hands, cleaners, and sex slaves.

It was at once heartbreaking and infuriating to hear how their dirt-poor parents had borrowed money, which they couldn't afford, to pay the smugglers to take their children across the border into America, to a better future than what faced them in Honduras.

The remaining four were all of European descent, like Courtney. Their stories were very similar to Courtney's. They were befriended by an idol who turned out to be nothing but a groomer who introduced them to a good-looking scumbag who seduced them and hooked them on drugs before selling them to the sex slave bosses.

Rex had all but wrapped Mr. Fuller from head to toe in duct tape before rolling him into one of the Persian carpets and securing the package with another roll of duct tape.

Fuller's mumbling became fainter with each new layer of wrapping. When Rex was done, he threw Fuller over his shoulder like a fireman and carried him up the stairs to the SUV, where he dumped him unceremoniously in the back. The man was a proven rapist. It was prudent to keep him away from the ladies in the main bedroom.

Another method to put people into protective custody thought Harris. *Quick, easy to execute, and no bureaucracy.* Harris was impressed. He'd decided that this whole thing about the fruit of the poisonous tree was overrated.

Nathan Fuller was screaming and crying and begging, but the sounds were too muffled to make out anything. He was ten to one, promising cooperation, money, and so forth, including not laying a finger on Courtney ever again.

Just as well, Rex couldn't understand him; he thought it would've been rather pleasing if the son of a bitch suffocated to death. He wouldn't; it would just feel to him as if he were. If his heart didn't attack him by the time he came out from under his carpet cover, he'd be ready to talk a lot. At the end of that, Rex was going to shoot him.

Courtney told them that all the girls had been off duty since yesterday.

That was great news. It meant they hadn't been raped in the past twenty-four hours. And Rex and the team didn't have to deal with more pedophiles.

Within minutes, the same team as the night before, plus Lieutenant Harris and Courtney Lloyd, started turning up at the doorsteps of Courtney's co-captives. It was difficult to pacify eight sleepy, scared, bewildered children. But with Digger's and Courtney's help, they managed to bring them all together in one of the houses. Courtney explained what was going on, and soon the children started to calm down.

The team stayed with the children, waiting for the FBI to complete their part of the raid on the rest of the buildings in the compound. The most important target was Dorset.

John asked Rehka to set up a secure call with Martin Richardson.

When he answered, without preamble, John gave Richardson the compressed version of the raid on Dorset's Vineyard.

"Dalton's daughter and eight children have been rescued," said John.

"Thank God," whispered Richardson.

"Nathan Fuller is a child rapist. Sidney Fuller is a Russian mole. Irina Kutuzova is her handler. And we've got them all in custody."

Richardson was quiet for a long time. Then he sighed loudly. "John, do you know what this means?"

"Other than war?" said John.

"Probably nuclear war."

"Yep. In the meantime, why don't you get the others on the line so—"

"Wait. What about the FBI operation?" said Richardson.

"Still in progress. Their team leader told me everything was under control. Dorsett and his girlfriend are in custody. They're busy interviewing all other occupants of the homestead while teams of computer and forensic professionals are collecting and confiscating every electronic device and other evidence they can find. They'll be busy for hours."

"Okay. Now get the president and the others on the line so I can tell it once to all."

Not long after, the president and the directors of the CIA and FBI joined the secured video call.

John told them what had happened while the president and others interjected choice words and phrases as they listened to him.

The president was white in the face when he spoke. "Charge them with murder, accessories to murder, rape, assault, child abuse, treason, espionage, and whatever else you can think of. Keep them in maximum security in separate prisons. I oppose bail. Now excuse me. I have a press conference to organize."

"Mr. President, the ladies will be asleep for another hour," said John.

"Okay, let me know when they wake up. Then we'll hold the press conference. I want the children taken care of immediately. "

Chapter Sixty-Five

PLEASE, DAD

Four hours later, Rex and Catia pulled up in front of Jessica's house with Courtney and Digger in the back seat. Digger was already her new best friend but became her hero with her dad when Catia told her how Digger was the one who'd led them to her when he picked up her scent and showed them where she was.

As the door to her mother's room creaked open, the soft glow of the afternoon sun filtered in, bathing the sterile room in a warm, golden hue. Courtney stood hesitantly at the threshold, her heart pounding with a mixture of fear and anticipation.

Her gaze fell upon the frail figure on the hospital bed, an IV drip snaking its way to her arm and various machines surrounding her, their quiet beeping punctuating the silence. She felt a lump form in her throat as she caught sight of Reece, seated by their mother's side, holding her weak hand in his.

The weight of remorse about the pain she had caused to her mother and Reece lay heavily on her sixteen-year-old shoulders. There were no words, no 'I'm sorry,' 'I apologize,' or 'I regret,' or any other words that would begin to right those wrongs.

She said, "Please forgive me." The regret in her voice was palpable, her heart aching for all the pain and anguish she had caused.

Her mother, despite her weakened state, opened her eyes and turned her head to face her daughter. A weak but genuine smile crossed her lips, her eyes glistening with unshed tears. "Courtney... my angel... we never stopped praying for your return."

Reece stood up and walked toward Courtney, enveloping her in a warm, protective hug. "We missed you so much, sis. You're back and safe. We thank God."

"And Dad," said Courtney. "And Digger." As she clung to her twin, her body shaking with sobs, she felt the love and forgiveness radiating from her family. In that moment, she understood that no matter the darkness she had faced, her mother and brother were still there for her; and her dad offered her unwavering support and love.

Rex, Catia, and Digger kept at a distance and quiet throughout it all. It was with indescribable joy that they looked at Jessica's and Reece's faces. At first, they had looked traumatized, but they weren't; it was a look of relief superseded by joy.

Rex mouthed to Catia, "Let's go." She nodded, but they hadn't fully turned when Courtney said, "Don't go away. Please, Dad, don't go."

"Please, Dad," said Reece.

Rex swallowed the lump in his throat and nodded as he turned back to them.

Jessica watched the emotional reunion unfold, her heart swelling with joy at the sight. Despite the emotional hardships that still lay ahead for her children, she knew that, together, they would find the strength to heal and rebuild their lives. She sighed.

She won't be in this realm; she'll be following their progress from the other side. The thought didn't upset her. From the moment Courtney stepped into the room, she was ready to meet her Maker. That's the promise she'd made Him. She'd done her part in the relay race of the children's care and education; it was time to hand over the baton to their dad. And she'd do so with the certainty that she couldn't hand it over to a better man.

I'm ready to meet you, Lord.

A FREE Novella from JC Ryan

vinci-books.com/no-doubt-free

Even paradise has shadows...

When a beautiful woman is found stabbed to death on the tranquil island of Olib, police quickly blame her boyfriend. But, Digger, a big black Dutch Shepherd, a trained military dog, and his alpha, Rex Dalton, a former black ops specialist, know the police were mistaken.

Fact and Fiction

All the characters in the story come from my imagination. As I have said in the foreword, any likeness to actual people, alive or dead, businesses, companies, events, or places, is entirely coincidental.

Visitors to Los Angeles will find downtown and Cliffside Street, but they will search in vain for the Pink Poodle, Cloud Nine, and Purple Pussycat. They don't exist.

While there are many vineyards in California, as far as I could establish, none of them is named Dorset's Vineyard. But if there is one by that name, I know for a fact it hasn't been visited by the Daltons, Digger, or any other employee of CRC.

I offer my sincerest and unreserved apologies to the port authorities of the Port of Los Angeles for conducting unauthorized fictitious spy operations within your area of authority.

As far as I could determine, the *TOMATS* has never dropped anchor anywhere in the Port of Los Angeles.

I've done my best to be factually correct about the child

sex slave industry in America. It was at once shocking, revolting, heartbreaking, and eye-opening to discover how little is being done about this unspeakable evil in our midst. Yes, I live in Australia, but my research shows this story could play out just the same in Sydney, Melbourne, or any of the other major cities across the globe. Don't be mistaken; this story is happening across the world every day.

Of course, the part about the Russians behind it is my imagination, but the child sex slave industry is not. I deliberately left out many of the goriest and most depressing details.

Pedophile statistics never make for comfortable reading, but it doesn't make them less true:

- About 67% of all victims of sexual assault are under the age of 18.
- More than half of those victims are under 12.
- Around one in five young girls and one in seven boys are sexually abused before they turn 18.
- There are about 780,000 people in the US's sex offenders' registries. Every state keeps its own registry. There is also a National Sex Offender Registry.
- About 4 percent of the population is believed to have pedophilic urges.
- Some psychologists now categorize it as a sexual orientation, no different from heterosexuality and homosexuality.
- With nearly 100,000 offenders, Texas has the largest list of registered sex offenders in the country. California ranks second with nearly 60,000. New York has the third-most registered

sex offenders, with about 43,000 people in its
state registry.

Onto more pleasant topics.

Readers often ask me about the technology and gadgets used by Rex and his team on their missions. Yes, they are real. The satellite phones, drones, GPS trackers, molar mics, turning a cellphone into a walkie-talkie, surveillance bugs, all of it is true, and they are being used by special forces, black ops operators, and spies across the globe every day.

What about the Pegasus spyware? Yes, it's real. Pegasus is a highly sophisticated form of spyware, originally developed for military use, that has been in circulation since at least 2016. It is considered one of the most advanced tools for hacking mobile phones and has reportedly been used to access the smartphones of at least 40 journalists in India, allowing for the extraction of sensitive data from these devices.

What about Digger's tactical vest? It's true. All of it. Just Google "special forces dogs tactical vests."

Is Digger really capable of doing all those things you describe in your stories? Yes, of course! He's a genius. On a serious note, though, yes, dogs can do what I'm describing and much more. But it's highly unlikely that one dog will be capable of doing all of it. Various breeds of dogs have capabilities unique to their breed. Some breeds are excellent sniffer dogs. Others are excellent guard dogs, military dogs, emotional support dogs, or just the best companion a human can hope to have. Digger has a combination of the skills of various breeds.

Can they read our minds? Probably not if you're not a dog lover. If you're a dog lover, though, you'd be convinced they can. The same with that smile on Digger's face. Dog lovers know their dogs smile and know what makes them smile.

Admittedly, I gave my imagination a bit of free rein in some scenes where Rex and Digger are conversing, but maybe I didn't go entirely overboard; just have a chat with police or military dog handlers and listen to them talking about what they think is going on in the minds of their canine friends.

How many words can they understand? Research by Dr. Stanley Coren, a psychologist and leading authority on canine behavior at the University of British Columbia, suggests that the typical dog can understand about 165 words, including a range of commands and signals. The most intelligent dogs—those in the top 20 percent—are capable of recognizing up to 250 words.

Dr. Coren notes that people are naturally interested in what their dogs are thinking, often trying to interpret the quirky, amusing, or puzzling things their pets do. He points out that dogs sometimes display surprising cleverness and inventiveness, reminding us that, while they may not be geniuses, they share more similarities with humans than we might expect.

Can Digger pick up a scent 12 miles away? Yes, he absolutely can.

Can he smell drugs wrapped in plastic inside a gas tank of a car? Yes, as many drug smugglers who've tried it can testify.

Is it true that dogs can smell our emotions and medical conditions? Yes, absolutely. I once met a lady with a support dog on the train, and she told me he was trained to detect when her blood oxygen levels drop, or her heartbeat gets too high. He was also trained to detect high sugar levels in people with diabetes and the onset of an epileptic seizure.

Dogs can smell cancer and have occasionally proven they can detect it on a patient's breath long before the laboratory tests can detect it.

And they can smell or sense when a woman is pregnant.

And I haven't even mentioned those amazing seeing-eye dogs.

vinci-books.com/the-message

The Line Between Peace And Annihilation Is A Single Click

As a corrupt Russian president and his ruthless mistress hold the fate of humanity in their hands, only one message can prevent annihilation. Rex Dalton and Digger must navigate a trail of espionage and betrayal. From California's vineyards to the heart of Kyiv and Moscow, they face relentless enemies and impossible choices. With the fate of millions at stake, the team must make the ultimate sacrifice to prevent nuclear annihilation.

Turn the page for a free preview...

The Message: Prologue

OVERTURE OF THE APOCALYPSE

The ancient Buddhist monastery, known as Zhelundung, sat perched precariously amidst the jagged peaks where the snowcapped mountains of western China bled into Russia's Siberian wilderness. For millennia, its labyrinthine tunnels and fortified walls had provided refuge to monks and lamas, weathering the ceaseless wars and political upheaval that raged across their ancestral lands.

On this late winter evening, Zhelundung's hallowed halls again played host to war talk. This time, not only how to survive it but to emerge victorious from the coming conflagration.

Over the next several hours, Zhelundung's ancient stones absorbed the whispered discussions and solemn assurances.

Nine nations cradled about thirteen thousand nuclear warheads in their arsenals, their combined power sufficient to wipe out all life on Earth many times over.

Russia's expansionism, Iran-backed proxy wars in the Middle East, and China rattling its saber over Taiwan had the world in such upheaval the Doomsday Clock—that grim harbinger maintained by the Bulletin of Atomic Scientists—stood at a precarious ninety seconds to midnight. Just one bullet or bomb away from the next Big War. That's exactly how the last two Big Wars started. However, this time, the war could be over in an hour or two. The survivors would be the ill-fated.

In America, political parties and the media were gearing up for their four-yearly blood sport, a presidential election. Politics was war, with fewer deaths than in a shooting war, but a war nonetheless.

In the grand tapestry of human history, rivers of consequence have flowed from the choices of generations past. But of all the rushing rivers, none could be compared with man's belligerent nature. Of all Earth's myriad species, none possessed quite the talent for violent chaos as Homo sapiens – 'wise man.' Yet, as the world teetered on the brink of annihilation, many questioned the appropriateness of that moniker. For what wisdom could be found in creating such peril?

Soon, the drumbeats of war, a faint and distant rhythm now, would pound through the world's citadels of power.

The emissaries of China, Russia, and Iran knew the seventy-eight years of relative peace since the end of WWII was a statistical anomaly, undoubtedly the longest reprieve from major conflict since humans were expelled from Paradise.

Everyone at the table was embargoed and isolated, yet each had something the others desperately wanted—the ideal conditions for pacts and handshakes amid a scenario of supply and demand.

Iran, with 12% of the world's oil, and Russia, with 13%, had no petroleum problems. Iran's issue was religious fervor —they had money but no nukes.

Russia had an abundance of nukes but not enough money; the war in Ukraine was ruinous. Banning his idiotic advisors to far-flung Siberian outposts didn't solve Krivkov's fiscal dilemmas. He was desperate to bring the war to an end but couldn't do so without assistance. He had been toying with the idea of using tactical nukes, but there were two major problems: The President of America and MAGMA. No one else around the table knew anything about MAGMA, and he would keep it that way. It would've been too embarrassing to admit a security failure of nuclear proportions.

China had money, military might, and an insatiable craving for oil, raw materials, and nuclear weapons. China's paltry 350 declared earthbound warheads were stashed in a 3,000-mile network of tunnels dubbed the Underground Great Wall. They were feverishly working to expand their stockpile, but never fast enough. They needed all the assistance they could get.

———

After years of nurturing terrorist networks and stoking hatred across the Middle East and beyond, Iran had a thriving arms industry, selling the latest instruments of war to anyone who would hasten the return of their savior, Muhammad Al-Mahdi (the Rightly Guided), the Twelfth Imam or Hidden Imam, destined to lead the forces of righteousness against evil, establish global justice, and convert all to Shiite Islam—the only true religion.

By Shiite accounts, the Imam was six to eight years old when he departed in 874 CE after foretelling his return during an era of worldwide chaos. According to Iran's ayatollahs, it's the duty of true believers to precipitate that chaos if they wish to witness their savior's second coming.

The ayatollahs deemed nuclear pandemonium the swiftest, most economical path to end-of-days kind of chaos. A few well-placed detonations "and Israel would be off the map," which would surely trigger World War III, aka the Second Nuclear War or Doomsday.

How much more chaos could the Imam possibly desire?

In the Bible, this apocalypse is called Armageddon, a term derived from the Hebrew "Hill of Megiddo," prophesied as the battlefield where God's forces defeat Satan and his forces at history's denouement.

As the first rays of dawn filtered through the stained glass, laying a crimson tint across the unlikely summit, a new geopolitical course had been charted. When the ashes finally settled, a new world order would emerge from the rubble. No longer beholden to outmoded concepts of democracy and archaic moral constructs.

The next Big War was in the cards.

The Message: Chapter One

THE NOXIOUS AND FESTERING SEWER

Langley, Virginia, USA

In Langley, sunrise was three hours ago. Martin Richardson, deputy director in charge of CIA operations, had been pacing around his office for the past two hours, sipping on his second extra strong black coffee from a one-pint insulated stainless steel mug.

Richardson never smoked, not even when it was fashionable. At university, he took two puffs of a cigarette and quit. But every now and then, a mission would come along that tested his willpower to the limits. Such was last night's mission—a vigilante raid by John's black ops operators, spearheaded by Rex Dalton and Digger, on a brothel and child-sex slave hellhole in downtown LA called Cloud Nine.

The victims, drug-controlled sex slaves, killed twenty-two of the lowlifes who'd been tormenting them for years; pimps, crime bosses, slave owners, drug pushers, and clients.

The mutiny at the den of iniquity was the prelude to tonight's raid. Ordered by the President of the United

States, on Dorsett's Vineyard in the countryside, about an hour's drive from downtown LA. It was owned by Robert Dorsett, who was worth three-quarters of a billion. He called himself an investment advisor, but, like an iceberg, ninety percent was below the surface. Sub rosa, he was the owner of Cloud Nine, a practicing pedophile, child sex slave trader, drug dealer, murderer, traitor, and a Russian spy.

No search- or surveillance- or arrest warrants were requested or issued. No one could be trusted. Not even the judges.

The raid in progress was authorized by the president.

All of that was the reason for Richardson's aimless pacing, shot nerves, and coffee-guzzling.

As the CIA's head of operations, he was one of only a handful of people who had a comprehensive understanding of the many existential threats posed by America's enemies —foreign and domestic.

The threat staring America in the face now was what unsettled his entire nervous system more than just a little.

The Russians were masters of the honey trap—the use of men and women to entrap a target for purposes of black-mailing. The Chinese were not too far behind them. But to be sure, it was a repulsive method that intelligence agencies across the globe employed regularly, including the CIA. The Russians and Chinese used it more often and were much better at it. By nature, the spy business was an ugly one. It couldn't operate properly without dishonesty, deceit, and underhandedness. Notwithstanding, turning children, minors as young as eight, into drug-addicted sex slaves to collect kompromat crossed the red line.

If this was not an act of war, what was?

But war with Russia was a spine-chilling thought. They had the world's biggest arsenal of nuclear weapons, 6,257.

The United States had only 5,550. It earned them second place among nine known nuclear powers. The two archenemies maintained around 1,600 strategic nuclear warheads in active deployment, mostly pointing at each other.

China had only around 400 weapons, according to them, at last count, but they'd promised to shift production into overdrive to catch up with the others.

A fraction of those nukes could do the total obliteration of each other. With the remainder, they could make our planet a lifeless wasteland and still have enough left to do it all over again a few more times. Mutually Assured Destruction—MAD. Indeed.

It was not as if the Russians didn't know all of that; regardless, they went ahead and implemented their diabolical plan to rape, addict, and kill American children so that they could set up one of the most detestable spy operations in human history. This egregious plan was born thirty years ago in the twisted mind of an ambitious KGB officer, a shrewd man, Stanislav Krivkov, now the President of Russia.

It was highly unlikely that neither he nor his advisors considered the possibility of war over this. It was more than likely precisely what they had in mind—war against a crippled America whose foundations were infested with the Judases, traitors, spies, moles, colluders, and vipers Krivkov had been recruiting and planting in their midst for many years. By the time America discovered the noxious and festering sewer, it would be too late.

The Message: Chapter Two

THE SECOND OPTION

Dorsett's Vineyard, an hour from Los Angeles, USA

Marissa gave Rex and company the clearance to go through the back door. Digger insisted that Courtney was in that house; therefore, he was in the lead. They first swept the house and confirmed that the drones were right; there were only two people in the house. Sidney Fuller and Irina Kutuzova, together in the king-size water bed in the master bedroom, both naked and engaged in the act of adultery.

A ketamine dart from Rex's gun assured that Ms. Fuller would sleep for two hours. The dart from Catia's gun had the same effect on Ms. Kutuzova. A minute later, their hands and feet were zip-tied, and their mouths duct-taped.

Harris said nothing. This gave new meaning to the concept of protective custody. The ladies were in sexual offenders' territory. It could be perilous out there. Better safe than sorry. Fruit of the poisonous tree? Absolutely, but that would only be relevant if they got charged with a crime. There were no arrests or charges yet. And, according to him, there was a very good chance that no charges would be laid, ever. The political reverberations would be too catastrophic.

Little did Harris know that the US Marshal and his big black dog were debating the same topic. If he knew, he wouldn't have been surprised; he saw enough of the marshal and his dog to know they talked to each other. He had no clue how, but they undoubtedly did.

Mate, need I remind you who these women are?

Rex shook his head and spoke inaudibly. "Nope. I know, and I'm working on options. This'll be the political upheaval of all time, at home and abroad."

I say, get rid of them. Now. They smell horrible. They're evil. They'll harm my pack.

"That's why I'm here; to stop *you* from doing things like that. We need information before we shoot them."

O-k-a-y, I know how to compromise. But don't let them live when you're done with them.

"Trust me, when this is over, I'll personally shoot them." He didn't explain what he meant by 'over'—Digger didn't ask.

With Digger out of his mind, Rex's thoughts returned to Russia. Their Director of Internal Intelligence was now in presidentially authorized custody in the US. Never mind the reason for her arrest or the manner in which she was arrested. No Miranda Rights. Krivkov wouldn't be very understanding about the arrest of his FSB Director of Intelligence and Chief of Staff.

Rex whispered a progress report softly into his molar mic to the rest of the team. "House clear. Two women neutralized and secured. Details later. Following Digger."

The subterranean area below the guesthouse was an extra-large bedroom, resplendently decorated and furnished, exuding luxury from every corner. The centerpiece was a majestic four-poster bed boasting intricately carved wooden posts supporting a sumptuous canopy of delicate silk. Rich velvet drapes cascaded down each side, creating an intimate and cozy cocoon. The opulent, hand-tufted bedding featured an array of plush, jewel-toned pillows. Glistening chandeliers cast a warm glow, illuminating the ornate, gilded moldings that adorned the high ceilings and the lush, patterned wallpaper that lined the walls. Elegant furnishings, including a gleaming antique armoire and a delicate, hand-painted vanity, completed the lavish scene, ensuring that this bedroom was a true sanctuary of sophistication and comfort.

Dorsett's recruitment room.

According to Greg and Rehka, this room and every room upstairs had been fitted with international espionage-level surveillance equipment, even the bathrooms. Dorsett's 'friends' who were privileged enough to be invited to spend a night in this guesthouse came out completely compromised and beholden to him—for life. The computers running the surveillance system were in a hidden closet in the hallway on the ground floor. Greg and Rehka were already making copies of all surveillance footage going back years.

On the bed were two people. Rex recognized both from their photos. He couldn't recall the name of the fifty-five-year-old naked man lying on his back. The naked sixteen-year-old child next to this man was his daughter.

She was shaking, on the verge of hysteria.

Rex could never describe to anyone the feelings that washed over him at that moment when he first laid eyes on

Courtney. In his subjective opinion, she was the most beautiful child in the universe. Auburn hair, her mother's deep green eyes, and a perfectly formed little nose. Even though he knew he wasn't going to see one soon, he didn't have to use any imagination to visualize what an angelic face she'd have when she smiled. The urge to rush to her, pick her up in his arms, and tell her that she was safe was nearly insuppressible. But he knew he would only scare her more if he did.

Since launching this operation, Rex and his team had learned that nothing could prepare them for the wickedness and corruption they'd encounter along the way. Apart from the vexing resentment, it was impossible to begin to understand how twisted a person must be to rape, abuse, and murder defenseless children.

Rex had promised himself if this mission led him to a situation like this, where he'd find the rapist in the company of his daughter, as he just did, that person was going to die.

Digger was on the villain's side of the bed, snarling and growling, begging Rex to let him execute the sentence.

Rex was tempted. He realized his finger was curled around the trigger of his pistol pointed at the man's forehead. Slowly, he let go of the breath he didn't realize he'd been holding and eased his finger off the trigger but kept the gun trained on the man's face.

No one would've blinked an eye if he'd emptied his gun into the face of the scumbag who had raped or was about to rape his daughter. However, he had two compelling reasons for breaking the promise to himself. Well, not break it; just delay it. He wouldn't shoot the man in front of his daughter. And this man's identity was bugging him. He had seen that face before. He had a gut feeling it was important to know who he was and hear what he had to say before shooting him.

Catia was the first to realize that Courtney's abject fear was because they must've looked decidedly alien in their night vision goggles and ski masks, not to mention the fear the guns must've instilled in her. She returned her gun to its holster, took the headgear off, walked to the bed, took her own jacket off, and covered Courtney.

Harris stood to the side, quiet. He'd also removed his night vision gear and ski mask. His gun remained in its holster.

Rex watched his daughter as he removed his face wear. He saw Courtney's eyes shoot wide for a fleeting moment and wondered why. But there was no time for questions now. He had to put her at ease first.

"Courtney, we've come to rescue you. Your mother and Reece asked us to find you. Please don't be afraid; you're safe now. We're taking you back to your family."

She nodded slowly, then said, "I... I... know you. You're... you're... my... my dad."

"Yes, I am. But how—"

"Reece looks just like you." She broke down in tears as relief washed over her.

Rex took two steps, picked her up from the bed, and held her in his arms like a baby.

Digger whined. Obviously, he was happy to finally see Rex and his daughter together.

The man on the bed made the first sound since Rex and the others entered the Hadean den of evil. His bladder had forsaken him and emptied itself on the silk linen. The loud sigh admitted defeat. Obviously, he'd figured it out; if this man with the dark eyes and the vicious big black dog was indeed this girl's father, he'd soon be a dead man.

Rex held Courtney for a while longer, whispering to her. "It's all over, Courtney. You're safe. You're going home with us."

He nodded to Catia. She nodded back. He whispered to Courtney, "I want you to go with Catia now. Our friends are waiting for you upstairs. I will join you shortly."

She nodded as Rex set her on her feet.

Catia put her arm around the child's shoulder and steered her up the stairs where Josh and Marissa were waiting for them. She spoke to Courtney in a soft and comforting voice, like a mother.

Digger's attention was flipping between the villain on the bed and the sobbing Courtney. He remained on his haunches next to the bed two yards away from the man. He groaned and growled and snarled and yapped, begging everyone who'd listen to let him rip this trash to pieces.

But Rex kept waving his finger.

Frustrating.

When Catia and Courtney were gone, Rex turned to the man on the bed. Gray hair rimmed his bald head. Rex knew the face, but the pictures in his photographic memory showed him with a luscious bunch of gray hair. He removed the man's hair in the picture. *Gotcha!*

He had absolutely nothing to say to the weasel on the bed. He spoke to Greg. "I take it everyone can hear me?"

"Yes, they can."

"Do any of you recognize this child rapist on the bed?"

Silence.

"No," said Greg after a few moments. "But I'm running a facial recognition query at the moment."

"Don't bother; this is Nathan Fuller, Sidney Fuller's husband. Look up the public pictures of him and imagine him without the wig."

Lieutenant Harris had a slack jaw. He sunk into the reclining chair two steps away. He'd climbed into Rex's vehicle an hour ago, fully expecting to see some bad guys go down tonight, but, in his mind, the bad guys had no names and no faces until now. This was not just trouble; this was a disaster. Sidney Fuller's run for the White House would end on the same night she announced her candidacy. *Unless... Nah, stop right there; too ghastly to contemplate. I'll be retired when she gets elected. Yeah, let's hope someone else will stop her before she can sell the country out to Russia.*

"Dear God!" sighed John.

That was how everyone felt.

"What a screwed-up family," said Josh. "Upstairs, Ms. Fuller is practicing infidelity and treason, while downstairs, hubby is raping a sixteen-year-old child. I wonder if they're aware of each other's extramarital activities?"

"Don't be surprised if they claim that all these years, they were unaware of what low-lives they were married to," said Christelle.

"Why don't we put them out of our misery and shoot them now?" said Josh.

Rex was also wondering if the president's pardon would include him shooting the vermin. There were two ways to find out if he'd get a pardon; phone the president and ask, then shoot, or shoot the bastards and ask the president after. He liked the second option better.

Grab your copy...
vinci-books.com/the-message

About the Author

JC Ryan is a bestselling author renowned for his intricate espionage, archaeological thrillers, and conspiracy mysteries. With over 30 acclaimed novels, including the popular Rex Dalton K9 Thrillers, Rossler Foundation Mysteries, and Carter Devereux Mystery Thrillers, Ryan has captivated readers around the globe.

Drawing from his diverse professional background—as a military officer, lawyer, and IT manager—Ryan creates compelling narratives that skillfully blend historical accuracy with thrilling adventure. He is celebrated as a master storyteller, known for crafting riveting plots, meticulous historical details, and engaging, multidimensional characters. Ryan's meticulous research lends authenticity and depth to each story, immersing readers in richly constructed worlds filled with intrigue, suspense, and adventure.

Fans of David Baldacci, Lee Child's Jack Reacher, Tom Clancy's Jack Ryan, Nelson DeMille's John Corey, Vince Flynn's Mitch Rapp, Mark Greaney's Gray Man, Gregg Hurwitz's Orphan X, Robert Ludlum's Jason Bourne, Daniel Silva's Gabriel Allon, Brad Taylor's Pike Logan, Brad Thor's Scot Harvath, James Rollins' Sigma Force, Steve Berry's Cotton Malone, and Dan Brown's Robert Langdon will find JC Ryan's novels equally compelling and unforgettable.

When not writing, Ryan enjoys spending time with his college sweetheart, whom he married in 1978. They are proud parents of two daughters, have two sons-in-law, and are grandparents to two grandchildren.